THE ROCKFORD FILES:
The Green Bottle

Also by Stuart M. Kaminsky in Large Print:

The Devil Met the Lady
Hard Currency
Poor Butterfly
Rostnikov's Vacation

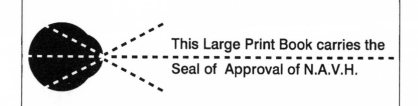

This Large Print Book carries the
Seal of Approval of N.A.V.H.

THE ROCKFORD FILES:
The Green Bottle

STUART M. KAMINSKY

Thorndike Press • Thorndike, Maine

Published in 1998 by arrangement with
Tom Doherty Associates, Inc.

Thorndike Large Print® Americana Series.

The tree indicium is a trademark of Thorndike Press.

The text of this Large Print edition is unabridged.
Other aspects of the book may vary from the original edition.

Set in 16 pt. Plantin by Al Chase.

Printed in the United States on permanent paper.

Library of Congress Cataloging in Publication Data
Kaminsky, Stuart M.
    The green bottle / Stuart M. Kaminsky.
      p.   cm. — (The Rockford files)
      ISBN 0-7862-1521-6 (lg. print : hc : alk. paper)
      1. Private investigators — California — Fiction.
    2. California — Fiction. 3. Large type books.   I. Title
    II. Series: Kaminsky, Stuart M.   Rockford files.
      [PS3561.A43R63   1998]
      813′.54—dc21
                                                    98-22575

To Anne and Bill Guisewite,
with thanks for their friendship,
hospitality and good humor.

PROLOGUE

Answering machine of Jim Rockford.

— *This is Jim Rockford. Please leave a message after the beep.*

— *Mr. Rockford, if and when you return from wherever you may be, this is Lawrence C. Tuttle reminding you that the bill of $412 for replacing the roof of your mobile home is now three months overdue and you have repeatedly promised to send us a check. You have my number. I would very much like to hear your story, though I would far prefer the promised payment.*

— *Jim, Angel. I've got a bit of a problem. Just a bit. Few hundred dollars and I was hoping what with the inheritance from Rocky and maybe business going well, you could see your way to helping your closest friend.*

— *Mr. Rockford, this is Fred Travis. You never seem to be home when I come by and you haven't responded to my flyer from the home owners association. I'll watch for you and come collect your dues when the missus or I spot you.*

7

— *Congratulations, Mr. James Rockford. You have reached the finals of the Statue of the Month annual competition. You and only a few others can win half a million dollars if you write to us immediately in the self-addressed envelope that should be in your mail today. Join Statue of the Month for only six payments of $19.95 and you are well on your way to that half million dollars, and you will receive your first statue, your choice of President James Madison or Barney of "Flintstones" fame. Please act immediately. We don't know how long this exciting offer will be available.*

— *Jim, Angel again. Where the hell are you? I need some help here or I may be walkin' around with two broken thumbs like Paul Newman in* The Hustler. *I told them they could have Rocky's pickup as collateral, so it may not be parked outside when you get this call and you may be considering calling 911 or Dennis Becker, but hold on and I'll get back to you.*

— *Jim, this is Janice. I got the box of mixed nuts. I'll eat the cashews slowly and think of you. I'll give you a call back when I get back from New York.* Damn Yankees, *here I come.*

— *Mr. Rockford, this as you certainly know, is Olivia Carstairs. You also know that I have*

8

now paid you $200 to find Douglas and I have not had a single report from you on your progress. I wish to discuss this with you in person. Perhaps I should have gotten Ace Ventura? Douglas is precious to me. He is not simply a valuable Self cat. He is a family treasure to whom I plan to leave all of my worldly goods. Call me or your services and my payments are terminated.

— This is Ms. Danforth at the telephone company. Your bill is $121.16 overdue. If it is not paid in full by a week from this Thursday, we will have to terminate your service. The address of your nearest payment location is listed in the telephone directory.

— Jim, I am a desperate man. They've got Rocky's pickup, but without papers they can only get a few hundred from a chop shop. Call me.

— Mr. Rockford, this is Dwight Cameron. I hope and expect that you are making progress in recovering the item we have discussed. Please call immediately upon your return.

— This is Dr. Lewiston's office confirming your appointment for tomorrow morning at ten. Please be on time.

CHAPTER ONE

It was raining in Santa Monica, a cold, driving, California winter rain, and I was crouched on the deck of a small but not inexpensive boat moored at the pier along with a few hundred other boats being tossed by the Pacific.

I was definitely soaked down to my underwear. I was definitely getting seasick. I was definitely not in a good mood. And, if my watch was still working and I was reading it correctly by the lights on the narrow white wooden pier, the people I was waiting for were late, at least ten minutes late. I wiped my eyes and kept them aimed in the general direction of one of the larger boats tied to the other side of the narrow pier. There was a dim light coming from the interior of the *Princess Louise.* It went out and a door opened and closed. A man in a hooded raincoat grabbed the railing and jumped from the *Princess Louise* to the dock. He was definitely better prepared for the weather than I was.

I wondered who Louise might be.

I was dressed in black: black jeans, black

pullover shirt, and a pair of black socks and shoes, my everyday-best walking shoes. They were probably ruined. I wiped my eyes. The ship I crouched swaying on was called *Gordo's Riptide*.

I didn't wonder who Gordo might be.

The man who had leapt off the *Princess Louise* stood in the middle of the pier, hands at his side, feet slightly apart. He stood straight up and looked relatively young, though his hooded face was shadowed. He stood straight with his hands at his sides. All he needed was a scythe in one hand to look like Death in Bergman's *The Seventh Seal* or Woody Allen's *Love and Death*. I had chosen the ship I crouched on because it was closer to the entrance to the pier than the *Princess Louise*. My plan was to cut off the escape of the man I was waiting for. He'd have to go through me or into the water. Going into the water on a night like this with bobbing boats was not a reasonable option. He would have to deal with me. I willed him to come soon. With each passing second, I grew wetter and angrier with this guy who I had never met. I soothed my anger — but not my queasy stomach — with the thought of the bonus check I would be getting from my client if everything went well.

And then he came. Slowly down the pier,

dressed in dark slacks and a zippered wind-breaker that I'm sure was waterproof. No hat. Light blond hair. I had no trouble rec-ognizing Jamie Hanson.

I had checked the weather report before I camped out on *Gordo's Riptide*. The rain was supposed to miss LA. My job was to be prepared, not to listen to weather reports, which had gotten me in trouble before. But my faith in the Channel Seven weather lady was only slightly shaken. She had the kind of voice that you believe in. She could ignore her mistakes; I could get killed by mine.

Hanson, coming down the pier, was near-ing the man with the hooded raincoat. He stopped when he was directly in front of the man; they said nothing. The man in the raincoat pulled out a pouch. The man in the windbreaker took a small package from his pocket. My cue.

I tried to stand. My knees refused to co-operate. I could hear the two men talking. I forced myself to stand, wincing, biting my lower lip to keep from moaning with pain. I had taken a bullet in one knee more than two years ago. It's hurt ever since. The other knee didn't feel all that great either. I had good days and bad, more bad than good; this was a bad one. I held onto a dangling rope and exercised each knee. They were working, but not as cooperatively as I'd like. At least they moved. I climbed off *Gordo's Riptide* slowly, painfully, hoping the hooded man didn't see me. The windbreaker had his back to me. They were cut off.

I brushed the sopping hair from my face and shouted into the wind,

"Hanson."

The windbreaker turned. I was a little over a dozen feet away. The package was still in his hand. The pouch was still being held open in the hands of the hooded man. The hooded man reached for the package in Hanson's hand. Hanson pulled it away. He didn't know who I was or what I wanted. He didn't know if the person who had hired him or the man in the hooded raincoat had double-crossed him.

Hanson shoved the package in the pocket of his windbreaker. I had watched him for two days. I was fairly sure he didn't carry a gun. I was definitely sure he carried a folding knife with a blade about four inches long. I also knew that he lived in a filthy house, which I had broken into, that he did not keep the package in the apartment, and that, according to a misspelled note near the telephone, something was to happen on Pier 6 in front of the *Princess Louise* at eleven the next night, which was right now.

13

I could have simply waited for Hanson at his house, but an hour crouched on *Gordo's Riptide* was preferable. I could have tried to get Hanson to tell me where the package was, but I had the feeling from watching him for two days and buying him a beer at Shuler's Bar on Melrose where I "happened" to make his acquaintance that Hanson had done hard time and watched macho movies. I had done time too, but I didn't watch many macho movies. My taste ran to old movie melodramas.

Tracking Hanson down had taken some time but had been relatively easy. I had a list of all repair and service people who had worked in my client's house or on his property over the last six months. The list had taken me to tree pruners, housecleaners, wall painters, an Italian painting restorer, a crew that put down expensive mosaic tiles in my client's dining room and a workout instructor named James Hanson my client had fired after two weeks when the man proved to be a fraud.

James Hanson had given my client his real name, Social Security number, even address. I got my friend Lieutenant Dennis Becker to check my entire list of people who had worked for my client. The list turned up three people with records. One had two

DUIs; the second had an outstanding on unpaid alimony; and James Hanson the bogus workout instructor had a printout as long as a football field. His favorites were grand theft, breaking and entering, and robbery. He had been convicted of stealing a painting from a private house and claimed he was hired for the job by a collector named Phillips, who vigorously denied the charge and walked away. Hanson was my man.

Now Hanson looked at me.

"The guy from the bar," he shouted. "Carson."

"Name's Rockford. Private investigator. Hired to return that package in your pocket to the man you stole it from. We do it easy. We do it hard. Man I'm working for doesn't care, but I'm wet and tired. *Princess Louise*, I suggest you put your pouch away, get on your boat, and plot some other deal."

I wasn't sure how much of what I said they heard. I had shouted, but the rain was coming down even stronger, hitting the bobbing boats like drums and thumping against the wooden pier.

The hooded man stood for a second or two, accepted at least temporary defeat, and climbed back on the *Princess Louise*. Hanson did not have surrender in mind. He rushed at me. I spread my legs and arms waiting for him, blocking his way, hoping he didn't send us both over the side and onto something sharp on *Gordo's Riptide* or the ship across from it, or into the white-capped waves.

Hanson didn't fight fair. I figured that I could take him. He was younger, in good shape, but I was smarter and bigger with a hell of a lot more experiences and aches to prove it. I figured him for macho hand-to-hand. When he ran into me, he suddenly bent his head, and his skull hit my chin. I toppled backward onto my back and didn't quite black out. I grabbed the side of the pier, took a small splinter in my palm and tried to sit up. Hanson was almost back to land. I managed to stand, shake my head, feel the pain in my jaw, and let the rain hit my upturned face. I was sure I had lost him.

When I looked, Hanson was on the shore where a muddy patch or slick grass gave way. His feet shot out in front of him and he went about a yard into the air and fell hard on his back.

I ran toward him on aching knees. At first he didn't move. Then he sat up, shook his head, remembered where he was, and looked back at me coming for him. I wasn't moving fast — my knees refused to cooperate — but I was moving, and Hanson was

16

having trouble catching his breath and getting to his feet. He managed to stand and gasp for air in the now-driving rain. He stumbled toward the boathouse where, when it was open, you could buy a beer and a Nestle's Crunch.

Hanson was catching his breath and moving faster. I did something I considered running but might have been viewed as a very slow tango step by anyone who might be dumb enough to be out on a night like this.

I ran in pain, knowing that once Hanson was himself again I had no chance of catching him. We were about fifteen feet up the slight slope leading to the boathouse when I caught him. He was wearing the wrong shoes for a night like this. Mine were better. I landed on his back as hard as I could and we went down.

There was enough fight in Hanson to push me off with a sudden push-up. I was standing. He turned over on his back. We were both covered in mud. I wiped at my arm. Something that might have been used for bait was crawling on it. I brushed it away and said,

"Just stay right there."

I pointed at Hanson's face and hoped I looked as miserable and angry as I felt.

Hanson kicked one of my already screaming knees. I tried not to go down but I knew I would. Hanson was trying to roll away. I managed to land on him and straddle him.

"Hanson," I said. "I am wet. My knees are hurting, my chin is very sore and I am more than a little angry with you. Put your hand in your pocket, pull out the package slowly and hand it to me."

Hanson tried to squirm out from under me. I hit him in the forehead with the flat of my right hand. I hit him hard. He stopped squirming.

"We can split," he gasped. "Guy back on the boat will pay."

"Don't tell me how much," I said. "I'm not in the mood for temptation in a tropical storm. I've got a client. You stole something from him. He wants it back. It's simple, Hanson. Even you can understand it."

Hanson didn't move.

I cocked my right hand, not wanting to punch him. I didn't need sore knuckles on top of my other pain.

"Okay," he said spitting mud from the corner of his mouth.

He reached into his pocket, pulled out a small box. I couldn't see it too clearly but I could feel that it was wood and inlaid with something smooth.

Hanson took a swing at my neck with an

open-handed karate chop. I blocked the blow with my arm, lifted myself on my knees, and dropped my weight on Hanson's chest. He let out a wet *glug* and lay still.

I opened the hinged box and took out the bottle that fit into my palm with plenty of room to spare. From what I could make out, it was what I had come for. I put it back in the box, closed it and put it in my pocket. Getting off of Hanson and getting to my feet in the mud, rain and pain was made even harder by my unwillingness to let Hanson see what I was going through. I got up, looked down at him, smiled and said,

"Go, now."

Hanson had no reason to put on an act other than to salvage whatever remained of his pride. He did his best. It didn't help when his left hand hit a patch of mud as he pushed himself up. I'll give him credit. He got to his feet and turned to face me, the fight definitely out of him, but with an anger in his eyes I had seen hundreds of times, both in and out of prison.

"I'm gonna come for you," he said.

"You don't even know who I am," I said wearily. "I gave you my name less than two minutes ago and I'll bet you don't remember it."

The rain had slowed to a hard drive.

"I'll find out," he said, pointing at me and trying not to stagger. He was a muddy mess.

"Hanson, just walk away from it and be thankful my client wants his bottle back and doesn't want to press charges if he doesn't have to. I said 'Go,' so please do before both of us are sick enough to be taken to the hospital, where they might put us in adjacent beds. I would be one angry roommate."

Hanson hobbled into the night toward the road while I stayed where I was, doing my best to look calm as I watched him. When I was reasonably sure he was gone, I moved in agony up the slope and toward my parked car. On a better night with a pain-free body I would have been tempted to go give the guy on the *Princess Louise* a lecture on buying stolen property. I probably would have resisted the temptation. I wasn't even tempted tonight.

I should have been feeling good. I had a bonus check coming that would cover my immediate bills, including my overdue phone bill and the repair of my trailer roof, which was being pelted with rain not more than ten minutes from where I was standing, providing the trailer hadn't been washed into the ocean.

I should have been feeling good but the seasickness was not quite gone, and though my sore chin wasn't as bad as it could have been, my knees were suggesting that I go into another line of work.

Fortunately, I had an appointment the next morning with Dr. Andrew Lewiston, an orthopedic specialist and surgeon, whose office visit I would be able to pay for when I collected from my client. Lewiston had been recommended by my client, Dwight Cameron. They were fellow collectors of rare Chinese snuff bottles painted from the inside.

I had long ago given up trying to figure out why rich people did the things they did and collected what they collected: women, 200-year-old bottles of wine or Chinese snuff bottles. I was getting $200 a day plus expenses with a bonus of $600 if I got this particular, very valuable bottle back. The plan was to "reevaluate" the arrangement if I wasn't making progress after two weeks.

Cameron had started in Bismarck, North Dakota, as a supermarket manager while going to night school. He had come up with a promotion idea; $50 in free groceries when the customer accumulated $1,500 in receipts. The free groceries were limited to fruit, vegetables, milk and other perishables that the store would have wound up throwing away if they weren't purchased by the end of a day or two. The president of the chain liked the idea and instituted it in all his stores, upping the receipts required to $2,000 and giving $100 in free groceries. Dwight Cameron was promoted to vice president of promotion for the Great Northern Supermarkets with headquarters in Omaha. Dwight, the youngest of eight brothers and sisters in a family of soybean farmers, was ambitious. He praised the boss, came up with idea after idea and slowly accumulated stock in the company. In six years, Dwight was the major stockholder of Great Northern. Two years later he packed a stockholders' meeting and became president, firing his boss after buying out his shares.

Great Northern stock went up. One year after he owned most of it, Dwight Cameron sold all his shares to a larger supermarket chain at a big profit. Now worth millions, Dwight moved to California, bought real estate no one wanted, and talked the supermarket chain he had sold out into becoming the cornerstone in his shopping malls. It worked. With the supermarket coming in, other companies — big companies, small companies — joined in. Dwight Cameron was even richer.

He started to produce movies — R-rated,

straight to video — starring someone who had once been a star and featuring blood, sex and what passed for a sense of visual humor and as little dialogue as possible. His cost was about $200,000 a movie. His worldwide profit: several million a picture.

He lived in a modest — at least for the area — brick house in Malibu not too close to the ocean, but high enough to have an unrestricted view of the sea from his bedroom and living room windows. When he heard that someone was about to buy the property between Dwight Cameron and the ocean, Cameron stepped in and bought it himself to retain his view. He had been instantly proclaimed a hero of Malibu, a protector of what remained of its natural beauty. He was named Malibu Citizen of the Year after he gave the land to the city on condition that it never be built upon. Cameron's tax write-off that year was astronomical.

When I got back to Canyon Cove in Malibu not three miles from my client Dwight Cameron's house, the rain had stopped, almost. I parked next to my trailer. On my small deck, I took off all my clothes, shook them out, including my shoes, and went through my front door in soggy underpants.

I had sunk some money into renovations

before I had been shot in the knee. I had managed to pay for the deck and a repainting. Now I could pay for the roof. When the changes had been made, I had the place cleaned and even made a few minor changes with the help of Rocky and his friend Lionel. Then I went to a Realtor and put it on the market. The Realtor had said I would get every nickel I had put into the house plus more. We almost had two buyers. One couple on the verge of buying had driven through the wrong neighborhood during the Rodney King riots and decided to head back for Santa Rosa. Another couple had backed out when the fires hit Malibu and actually made it as far as my place. I had to douse my roof with a hose when the fire jumped the highway. And then there was the earthquake, a little one, but when you live in a trailer . . . I had spent what little money I had inherited from my dad, Rocky, to put the trailer back in living order and was now resigned to staying on this piece of "choice" property. I had been burglarized five times in twenty years. Not bad compared to my dwindling number of neighbors, but bad enough.

The lights were on when I stepped into the trailer carrying my soggy clothes. Sitting behind my desk reading or looking at the pictures in a very old issue of *Playboy* sat Angel Martin. Angel and I went way back, back to prison, where I'd been given a bad sentence and spent some very bad years behind bars till they found out I hadn't done the crime. Angel had done his crime and more. He was a pack rat — a little mouse, really — who picked up bits and pieces, information and goods, and shared a cell with me. There had been times he had helped me and other times when he had come close to getting me killed. Without my knowledge, he had told other inmates that I was his "enforcer." In fact, I was a bitter, cynical man who wanted to be left alone to feel sorry for himself. Eventually, I had to admit that Evelyn "Angel" Martin had helped to pass the long days and noisy prison nights and we became something like friends.

Angel looked up at me — his feet on my desk, sitting back in my chair — and shook his head. Angel has changed little over the years. Less hair on top compensated for by a full beard. Curly hair and beard had more than a touch of gray in them. He wore a pair of tan trousers and an off-white shirt unbuttoned to show a hairy chest and a silver cross that, supposedly, had been given to him by his mother.

"Jimmy," he said with something approaching disgust, "you look awful. You don't go swimming in the ocean during a storm."

"Angel," I said, digging a plastic bag out from under the sink and filling it with my clothes, including my wet underwear, "you are risking your life by coming in here."

"Nah, Jimmy," he said as I went for a towel and wrapped it around myself. "They don't know where you live, and I promised them the money tomorrow. You've got it, don't you?"

"Angel, the risk is not from whoever you owe money," I said. "It's from me. You put my father's pickup truck up for collateral. You break into my home. You put your feet on my desk, and you've probably drunk the last bottle of beer in the refrigerator."

"That was the last bottle? Sorry, Jimmy. I'll borrow your car and go get some," he said, taking his feet down and starting to get up.

"Borrow my — you don't have a car?"

"You see I was leasing, and . . ."

"How did you get here?" I asked, not sure I wanted to know.

"Bus and got a hitch with a trucker," he said. "Almost got caught in a mud slide. I've had a bad night, Jim. I could use a little succor."

26

"Succor?" I said. "Bad night?"

"Right, Jimmy," he said, coming around the desk and placing the old *Playboy* down so he wouldn't lose his place. "Just give me the keys. I'll find an open store, bring back some brews and . . . You've got the money, haven't you?"

"You can't have the keys to my car," I said. "I've grown fond of that Firebird. I'd like to see it again, drive it again, not wonder if parts of it were in a passing Oldsmobile."

"Have I ever let you down, Jimmy?" Angel asked, his hand on his heart, a tear in his eye.

"Almost every chance you've had," I said. "Now, I'm going to make a phone call to my client, take a shower, and drive up to make a delivery and collect a check, which I can cash tomorrow — when I'll loan you two hundred dollars. After I put that two hundred in your hand, I want Rocky's pickup parked outside by the end of the day. Then I don't want to see you at all till you're ready to put two hundred dollars in cash in my hand. Clear?"

Angel nodded sadly.

"Can I sleep on the couch?" he asked, pointing to the small sofa next to the window.

"Okay," I said.

"Great," Angel said. "You won't regret this, Jimmy. As God is my judge — and he surely is — I'll get Rocky's truck back and have two hundred in cash for you in less than two weeks."

"Go to sleep, Angel," I said, heading for the desk and phone.

"I think I'll read awhile," he said, going for the *Playboy*. "May I suggest you get cable?"

"They won't let me have cable." I was standing in my towel and dialing Dwight Cameron.

"Then a nice little satellite dish," Angel said, showing me with his hands how little a satellite dish could be. "They're cheap, work good."

"And you can't get local stations," I said as the phone rang once before Cameron picked it up.

"Rockford," I said. "I've got it."

"Problems?"

"Minor," I said. "I've got to shower and change and I'll bring it right over."

"I'll have the check ready," he said. "My memory and appreciation for services are long, Mr. Rockford. You could have stretched this out."

"I don't work that way," I said.

I took the box and the bottle inside it into

the shower and placed it on a shelf above the shower head. I didn't want Angel finding it. I knew he'd go through my wet pants. I had already removed my wallet and car keys. They were on the shelf with the green bottle.

After a soapy shower and shampooing twice, I felt better. Jaw simply tingled and was sore to the touch. I wiped off the mirror. It didn't look as if it were changing color or swelling. My knees were a different tale.

I dressed in slacks and a sports jacket, pocketed wallet, keys and box, and moved past Angel, who had found a pillow and was lying back with one hand behind his head reading *Playboy*. He never looked up as he said,

"Hope you didn't use all the hot water."

I didn't answer.

"And don't forget you're out of beer. Hell, you're out of just about everything but Pepto-Bismol."

"Good-bye, Angel," I said and went outside. It was no longer raining. I drove to Dwight Cameron's house. No dogs. No guards. No big gate. A few tasteful outdoor lights.

Thunder clapped over the water. I parked in the driveway. He answered the door of the big brick house himself. It was nearly two in the morning. He was dressed completely though casually in designer jeans, a green button-down short-sleeve shirt and a look of anticipation, his eyes going immediately to my hand. I gave him the package and closed the door behind me.

I had heard there was a Mrs. Cameron. I had never seen her, but then again, I had only seen Cameron once before. I don't remember how the subject of knees came up, but it had. Cameron, who was now somewhere in his fifties and looked about ten years younger and twenty years fitter, had had some kind of procedure early last year. He recommended Doc Lewiston and even made the call asking for an appointment for me as soon as possible.

Cameron was tall, lean, tan and fit. His white hair was cut military short and his teeth were a white marvel of modern care and dentistry. We stood in the entryway to the house. I could smell a fire burning and hear the crackling of wood somewhere to the left. Air-conditioning and a burning fireplace. California. There was a chandelier high overhead ready for the Phantom to cut down. The lights of the chandelier were out.

Cameron opened the box and took out the bottle. His tough eyes fought back tears as he held it up to the light.

"Perfection," he said. "Mr. Rockford, this

is perfection. The greatest master of the art of bottle-painting did this small garden scene more than sixty years ago."

He showed it to me. I nodded appreciatively.

"It took him almost a year to paint it with brushes, some of which had only a single hair, a human hair, his granddaughter's hair, painting from inside the bottle where even the slightest movement could be a disaster, destroy months of work. Mr. Rockford, there is only one bottle like this. Thousands of cheap ones are flooding the market from China, done quickly by students who take no great care and have no skill, nothing like this. If I could find a Chinese artist who could do work like this . . . Would you like to go to China, Rockford?" Cameron said with a smile.

"No, thank you," I said.

"Great acupuncture," he said, reluctantly putting the bottle back in the case, closing it, and placing it on the table near the door.

He produced a checkbook, filled out a check and handed it to me.

"Satisfactory?" he asked.

"Very generous," I said.

He held out his hand and we shook. Good grip.

"A little security around here might not be a bad idea," I suggested, tucking the check nonchalantly in my shirt pocket.

"I suppose so," Cameron said with a sigh, running his hand across his brush of white hair. "One hates to think it's necessary out here. But I'm a realist and I'll do more than take it under advisement. Hanson?"

"I've advised him strongly that he give me no more cause to look him up," I said with a smile.

Cameron smiled back. His smile was better than mine.

"Thank you, Mr. Rockford."

"Thank you, Mr. Cameron," I said, patting the pocket with the check inside.

Something stirred in the darkness at the top of the stairs. It was white, billowy, and I saw or imagined I saw a bare woman's foot reach down to the stair below. Then I was gone.

Angel was asleep and snoring when I got back with a six-pack of beer and a bag of Doritos. I had enough cash for gas to the bank in the morning. The *Playboy* was on Angel's stomach. He was wearing my favorite robe and his hands were crossed protectively over the magazine. I put the beer and Doritos away quietly, turned out the lights and went into my small bedroom. I hung

32

my clothes up, tucked the check in my wallet and put them both under my pillow and then collapsed after taking four aspirin. I could hear Angel's snoring through the door. The trailer was not built for privacy. I would have covered my head with my second pillow, but Angel had it. I rolled my pillow over my ear, thinking I would spend half the night listening to Angel and feeling my knees, especially the one Hanson had kicked. I fell asleep almost immediately.

I dreamt that Rocky and I were fishing, hip deep, reeling in salmon in a narrow-running river with deep green trees on both banks and a bright sun in the sky.

"See, sonny, I tole you," Rocky said, flashing his smile, adjusting his cap and reeling in a big one.

I woke up. The sun was coming in the window. My knees didn't ache quite so much and my wallet and check were still under the pillow. Angel was awake, finishing the bag of Doritos. He was dressed and nursing a beer.

"I thought you were gonna sleep all day," he said with irritation. "And you should have some breakfast stuff in here, like cereal or eggs or something. This isn't healthy. You got the money?"

"I got it, Angel," I said. "And you are

never to wear that robe again."

"I understand," he said, reaching for a Dorito from where he sat on the couch. He munched, dropping crumbs. "Sentimental value?"

"No, Angel. It's just mine. And I don't want you to wear it."

"Don't be touchy, Jimmy," he said. "Get yourself shaved and dressed and we'll go over to the bank, get some money, have us a decent breakfast and you can drop me off somewhere."

"I'm going to town," I said. "I've got a doctor's appointment."

"I don't trust doctors, Jim," Angel said, drinking more morning beer.

"I'll bear that in mind," I said.

The rest of the early morning went reasonably well. I shaved, dressed, took a few more aspirin with water, brushed my teeth and my hair and was ready to go in about fifteen minutes. The *Playboy* was rolled up in Angel's back pocket.

The bank deposited my check, too late to catch a couple of checks that had bounced. I paid what I owed on them and found out to whom they had been written. I gave Angel the two hundred dollars, kept out two hundred for myself, bought him breakfast at a seaside diner and listened to his plans for getting rich as a video producer. I now had about a thousand and six dollars in my bank account and bills totaling somewhere in the vicinity of the annual interest on the national debt.

I dropped Angel on Hollywood Boulevard and reminded him that I wanted Rocky's pickup back in front of my trailer by nightfall. And I wasn't forgetting about the two hundred dollars.

He was standing at the curb as I pulled away and headed for the Hollywood office of Dr. Andrew Lewiston, orthopedic surgeon. My muffler rattled just a bit. I tried to ignore it.

CHAPTER TWO

Andrew Lewiston looked way out of my league, from the big reception office to the teenage receptionist who should have been on the cover of *Sports Illustrated* but was dressed in a tasteful green dress and the perfect pearls. The nurse, dressed in white, reminded me of the well-groomed and smiling middle-aged ladies who took their grandchildren shopping at Saks and smiled benevolently at all who gazed their way.

She told me her name was Miss Caples and took me to a third employee, named Albert, who took X rays of my knees after having me put on a white gown and hanging my clothes in a locker.

Then Miss Caples took me to a small white room, took two vials of blood and, X rays in hand, led me out of the room and down the narrow, carpeted and clean-smelling corridor.

"Private investigator?"

"Yep," I said, wondering if the paintings in the hallway were originals.

"Is that interesting work?"

"Sometimes. Sometimes you have no clients for weeks or have to take jobs you weren't exactly trained for."

"Such as?"

"Right now I'm in search of a rich lady's missing Self cat. Ace Rockford, Pet Detective, that's me," I said with a smile.

She smiled back as if I were the funniest human to walk the surface of the planet.

"That could be interesting," she said, reaching out to knock at the doctor's door. "I have a cousin back in Moline who owns a Self. I'm allergic to cats."

"I'd like to get dressed now," I said.

"When the doctor is finished with you," she said with a smile I didn't believe for a second.

She knocked softly at the door in front of us.

Lewiston called to us to come in. Nurse Caples disappeared. Lewiston shook my hand, smiled. He had a good, solid grip.

Andrew W. Lewiston, MD, with plaques and certificates on his wall from the University of Illinois and Harvard Medical School, plus several certificates of residency and advance residency, placed my X rays on one of those light boxes.

I was sitting in one of the two comfortable green suede chairs across from his desk. He was seated in the other suede chair, his back to the wall full of honors and evidence of his skills. I turned around slightly. The office was impressive. Big, expensive furniture, a pitcher of lemonade on his desk with clean thin-sided tall glasses beside it. The lemonade had both ice and slices of lemon in it. I wondered if Doc Lewiston had an assistant whose job was to keep those glasses clean and that pitcher full.

He was wearing a lightweight light blue silk suit with a tie that carried the motif of stripes along with a rainbow of other stripes.

Andrew Lewiston could have been Dwight Cameron's brother. He was a little bigger than Cameron, a little heavier, a little older, but both were in good shape. Lewiston's hair was just a tad longer, with not a strand out of place, and his white had definite overtones of the dark strands of his earlier days. He was handsome, completely confident, very affable and I didn't like him.

I was in a bad mood. Getting undressed and putting on a white gown that tied in the back hadn't helped it any. Lewiston probed my knees, took my pulse, listened to my heart and stood back.

"Dwight called last night," he said. "Like a kid with his first BB gun. That bottle is almost priceless. Dwight has one hell of a collection, probably the second best in the United States."

"Let me guess," I said.

Lewiston smiled and said,

"Right. I've got the best. That's how Dwight and I met a few years ago. We'd both heard of each other and found ourselves bidding for the same bottle at an auction. As I recall, it was a head of Andrew Jackson. I already had an Andrew Jackson, but it's good to have a backup, don't you think?"

"A backup is a good idea," I agreed, putting my hands on my aching knees.

"Well, as I said, I had a full collection of the presidents done in the twenties. Not the highlight of my collection, but an eye-catcher. You should come and see my collection sometime."

"I'd love it," I said, knowing that an invitation like that was no invitation at all. Besides, I was there to get my knees examined.

"I gave Dwight that Jackson two weeks after we met," he said.

I looked up. He laughed.

"No, we're not gay. We just became friends, fellow collectors and tennis partners. His wife and mine are friends, too."

"That's nice," I said.

"Let's talk about these X rays," he said with a smile, right hand on my shoulder.

Things were looking decidedly bad.

"Jim," he said, pointing to a place in the X ray where two bones met, "what do you see here, between the bones?"

"Nothing, Andy," I said, wondering if he would take the familiarity any better than I was. He did. He was going to get paid. And what could he do? Ask me to call him Dr. Lewiston? I planned to compromise in the future and call him "Doc."

"Nothing, Jim," he agreed. "There should be a layer of cartilage between those two bones where your knee is. On both pictures, there's nothing, only that ghostly thin remnant in your right knee, which is doing you no good."

"So?"

"Without that layer," he said, looking at my X ray with compassion, "your bones grind together. Arthritis. The pain you're feeling in that leg is that grinding. If you walk moderately, you should be fine. If you try running or doing exercises that slap those two bones together, you not only wear them down, it will hurt like hell. Your other knee . . . That's a different story. What happened?"

"Like I said on the form your receptionist

had me fill out, I was shot about four, five years ago," I said. "Had surgery. Now I have pain, and a big flight of stairs looks like Mount McKinley to me. Give me some choices, Doc."

Now he turned to me and smiled with hope. I watched him walk around his desk and sit behind it in a green swivel chair that matched the one I was sitting in.

"First, we can give you knee replacements. Simple operation. You're off your feet for two to six weeks and then you can frolic again. However, you're a little young for a replacement, though we really don't have much choice with the knee that took the bullet. Whoever did the surgery was adequate, but . . . I don't see any way past a knee replacement. However, at your age, my guess is you'd need another one in about ten or twelve years."

"Other choices," I said.

"You could just live with it. Many do. I can prescribe pain medication and advise you not to do any running, which, given your profession, I assume might be a problem. Or we can do a new procedure on the left knee while I replace the right one," he said. "Well, not so new a procedure anymore. We take the cartilage of a cadaver and insert it in your knee. It's fast and you could

41

be up, walking, playing tennis, in days. I did it for Dwight and he's on the court running painlessly. The problem is this."

He pointed at the X ray of the knee that had taken the bullet. It looked like pieces from a puzzle put together with pieces of metal, which is what it was.

"I don't play tennis," I said. "But I can live with a little cadaver cartilage in my knee."

"Good," he said. "There's a waiting list, but because of what you've done for Dwight, I'll see to it that you get moved up. You'll be in bed for a few days in physical therapy, out on crutches a day later and a new man in a matter of weeks."

"Thanks," I said, finishing my lemonade and knowing my glass would disappear the second I went through the door. I stood up and said, "About the cost of this. I don't have insurance, and . . ."

"I don't talk money," said Doc Lewiston, pouring himself a refreshing lemonade. "I leave that up to Miss Caples. I've told her, however, that you are to get a twenty-five percent discount on any office visits and surgical procedures or treatments."

He pushed a button on his phone, still holding the glass of lemonade. Then he came around the desk, took off his half-glasses, laid them carefully on the corner of the desk and shook my hand.

The door opened and the smiling Nurse Caples stood aside to let me pass. Doc Lewiston was taking down my X rays as we left and Nurse Caples closed the door. I followed her down the antiseptic wooden inlaid floor, past the paintings that might have been authentic and into an office that read: JANET CAPLES, RN.

It was about a quarter of the size of Doc Lewiston's but it was no-nonsense and the furniture looked severe, black metal and recent.

"Your bill for today's visit is $234," she said, tearing a prepared sheet from the pad in front of her. She handed me the bill. "You got a twenty-five percent discount from the doctor. He must really like you."

"We're considering moving in together and maybe adopting a baby," I said. "Can I get dressed now?"

Nurse Janet Caples didn't smile. She nodded to acknowledge that I had spoken. My payment from Dwight Cameron was almost gone the minute I paid this bill.

"I'm sure your insurance will cover most of this," she said.

"I have no health insurance," I said. "No one will insure me. I pay cash and I hold the receipts for my accountant."

She nodded and looked worried.

"Even with the twenty-five percent discount," she said, "the cost of a cadaver procedure will be six thousand dollars."

"Six thousand?"

"Maybe a hundred dollars more or less," she said, her hands folded in front of her as I counted out the payment for today's visit.

"How much is a knee replacement?" I asked. "With the twenty-five percent discount for old buddies?"

Nurse Caples shook her head and smiled at my naivete.

"The surgery alone is four thousand dollars."

"For both . . . ?"

"Per knee," she said. "And then hospital costs. My guess is we're looking at close to ten thousand dollars."

"Lady, I've got one hundred and eight dollars and some change in my pocket, and the only case I've got for sure is a missing cat."

"Doctor Lewiston can recommend a surgeon who might be able to do it for a bit less," she said. "Mr. Rockford, you came to the best. You must expect to pay for the best."

Dwight Cameron had sent me here.

44

Dwight Cameron had enough money to have the surgeon general operate on him.

"I'm sorry, Miss Caples . . ."

"Janet will be fine," she said with a knowing smile.

"Janet, there's no way I could ever come up with that kind of money. I'll just have to learn to live with a little pain and take the medication Dr. Lewiston said he would prescribe."

She reached over for another pad neatly laid next to the one that had the bills. She had a whole row of pads of different sizes and colors. She tore off the top sheet of one and handed it to me. It was a prescription.

"I can give you a small supply at no charge," she said. "Manufacturer's samples. But then . . ."

I took the prescription, folded it and tucked it in my wallet as she opened a drawer and came out with a small box that rattled as she handed it to me. I opened it to take a look. There was a little bottle with white capsules inside.

I started to get up, telling myself the pills would work miracles, that my running and jumping days were not over, that if I could just control or get rid of the pain, I'd be on the road to being a happy man.

"Wait," Nurse Caples said, holding up a

hand. "Maybe Dr. Lewiston has an idea. Why don't you go get dressed and I'll take you back to his office."

I didn't like the way she had done that. It definitely looked rehearsed, but I had no choice. She picked up her phone, pushed a button and almost immediately said,

"You have ten minutes till your next appointment, Doctor. Could you give Mr. Rockford a minute or two more of your time? It seems he has no insurance and little prospect for immediate or even long-term income."

She was silent, listening, and then she hung up.

"When you're dressed, please come back here," she said.

After I had my clothes on and felt a lot less vulnerable, back we went to the office of Doctor Andrew W. Lewiston. Nurse Caples knocked. I entered, and she disappeared. Lewiston was behind his desk looking at a file with furrowed brow. He might be able to fix a bad knee or a broken neck but I was better at the game we were now playing. I'd been playing it for a long time.

"What's the deal, Andy?" I said.

Lewiston looked up from the intriguing file and his serious look turned to a small, sad smile.

"I understand that you have no insurance and you can't pay for either procedure," he said. "I could come down a little, but not much."

"You set me up," I said, not sitting. "Want me to figure it?"

"Figure . . . ?"

"You knew from Dwight Cameron that I was a private investigator," I said. "I did a good, fast job for him and when I made my appointment, you checked on my income, bank account, insurance and worldly goods. Not hard to do, especially for a doctor."

"Those really are discount figures," he said, putting on his half-glasses and leaning forward to fold his hands on the desk.

"I believe it, Andy," I said. "But this is way out of my league and you know it. What do you want?"

"Well," he said, pouring himself some lemonade, "my niece is missing. I've informed the police. They tell me she is eighteen and has a right to disappear. They promised to look into it, but, Mr. Rockford, I don't think they have any intention of doing so. Los Angeles must have more missing girls than the total population of Fresno."

"You want me to find your niece?"

He handed me a laminated wallet-sized photograph from the file that he had been studying. She was young, pretty, long blonde hair, even teeth. She looked like half the girls in Los Angeles.

"Her name is Barbie, Barbie Lewiston," he said, studying his glass of lemonade through his half-glasses. "My brother's daughter. He's a urologist in Little Rock. Very successful practice. My brother asked me to look after her while she took acting lessons, and he asked if I could set up interviews for her with producers or people I know in the business. I said I would. I got the idea that he probably preferred that Barbie fail and return to Little Rock, but Barbie just got out of high school and is . . . let's say, a bit unpredictable."

"I'll bet she was a cheerleader," I said, still holding the photograph.

"Yes," he said. "And she acted in school plays. I actually saw her in one when I visited them for a few days last spring. She played the girl in *The Glass Menagerie*. To say that she was awful is giving her the benefit of the doubt. I'll give her 'enthusiastic,' but that's the best I could do. So, she came out here. I set up some appointments, expecting the people I sent her to to let her down gently. Four days ago when she didn't come down for breakfast, I went to her room and found this."

Lewiston handed me a piece of lined paper torn from a steno notebook. Printed in ink was: "Uncle Andy, One of the kind people you sent me to is going to take care of me and my career. I'll be in touch soon. Thank you for all your help."

It was signed "Barbie."

"The police had no interest in seeing the note," said Lewiston, downing what was left in his glass and considering a nibble on the lemon at the bottom by playing with it with his long fingers.

"And the deal?" I asked.

"Cartilage in both your knees. No charge."

"Hospital?"

"No charge."

"That's a generous offer, Doc."

"Dwight says you're a good man and that you work quickly."

"You've got a deal," I said, reaching over to shake his hand. "I may need a few hundred dollars to stay alive."

"I'll have Nurse Caples return the money you paid for this visit," he said.

I shook my head and he handed me a sheet of paper from the file.

"It's a list of all the people I sent Barbie

to, mostly former patients and people I know socially. The addresses and phone numbers are there, too."

"And when I find her?" I asked, taking the file and putting in the note and Barbie Lewiston's photograph. "She's eighteen. Legal age."

"Just find her, tell me where she is and with whom," he said, deciding definitely to nibble the lemon. "I'll take care of getting her back to Little Rock even if I have to have my brother and her mother come and get her. But I accepted responsibility for her, and . . ."

"I've got the picture," I said, holding up the file. "And you've got me. It's a fair deal, but you think you might put it in writing and get a signed copy of the agreement to me by the end of the day? You have my address."

He dropped what was left of the lemon back in his glass and said,

"That can definitely be arranged. Keep me informed."

"One more thing," I said. "Have all the people listed in this folder had knee replacements or knee surgery from you?"

"I don't see how —" he began.

"You fix knees. I do investigations," I said. "I won't operate on you and you don't tell me how to find a missing person."

"You're right," he said. "Yes, most of them have."

I handed the folder back to him and told him to mark whatever procedure or operation he did on each name on the list. He sat, opened the folder, wrote quickly and handed the folder back to me.

"I may have to push the truth a little when I talk to these people," I said. "I'll protect your good name, and you have your staff confirm that I'm a patient if anyone on this list calls to check on me. You don't know I'm a private investigator. You don't know what I do for a living. Can you live with that?"

"Surgeons learn to make compromises with everything but the patient's health," he said somberly.

I waved the folder at him and went out of the door to Nurse Caples' office. Her door was open. She had an envelope in her hand. I took it and waited till I was back on the street before I counted it. There were six fifty-dollar bills. I'd made a profit. Finding Barbie Lewiston should have been easy money. But you'd think after all the years I'd put in being a private investigator, I'd know there isn't any easy money.

When I got back home, the surf was up

and a few bleached-out kids were riding it and saying, "guy" to each other a lot.

That was the first thing I noticed. The second thing I noticed was that Rocky's pickup wasn't back. Third, but not least, I noticed a recent-vintage blue Lexus parked right in front of my door. I got out of the car with my folder trying to come up with a story for my client with the Lexus. She saw me and got out of her car.

Her name was Olivia Carstairs. She was sixty-five, wearing a dress that would have been perfect for a 1920s masked ball. The dress was green, sequined and just a bit revealing. Her black shoes had heels just shy of a fetishist's dream. As for Olivia, she was still a handsome woman, with white hair and too much makeup. Her earrings glittered like her dress. She clutched a small purse and did not look happy.

"I've been waiting for fifteen minutes," she said.

"I had a doctor's appointment," I said.

"We had an appointment."

"An appointment? I said I'd call you this morning. That's not an appointment, Mrs. Carstairs."

"Let's go in," she said, shaking her head at my inability to maintain a calendar.

She glanced at the boys on their surfboards and then led the way to my door. She smelled of some ancient, sweet and expensive perfume as I inched past her and opened the trailer door.

The place could have been in worse shape. I did not normally meet clients here. In fact, it was my policy not to meet clients here, but sometimes it couldn't be helped. My clients came from referrals. There were seasons when I was reasonably flush and on a retainer from two separate insurance companies. There were seasons I wasn't on a retainer from anyone, and when I panicked in a bad month I took on a client like Olivia Carstairs, who looked disapprovingly around the room. The pillow Angel had borrowed was still on the couch. The blanket was folded, but not neatly on top of it. No stray items of clothing littered the room but yesterday's newspaper was on the floor opened to the sports page.

Mrs. Carstairs checked the chair across from my desk for dust mites and elephants that may have come there to die and then she sat down, purse in her lap, waiting for me to sit across from her. I did and put the list from Doc Lewiston on the desk in front of me.

"Have you made any progress in finding Douglas?" she said as I eased deeper into

53

my chair, the pills from Nurse Caples jiggling in my shirt pocket.

Douglas was Olivia Carstairs' cat. She had named him for her long-dead husband, Douglas Carstairs, who had put together a fortune as a talent agent. He had picked beginners carefully, traveling around the country to little theaters in Davenport and points north, east, west and south. He had signed the talent, pushed them at the studio and sat back with ten percent. Some of his clients became big stars. Some became small stars. Almost all of them worked, sometimes as bellboys in a TV soap with a single line, "May I take your bags, sir?" Doug Carstairs got ten percent of that, too. He invested in coffee shares, oil shares — shares of anything except television or movies. He knew too much about them and he wasn't about to take risks. "When you make movies," he had once been quoted in the *Hollywood Reporter*, "you win one and you lose six. You don't talk about the six, the six that make the one big picture an almost break-even." So he had invested in actors and hard goods using a smart broker who took ten percent of Doug. When Doug finally had one cigar and three heart attacks too many, he died and left Olivia — whose career on stage, screen and television had lasted two years back in the fifties — enough money to buy a fleet of aircraft carriers plus the island of Guam.

Olivia lived quietly, unpretentiously, in a ten-room villa in Beverly Hills on the interest from her husband's investments. She sold her husband's agency and, therewith, the contracts of her husband's clients, in a semi-legal deal with a group called Talent Investment Marketing, or TIM as they were known and hated in the industry.

"Douglas," she said, looking at me with green eyes that were not about to turn away.

"I'm working on it," I said. "I'm following several very good leads. I'd say I should have Douglas back to you in a week."

"I find it difficult to believe you," she said.

"It's true," I said with a confident shrug, leaning forward with a knowing grin. "My guess, from what I've put together, is that someone took Douglas with the idea of asking for ransom, and . . ."

"I would pay," Olivia Carstairs said immediately. "Even if the sum were mildly outrageous."

"I think they lost the cat, Douglas," I went on, making the damn thing up. "Douglas wandered the streets of Los Angeles looking for you. A man picked him up and took him home as a pet. That much, and the first name of the man and the area in which he lives, I know. I'm in the process of having one of my operatives finish tracking down the man and Douglas and offering him a modest reward for your cat's return."

"You have operatives?" she said, looking around my less than palatial trailer-office-home.

"Several," I said. "I pay them by the job."

"I expected you to find Douglas personally," she said. "I am paying for you upon recommendation of Helene Kovonovich."

"I'll be right there at the end to handle the final negotiations," I said reassuringly.

"One week?" she asked suspiciously.

"Let's say five days, probably less," I said with confidence and a nod of my head.

"I pay you no more till you put Douglas in my arms," she said.

"Your initial payment was adequate," I said.

Actually, she had paid very well. The problem was I had spent it just as well on repairing the transmission of my Firebird.

Helene Kovonovich, the Countess Helene of the Romanov line, was actually a refugee from Poland who had hired me to find and put an end to a man named Victor who threatened to expose her and take away the round of wealthy friends like Olivia Carstairs upon whom she lived. The movie-industry rich and those who had made their bundles in other ways, some quite legal, also sought the lovely countess, who was supposedly twelfth in line for the throne of Russia. I found Victor, told him the countess was prepared to press blackmail charges and accept her exposure. I had told Victor that she was on her way back to Europe in the next few weeks. I had told Victor, who was no more than five-two, to accept defeat. He did, and I gave him a hundred dollars for his time and trouble. Now Helene sent me an occasional client, like Olivia Carstairs.

Mrs. Carstairs rose elegantly.

"If you find the man who actually took Douglas initially," she said, "I want him beaten savagely and ordered to leave the state."

I didn't like this new Mrs. Carstairs. I didn't know where she had come from, but if she could say this about a kitten-napper who may not have existed, she might say something like that to someone else about me.

"I don't do things like that, Mrs. Carstairs."

"I'd pay well, Mr. Rockford, and you are a big man," she said, determined not to let the idea drop.

"I'll find Douglas and bring him back to

you," I said, standing with her. "Hurting people was not part of our agreement, nor was my giving you the name of the person or persons responsible. The deal was I find your cat. I return your cat. I get paid. Is that still the deal, or do you want to search the Yellow Pages for a new investigator?"

"Five days," she said, moving to the door and pausing. "But I think your story is a fabrication and you have no idea where Douglas is."

"Fabrication?" I said, showing that I was surprised and deeply hurt.

"*Bull shit,* if you prefer that language," she said.

And she left, closing the door quietly behind her.

I waited till I heard the Lexus's engine purr away. The surfers were laughing hysterically. I went to the sink, rinsed a cup, took two of the pain pills, and washed them down with tap water. Then I made a fresh pot of coffee and just stood there waiting for it to finish perking. When it was done I filled my yellow cup, the one with DENTAL MANAGEMENT CLINIC printed in black on the side, and went to my desk.

My knees seemed much better. I doubted it was the pills; too soon. But whatever the reason, the pain was hiding and ready to strike when I least or most expected it.

I took a sip of coffee and pulled out my desk drawer. I removed a brown eight-by-ten envelope and dumped the photographs of Douglas the Cat on my desk. Olivia Carstairs had given me dozens of pictures of the cat, a long-haired orange cat with a flat face. Douglas was a good-sized cat. He had an imperial air about him, or Olivia had simply waited to catch him that way. There were a few photos of Douglas playing with a variety of objects — balls, a leather mouse, a box of cereal — but mostly I had Douglas before me with competition ribbons and silver cups surrounding him.

I didn't have the damndest idea where Douglas was. I had spent two hours calling animal shelters and describing the cat. No such inmate. I had called Animal Control, which usually waits a while before exterminating strays because Beverly Hills strays often prove to belong to some pretty important people. Animal Control didn't have Douglas.

I could run around Beverly Hills calling out, "Here, Douglas. Here, kitty, kitty." I could knock at doors and ask people like Demi Moore, Larry Gelbart, and Don Johnson if they'd seen a cat with long orange hair and a pushed-in face. I was fairly certain neither approach would yield me a cat. I left the photographs on the desk to make me feel guilty and try to think of something to help me find the cat.

I opened the Lewiston sheet and looked down a pretty impressive list of names, movie and television names, at least the ones I recognized. There were neatly typed phone numbers and Lewiston's handwritten notations next to each name — broken arm, knee replacement, slipped disk, cartilage insertion, etc.

I checked my machine for messages. There were four of them. The first was from Olivia Carstairs, who said she was on her way for our appointment. The second was Vince Tremonis of Northern Casualty, who said he might have some work for me in about a month and to let him know if I was interested. It would take me out of state for a while. The third call was from a credit card company, my only credit card, telling me to send in a payment immediately; the card was now over the limit. The last call was from Angel, his voice filled with genuine anguish:

"Jimmy, it's me. Things didn't go right. Those guys. They said I owed them interest. Another hundred. They won't give me Rocky's pickup till I come up with the money. I'm desperate. I'm distraught. I'm considering suicide. You gotta help me. Just one more time. They gave me three days. Then they're gonna keep the pickup and do something unpleasant to me. I'll get back to you real soon."

Those were the messages. I started on Lewiston's list. There were eight names. I began to make calls starting at the top. The odds were against striking it rich on the first one, but all eight had to be called. The first was a producer named Carl Corbin. I'd seen him once at a restaurant. Heavy-set guy with a trim white beard and a confident white suit. His gold mine was an actor named Richard Lamotta, a karate champion — who you could buy by the busload in Hollywood. Corbin had parlayed Lamotta into a television series that had been top 30 for four years. He had also made two features with Lamotta, a young, good-looking Mexican who did his best to sound like Ricardo Montalban but sounded more to me like Cheech Marin.

I tried the office number first and got a bingo.

"My name is Rockford," I told the woman who answered. "I'd like to speak to Mr. Corbin. He was recommended to me by Dr. Lewiston."

"Dr. Lewiston," she repeated as if she were writing the name.

"Please give me a number where he can reach you," she said politely.

"I'm afraid I've got to leave for an appointment," I said, sounding disappointed. "I won't take a minute of his time, and Dr. Lewiston did say I should speak to him."

"One moment, please," she said and put me on hold.

A man's voice came on about a minute later.

"This is Carl Corbin," he said evenly. "You say Andy Lewiston told you to call me?"

"That's right," I said. "I'm contemplating some surgery from Dr. Lewiston and he said you were a satisfied patient. I'm due for the knee transplants just like you."

"Lewiston is great," said Corbin. "Overcharges, but so do I. That answer your question?"

"Almost," I said. "But I'm a cautious man, wouldn't have gotten where I am without being cautious."

"And where are you?" Corbin said with an almost imperceptible sigh.

"Riding fast on the information superhighway. I'm the president of R&R Supergraphics. Software, CD-ROMs. Moving into live-action interactives right now."

"Maybe we could do some business, Mr. . . ."

"Rockford. James Rockford. I can have one of my associates set up a meeting. Carl," I said softly and slowly, "right now I simply want a few minutes of your personal and valuable time to see the results of Dr. Lewiston's operation. I'm a cautious man and I like to think that my time too is valuable, and lying in bed or walking on crutches for a week or two can cost me deals and dollars. You understand?"

"How are you fixed for brunch today?" he said. "I've got a client I'm brunching with, but you can join us. Little Thai Palace, on La Cienega. You know it?"

"I know it."

"Eleven o'clock. Reservations in my name. Maybe we'll be able to talk a little business."

"I look forward to it," I said.

"Andy Lewiston is a great doctor," he said and hung up.

I marked the time and the location of the lunch in my notebook. With seven more to go and I don't know how many lunches, dinners and drinks, I hoped Corbin was planning to pick up the tab. I wanted to take it easy on expenses.

I finished my second call, having no great

success in getting anyone to answer the single phone number given to me by Lewiston, when I heard a car pull up outside and park.

I was about to make my third call when I put down the phone and waited to see who it was. It might even be a lost surfer.

It was Angel.

"I know what you're thinkin', Jimmy, but you've got it all wrong," he said, bursting through my door without knocking.

"Knock, knock, Angel," I said.

Angel stopped bewildered.

"This is no times for games, Jimmy," he said. "But okay, who's there?"

"No game, Angel," I said. "You come to my door. You knock. I say, 'Who is it?' or 'Come in?' or I don't answer."

"Jimmy," he said, plopping on the couch and putting his arm over his eyes. "These guys are vultures."

He sat up suddenly.

"You got something to eat? I couldn't find the *TV Guide* last night."

"You're not staying here tonight, Angel," I said. "I want Rocky's pickup. Do you have it?"

"Boy, you are in a bad mood," said Angel, looking at me.

"I've got reasons. Just answer the question."

"You mean . . ."

"Yes, I mean . . . ," I said.

"Well, the God's truth, Jimmy, is that I don't have Rocky's pickup, not yet. I called you. Left a message. These guys want another hundred."

I started to get up from my chair, and Angel's hands came up to stop me from whatever I was going to do.

"Look," he said. "I'm here in good faith. I could have hid away somewhere."

"You want me to give you the hundred, Angel," I said.

"Need, Jimmy. Need. *Want* is too weak a word. It's simple. The guys I owed the money to want another hundred bucks. A lousy hundred. They say it's vig, interest. A hundred bucks in three days and I get Rocky's pickup back."

"I've got a better idea, Angel," I said. "I call the pickup in as stolen and you tell me who these guys are."

Angel laughed, the kind of laugh that said what I was telling him was beyond funny. It was well up in the stratosphere of suicidal.

"They're not in the big leagues," Angel said, "but they've got friends and sharp tools. Jimmy, a little heart here for an old friend."

"Father, can you spare a quarter for an

ex–altar boy," I said, going to the refrigerator for a beer. I had stopped for a six-pack at Angelo's on the way home. I threw one to Angel.

"Thanks, Jimmy, I can use this."

We opened cans, drank for a minute and he looked at me hopefully.

"Tell you what I'll do, Angel," I said, handing a folder across my desk.

He held his beer in one hand, eyed me suspiciously and took the pile of photographs of Douglas the Cat I handed him. He put the beer can on the floor on top of yesterday's *L.A. Times*.

"These are cats, Jimmy," Angel said, looking at me with a squint and a tilt of the head that showed he wasn't keeping up with where we were going.

"Wrong, Angel," I said and took a drink. "That is one cat, a Self cat with long, orange fur. Self cats have been bred to have pushed-in faces and little noses. Now you know as much as I do. Here are some pictures. The cat's name is Douglas. He is owned by a very wealthy lady who wants him back and will pay generously. Not stupidly, but generously."

"I know how these rich old ladies can be about their pets," Angel said, interested now. "Who is she?"

66

"Sorry, Angel," I said. "I'm going to give you a general neighborhood and assume you've got or will find contacts in the pet-nabbing business. You find Douglas —"

"Douglas?"

"The cat, Angel. You find Douglas and I give you the hundred, plus an additional two hundred the minute I see Rocky's pickup outside my door."

"I'll need some working capital," said Angel. "I've got to go to animal shelters, pet shops, the kind of people you mentioned. I might have to fork over a few dollars and maybe even pay a ransom."

"So you agree?"

"The job intrigues me," said Angel. "Let's say a hundred in advance and the other two hundred when I hand you the cat. Shouldn't be too hard."

He looked at the pictures of Douglas.

"What kind of cat you say he is?"

"Self," I said. "They're rare. You can't mistake them for any other cat. You can stop at the library and do some research. You can also call in every day and tell me what you've found."

"Got you, Jimmy," he said standing up, finishing his can of beer and putting the empty on my desk. His hand was out. I fished six twenties from my pocket and handed them to him.

Angel grinned.

"I want you looking for that cat," I said.

"Jimmy, I don't want those guys hurting Rocky's pickup," he said, pocketing the bills. "You know that."

"Then why did you put it up as collateral, Angel?"

"Desperate, Jimmy," he said. "A desperate man will consider digging deep into his own mother's life savings."

"You already did that, Angel," I reminded him. "One more question before you leave."

"Can't I just . . . ?"

I didn't speak. I gave him my best exasperated look and folded my arms.

"What's the question?" he asked defeated, reaching for the door.

"Where did you get a car to drive out here?"

"You don't want to know," he said with a sickly smile.

"Probably not," I said, "but I'm considering a whole list of options, none of which appeals to me."

"Rental," he said so softly that I could barely hear him.

"Say again?"

"Rented it," he said.

"You don't have a working credit card,"

I reminded him. "If you did, you'd go to a cash machine and pay these guys off."

"Well, Jimmy," he said, the door open now, "I don't have a working credit card, but you do."

I knew my card was in my pocket tucked inside my wallet, but I also knew Angel.

"What kind of car am I renting?" I said through clenched teeth.

Angel ran out the door. I followed him to the top of my steps. The sea was dark and the waves were splashing high and noisy. Angel leapt into a blue convertible, unknown vintage, a gas addict.

"Got it from Abe's Broken Bumpers," he called, turning the ignition and backing out as I came toward him. "See, I got a cheapie. Don't want to waste your money. Pay it all back. Every penny. And I'll find Dominick."

He held up the folder full of cat photographs.

"Douglas," I shouted.

Angel waved and was gone. The one thing I believed, that I clung to as he clanked away, was that he didn't want anything to happen to Rocky's pickup. He knew that was a big one that wouldn't be forgotten. At least I hoped so. I had no idea if he could find Olivia Carstairs's cat, but if anyone could, it was probably Angel.

I went back inside, threw away the empty beer cans, cleaned up the floor, took off my pants and lay down for a nap and to rest my knees. What happened to the Hippocratic Oath? Didn't it apply to knee surgeons?

The machine could take my calls. When I got up, I'd set up the rest of the appointments I had to make to find Barbie Lewiston.

I fell asleep. The night before had been long and Angel had been loud. Normally the sound of the waves puts me to sleep no matter what, but Angel's snoring, weeping in his sleep, and laughing as if in the throes of some sensual ecstasy had been too much even for me.

It was early. I still had a pretty young blonde to find. Considering this was Los Angeles, there couldn't be a better place to find one generically and a worse place to find a specific one.

CHAPTER THREE

I was late for my lunch at the Little Thai Palace on La Cienega. I hadn't overslept. I had been up early, showered, shaved, shampooed, returned a few calls and decided what to wear, figuring twenty minutes tops with parking to get to the Little Thai Palace.

I settled on the confident look of an out-of-towner who had heard how laidback Los Angeles power brokers were. The laidback look was actually on the way out, except for actors. I put on my best blue jeans, a white shirt with a button-down collar and no tie, and a lightweight sports jacket with a casual tweedy look.

Then I finished setting up meetings with the people on Doc Lewiston's list. Some of the names I recognized. Lewiston's name got me through to them or a promise to call me back and leave a message. The ones I reached all seemed satisfied with the good doctor's work, though many found a way to make it clear that when you get the best you have to pay for the best.

The knock at the door was insistent. I was checking my pants, my story and my business cards when the knock came. I had decided to be early. I had just hung up the phone and checked my watch.

The knock came again.

It was Mr. Travis, the president of the trailer park owners association. He prided himself on his resemblance to Hume Cronyn, a resemblance that existed primarily in the mind of Mr. Travis. Mr. Travis was a determined man, though the world had long passed him by. There had been several dozen trailer homes in the park when I moved in shortly after getting my pardon and setting up shop as a private detective. I had gotten the place as payment for my first big case.

At the time, the association had decided to petition the city of Malibu to have my trailer torn down. It hadn't been lived in for two years and looked it. With the help of my father and a few of our friends we put it back together, scrounged some furniture, bought some paint and made it livable. After we were finished, in fact, a few of the already existing trailers looked a little shabby and were visited by the committee.

That was almost two decades ago. Fred and Connie Travis were president and vice president of the owners association back then, when they had their teeth and their kids still visited them. Now the association was just the Travises, whose place looked like it had just been plunked down and rested next to the rocks on the other side of the lot surrounded by plants, flowers and a fence with a KEEP OUT sign.

In addition to me and the Travises, there were the Websters, who had bought their place a few years ago unable to believe their luck: living in a real cove in Malibu on the water for just five times what the trailer was worth. They had one little boy about six and Mr. Webster had a good job as a chef in town. Mrs. Webster, Laura, had all the backbone, and plenty of it. Normally, the Travises and Laura Webster were at each other over driveways, public access, my late hours and strange guests, noise, and proposed improvements.

"Fred," I said with a broad false smile. "Good to see you. Been a while."

"We must talk, Mr. Rockford," Fred said solemnly.

He was white of hair and tan of face, which had given him a few skin cancers, which he had dealt with quickly and efficiently. Now he wore a wide-brimmed cowboy hat to keep his face in shadows. The man from nowhere seeking truth, justice and the American way.

"Fred," I said, stepping down and closing

the door behind me, "I'd love to. Tonight. I've got an appointment, and —"

"Now," said Travis. "I must be insistent."

It was then I stopped, put my hands together in front of me, squinted into the sun at the shadow of Travis's face and waited.

"Your dues are overdue," he said.

"Fred," I said. "There are no dues. There is no longer an association. The Websters won't pay and I won't pay. I never joined the association. I never attended a meeting. Your bill came under my door every three or four months and I paid it. I wondered what it was being spent for, but I was a good neighbor. I paid. Now, with just three owners left, our fees have gone up to two hundred dollars a quarter. Fred, old buckaroo, I just ain't paying."

"We have fewer home owners. We need more money," he said in exasperation, taking off his hat and whacking it against his side just like Ward Bond used to do. "We've got landscape to maintain, custodial care, intangibles."

"I pay my own water and electric bills," I said. "I've got a company that overcharges me to maintain my toilet. The city repaves the lot every five years. There's a beach right-of-way so we can't put up fences to keep people out of the lot. Whatever insurance I need, I've got when I can make my payments. I'm sorry, partner. No hard feelings, but I'm no longer a member of the Canyon Cove Trailer Owners Association."

"Webster's said the same," Fred said with a sigh, putting his hat back on and looking toward the water for an answer. "We had hopes for this place. You know, ads in papers back East inviting people to consider moving to this choice location and living in a trailer home. Someday Rockford, if we don't rebuild this place, the city's gonna take it from us. Then where do Connie and I go?"

"Fred, I wish I knew. Why don't you sell now and go live with one of your kids or in a small condominium?"

He shook his head.

"We like it right here. It's home."

I wasn't quite sure of the comparison Fred wanted me to make, but I was sure it was from old Westerns. We were the original cowboys and we were being threatened by greedy land developers, sheepherders, competitors ignoring us and using our water. I patted him on the shoulder. There wasn't much there to pat and I said,

"Buena suerte and *adios, amigo."*

I got in my car, gave the old rancher a wave and drove off away toward the high sun. I was late.

75

Twenty minutes later, missing every light and driving behind the mad, the ancient, and the indifferent of Los Angeles, I made it to La Cienega and found a parking spot that demanded lots of quarters. I didn't have lots of quarters. I drove around the block and found a space in the loading zone of a bootery shop that was definitely closed and for sale.

Carl Corbin was easy to spot the instant I stepped through the red doors of the Little Thai Palace. The lights were low, but there were very few tables and only four booths. I had heard that it was one of the newly rediscovered places for the rich and infamous to be seen. The Little Thai had responded by jacking up its prices as high as a Siamese elephant's eye. They were riding the waves while they were rolling with them and not over them.

Corbin was in a booth. A man sat next to him. I recognized Richard Lamotta and would have even if he weren't wearing dark glasses inside a dark restaurant, the celebrity wanting to be spotted.

"Sorry I'm late," I said, easing into the seat across from them. "I'm Jim Rockford, R&R Industries."

I fished out an all-purpose R&R card that said I was the president of the company and handed it to him. The number was Angelo's Pizza and so was the address. Corbin looked at the card, placed it on the table and said,

"Carl Corbin. And this, as you probably know, is Richard Lamotta."

Corbin held out his hand. We shook. Lamotta simply nodded, still incognito, though there were only four other people in the restaurant and they didn't seem to be looking our way.

"I took the initiative and ordered for us," said Corbin. "Hope you don't mind."

I shrugged. "I was late. You were being polite."

"Andrew Lewiston is a great surgeon," Corbin said.

I nodded and looked at Lamotta, who didn't look back. He was dressed in black from shoes and socks to slacks, turtleneck shirt and silk zipper jacket.

"I guess that basically ends our conversation on the subject," I said as a waiter, who had obviously been told to wait for me to arrive, suddenly appeared with a tray full of food. "I trust your recovery was complete."

"Complete, and rapid and expensive, Mr. Rockford," Corbin said, checking each dish as it was placed on the table.

The waiter stepped back. He looked Chinese to me. Corbin nodded that all was well and the man disappeared. I drank some water and Corbin said,

"Allow me."

He served himself and me. The waiter returned with a plate he placed in front of Lamotta. It looked like a piece of broiled chicken breast with a green salad and some rice.

We ate and spent a minute or two more on Dr. Andy Lewiston's right to sit at God's right when the horrible moment came for him to leave the realm of the living and the kneedy.

"R&R Industries," Corbin said, looking down at my card as he paused in his eating.

"Electronics, looking to branch out," I said. "Good studio back in Texas."

"And what did you think you and I might work out?" Corbin said.

I've spent a lifetime reading people in an effort to stay alive, healthy and out of jail. I didn't like a slight tone I was catching in Corbin's voice.

"Well," I said. "By the way, this is delicious."

"I'll tell the chef," said Corbin without a smile.

He looked a bit like a slightly undersized, well-groomed Ernest Hemingway. There's a contest each year in Key West for the best

Hemingway look-alike. I considered briefly suggesting it to Corbin, but he didn't look as if he would be interested or amused. The food was much too spicy for me but I ate and watched Lamotta cut his chicken into tiny pieces and chew them forever before swallowing. It was a wonder he could get movies and a television series done with the time it must take to eat a simple meal.

"Interestingly," I said, reaching into my jacket pocket, "when Andy Lewiston examined me, he told me he had a niece who was starting out in show business. I wasn't interested, but there's no point in antagonizing the man who's going to be sticking sharp knives into your legs. So I looked at the photograph he had of her. Not bad."

I handed the photograph of Barbie Lewiston to Corbin, who looked at it and showed it to Lamotta, who glanced at it and nodded.

"She'd be perfect for the CD-ROM I'm planning to produce," I said, taking the photo back and pocketing it. "I've got a big-name writer, an Edgar Allan Poe award-winner, and a director with credits two feet long. This girl would be perfect."

"But . . . ?" asked Corbin, continuing to eat.

"Andy doesn't know where she is," I said with a shrug. "Say, you find this curry just a little too bland?"

"There is no such thing as curry," said Corbin. "That's a creation of the English to describe a variety of spices commonly used and often varied in regional cooking."

"Sorry," I said. "You haven't see her?"

Corbin smiled and closed his eyes for an instant, shaking his head before looking up at me.

"Listen closely, Mr. Rockford," he said. "I'd like to complete what I have to say so I can continue to eat while my food is still reasonably hot. Barbie Lewiston came to see me. Used her uncle's name. Dr. Lewiston had called in advance and I was happy to do him the favor of talking to her. Rockford, the girl is remarkable. Her lack of talent is unmitigated by her beauty. And, in fact, as far as beauty and youth are concerned, in this town she is run of the street. Plenty out there just as good-looking who can actually act."

Lamotta made a sound. I thought it was a snicker. Corbin went on.

"You are, in spite of your years, a bit of an amateur. You are listed in the telephone directory under 'Private Investigators.' My guess is that Dr. Lewiston has engaged your services to find his niece and you are going around to everyone he sent her to to see if

80

you can find her. So far?"

"Right," I acknowledged. "But I do have bad knees."

"For that, I am sorry, but what possible reason would I have for harboring or taking in Barbie Lewiston?"

"The obvious," I said.

"Rockford," he said with a sigh. "I am gay. It is common knowledge. I was present for some of the momentous gay verbal battles between Cukor and Cole Porter when I was a boy."

"And the shadow?" I asked, nodding at Lamotta.

"Let's say that to a great degree, Mr. Lamotta's success is due to a high regard we hold for each other and have ever since I plucked him from a storefront karate shop in Pasadena."

Lamotta kept eating.

"You might want her around for people you need favors from," I said. "People who don't share your preferences. People who like little girls and make deals with you."

Corbin stopped chewing and looked at me. No anger. Nothing.

"You have succeeded in provoking me, Rockford," he said. "I am rich. I am successful. If our ratings go down and we're in the low nineties next week and our next feature is a box-office disaster, I will still be rich and respected. That's the way this town works. I don't need to sell little girls or buy little boys."

He put down his napkin.

"I've had enough," he said. Lamotta stopped eating and put down his fork. "My appetite is gone and I find your presence offensive. I plan to call Andy Lewiston and complain strongly about your tactics."

"I'm doing my job, Corbin," I said, putting down my napkin.

"R&R Industries, CD-ROMs, looking for a perfect actress," he said softly, shaking his head. "Weak. You could use a few of the writers on our series."

"I've seen the series," I said. "I'm better off with my own material."

Corbin rose and Lamotta slipped out to stand next to him.

"I know nothing of Barbie Lewiston's whereabouts," Corbin said. "I care nothing about her whereabouts. I have a strong impulse to suggest to Mr. Lamotta that he cause you some pain before we leave so you won't have the urge to call me again with insults."

I stood now. Lamotta at a little under six feet tall was about half a foot shorter than I was, and I didn't doubt that he could and would do what Corbin told him to do.

"I'm a determined man when I feel threatened or demeaned, Corbin," I said. "I have a feeling that before your Academy Award prospect here could break most of my bones I'd get a shot or two at his face with this."

I held up the water pitcher.

"I can recover from what he does. I've been worked on by the best, but I've learned that no matter what shape they're in or how many black belts they have or concrete blocks they can break, actors don't want their faces broken. It's their living."

Corbin nodded and put out a hand to hold Lamotta back.

"You've regained a bit of my respect," Corbin said, looking so much like Hemingway that he must have been aware of it. "Let's leave it at that."

He turned his back to me. Lamotta removed his sunglasses and looked angrily with his famous gray eyes and the threatening look that told stunt men and whoever the camera operator was that he was angry.

"*Temple of Blood Warriors*," I said, pointing at his face and smiling. "Same look you gave the evil head priest before you started kicking his turbaned warriors into the pit of snakes. I always wanted to ask someone in movies why the bad guys, when there are two or three dozen of them, only attack the lone good guy in groups of two or three."

"Richard," Corbin called.

I held up the water pitcher in a mock toast and Lamotta turned away and followed Corbin, who called back to the man who had waited on us:

"Mr. Ampur, the lunch is on my bill for the week."

Then they were gone. The people at the other tables still hadn't looked up. I sat down, poured a glass of water and drank it, knowing I had screwed this one up. Mr. Ampur appeared and began to clear the table.

"Mr. Corbin said this was on his weekly bill," I reminded him.

"Sure did," said Mr. Ampur.

"In that case, I'd like a quart of four of your own personal favorite dishes to go. Extra mild. And give yourself a generous tip."

Mr. Ampur nodded, happy to oblige. Lunch had not been a total loss.

I took my Thai specialties home. The parking lot was full and the surf was fair and there were some hearty blond young men riding the waves. The water was cold. I remember only a handful of days in the past twenty years when I had found it warm enough to actually find my old trunks and step into it. Once I stood waist high for about ten minutes drinking coffee and then used the cup to pour water on my head and body. I did not remember it as a positive experience. I had been trying to wash away a bad memory and had failed.

My trailer door was open. Definitely a bad sign. I hoped they had left my refrigerator this time. I expected the television, an Angel special that may have been hot and taken from someone else's home, to be gone. They usually went for the easy electronic and mechanical stuff. I had lost as many telephone answering machines as televisions. The neighborhood was fine. It was just easier now for burglars to get in and out of.

There were two men standing in front of my desk, arms folded, waiting like soldiers or prison guards. I knew prison guards. The third man sat at my desk making holes in the wood by tapping it with my class reunion memorial letter opener.

The two standing wore chinos, stone color, and lightweight cotton pullover shirts, one blue, one green. They could have been posing for a page in the L.L. Bean catalog. Both had muscle. Both looked foreign, dark and probably Hispanic. The man making holes in my desk definitely looked bored. He was older, heavier than his friends and wearing a very lightweight tan suit with a tie that should have come out only on Halloween. I wondered if he was making a pattern or picture or just randomly destroying my property.

"Rockford," the man behind the desk said.

"Yeah," I said. "Would you mind practicing your desktop art somewhere else with your own tools?"

"That supposed to be funny?" asked the man behind the desk.

I could see now that he was a lot older than the other two, had slightly shorter well-groomed hair and a bad complexion.

"What do you want?" I asked as one of the two prison-guard types moved behind me and began to pat me down.

"Two hundred dollars," the man behind the desk said, pointing the letter opener at me. "Right now. We've got other stops and this is small change."

I put my package of Thai food on my marred desk.

"I owe you two hundred dollars?" I asked as the guy who had searched me stayed behind to block the door. Obviously, he knew nothing about my knees.

"Angel Martin owes me. Paid back the principal. Owes on interest. One hundred a day," said the man in the suit, laying the letter opener gently on my defaced desk and leaning over to open my bag and peer into it at the white boxes of Thai food.

"Then get it from Angel," I said.

"We've got your old man's pickup," the man behind the desk said, now folding his hands like a judge. "Angel says you have a sentimental attachment to the truck. You keep it in good shape."

"Thanks," I said.

"I've decided that you are going to pay me the two hundred," he said. "I will return the pickup and you can collect from Angel."

"Who pays for my desk?"

The man sitting behind it shrugged.

"Fortunes of war," he said. "Let's be quick here." He checked his watch. "We've got stops all around the coast and a couple on the way back in the Valley."

"And if I don't pay?" I said.

"Pickup gets turned into a two-foot by two-foot very heavy paperweight and Angel still owes us," he said.

I went into my wallet, took out the two hundred and handed it to him. I'd have to go back to the bank if I could get there before it closed. The man behind my desk didn't bother to count it.

"You look pissed," he said. "Get a drink.

Sit down. Calm yourself. It could have been worse, a lot worse. You have any idea of who I am and who I work for?"

"I've got an idea," I said.

"Good," said the man in the tan suit and Halloween tie, getting up.

He walked around the desk, stepped next to me, patted my shoulder and said,

"My old man was a car thief. And a rapist. He didn't leave me anything but a few glitches in my personality, and I didn't even want them. That your old man's picture on the desk?"

I shook my head "yes."

"Looks like a nice old guy," said the tan suit.

He motioned to his casually well-dressed pals, picked up my bag from the Thai Palace, handed it to one of his hippos and exited behind my back, closing the door softly. I went to the bank for another two hundred and then home again. Rocky's pickup was already back.

I spent the next two hours sanding down and refinishing the top of my desk. The smell of stolen Thai food lingered the whole time. I stopped long enough to double-check on my appointment with the next person on the list I had been given by Dr. Lewiston. I reminded Miss Crystal Fontaine's personal secretary that I had an appointment at four and that Dr. Lewiston had suggested that Miss Fontaine and I chat.

"You're on the schedule for four to four-fifteen," he said.

"I'll be there," I said and hung up, almost putting the phone back on the desk, which wasn't yet dry. I put the phone and answering machine I was holding back on the floor.

I'd worked up a sweat working on the desk. At first I had attacked the little holes with rage and then had settled in. As I started to get into the job I calmed down and began to see life as a series of random bad jokes, the point of which very few people got. I was sweating. I hadn't changed clothes for the job. Now I had to shower and put on whatever I had that was right for seeing a movie star whose career was definitely on the way down. I had read that Crystal Fontaine was one of those being considered for the lead in a road company production of *Sunset Boulevard*. I couldn't remember her ever singing, at least not with her own voice. She had done a "guest" year on a prime-time soap as a wealthy seductress. Word was she expected to be picked up for the role the next season, but the writers and producer killed off her character in a mountain resort buried by an avalanche. The character could always come back later but now Crystal was faced with dropping out of show business or taking third leads in anything she could get and announcing to *Variety* that she was enjoying the new challenge of character parts.

She had also enjoyed three husbands. Number One had been a movie star, a few years younger than she was and on the way up. When he made it all the way there, they had split. Then his career, with the help of drugs, had fallen into a deep hole. She had managed to hold on. Her second choice was fiscally better, an independent producer much older than she was who gave her five films, one of which actually got people talking about a possible Oscar nomination. She didn't get the nomination and her producer husband died, leaving her — along with a few good real estate investments in Connecticut — more than comfortable. Husband Number Three had been a windfall, an over-seventy star-struck sole owner of more than eighty supermarket hardware stores across the country. He had a bad heart but a will that gave Crystal one-third of his estate. The other two-thirds went to her husband's daughters. Crystal was gracious to the grown daughters and their families and one-third of Husband Number Three was quite enough to make her even richer.

Her house was in Beverly Hills, well protected along with other rich and famous people's by guards and dogs and cameras and wired gates, doors and windows as sensitive as the trigger had been on Bugsy Siegel's favorite gun.

I got through the gate and guards, found the house, which was within a couple of tennis courts of Sally Field's, and went through the gate that opened after I announced myself on the intercom.

The house was very modest for Beverly Hills and a woman as wealthy as Crystal Fontaine was reported to be. It was, I understood from an article in the Sunday *LA Times* by Charles Champlain, the new trend: modesty. The house was a two-story brick with a well-kept lawn. I'd guess it for no more than three or four bedrooms.

I walked up the brick path and saw the door was open. A young man stood before me. He wore black denims and a white pullover shirt. He also wore sneakers and had his hand out and a ready white smile on his handsome face.

"My name is Mark Oshana," he said, taking my hand.

"Cherokee," I said, shaking back.

"Two-thirds Osage," he said.

"I'm one-eighth Cherokee," I said.

"You're qualified," he said, letting go of my hand.

We walked into the house. The interior was modest and the furniture eclectic, with pieces from all periods from eighteenth-century French to contemporary authentic ranch. Mark Oshana told me this as he ushered me into the living room, which looked comfortable and intimate with furniture that invited you to sit in it. The basic colors were all over the place, but everything seemed to fit. Crystal Fontaine had quite an interior decorator. Looking this casual, comfortable, and what-the-hell-do-I-care took a good eye and cost a lot of money.

"Something to drink, Mr. Rockford?" Mark asked, inviting me to sit wherever I might be comfortable.

"You're . . . ?"

"Miss Fontaine's personal assistant," he said. "I have an MBA from Northwestern University with honors and I plan to be a television and movie producer. I'm working on a project now."

"Which," I said, taking a plaid-covered chair with wooden arms, "Miss Fontaine is considering backing."

Oshana laughed. The laugh was small but looked real enough.

"Miss Fontaine doesn't put her money in

movies, not even her own," he said. "Too big a risk. No, I'm on my own with it, though I have her permission to use her name and her promise to read it if and when someone is ready to produce it and it has a role for her."

"Does it?" I asked.

"It does," he said. "A good one. Tailored for her. Sometimes things aren't what they seem, Mr. Rockford."

I felt that one personally but kept my smile.

"Miss Fontaine and I have a relationship that means a great deal to me," he said. "She hired me when I was waiting tables on Melrose. MBAs who want to get in the movie business are almost as easy to find as actors out here. She didn't buy me. She didn't demand anything of me. I do a good job for her and we are . . . close. Have I answered your questions?"

"One more," I said, reaching into my pocket. "And you can bring me a glass of ice water."

I showed him the photograph of Barbie Lewiston. He looked at it as if trying to remember and handed it back to me.

"You recognize her?" I asked.

"Yes," he said. "She's been here twice. Miss Fontaine treated her kindly, invited her back for lunch to try to talk her out of wanting to get into the movie business. Those were the only times I saw her."

"She's pretty," I said, taking the photo back.

"Very," he said, standing in front of me. "She's also very young, and at the moment I am very satisfied with my relationship with Miss Fontaine."

"Well put," came a husky, familiar woman's voice from the doorway.

Crystal Fontaine, wearing casual designer jeans and sneakers and a blue silk blouse, stood holding her hands together like a schoolteacher. Her blonde hair was tied back with not a strand out of place and her makeup was perfect, casual. The first thing I noticed was that she was thin. Most actresses were thinner than they photographed and worked hard at keeping the weight down; even the character actresses in their sixties and seventies watched their diets and only gained weight if they had a part nailed down and the director told them to put on twenty pounds.

Crystal Fontaine breezed in. I don't know for sure how long she had been in the doorway. Not long or I would have noticed. I got up; my knee, the one that had taken the bullet, slowed me down but reminded me what I was here for.

Crystal moved to Mark Oshana's side and held out her hand as she smiled. Great teeth. Great mouth. I had the feeling both were authentic and original, but it's impossible to tell these days.

I took her offered hand. Her nails were short and painted pink. Her skin was soft. Nothing about her showed her age. She was the rare beauty who looked better in person than on the screen. I thought she'd be a great Norma Desmond if she let herself show a little more of her age.

"What is Mr. Rockford drinking?" she asked Mark, smiling at him.

"Ice water," Mark said.

"Let's have a pitcher," she said, hugging his arm.

She let go and he departed to get the drinks.

"Dr. Lewiston told you that he had performed surgery on me," she said sitting back, arms resting queenlike on the arms of her chair as she did so.

"He did," I said.

"That may be a violation of medical ethics," she said. "Not that I would press the issue, but then again, maybe he has the right to refer new patients to satisfied patients. What did he tell you about my operation?"

"Nothing," I said, not sitting back. "My problem is my knees, but I'd like to know simply what you thought about whatever Dr. Lewiston did for you."

"Cured me," she said with a smile. "I don't think I want to go into any further details about it. Gossip columns, supermarket magazines. You understand?"

"Fully," I said with the Rockford family grin as Mark returned with the water and poured a glass for Crystal and me.

"You are a . . . ?" she said after a sip.

Mark was standing next to her. She raised her free hand to touch his arm. She looked as if she might be purring.

"Producer, back in Texas," I said, pulling out an R&R Industries card and hoping that Mark and Crystal weren't as prepared as Corbin had been. They didn't seem to be, so I went on. "Very successful in computer software and experimental projects — CD-ROM, virtual reality," I said, not knowing what the hell I was talking about. "All computer tie-in, IBM, Macintosh. We're going into production of CD-ROMs with story lines, actors, giving the user an opportunity to select different directions in stories. The really big guys are hiring people like Dennis Hopper for their product. We don't want to be left behind, but we don't want to take a big risk just yet."

"And you want me to do one of these?" she said, looking up at Mark to smile at the very absurdity of such an idea.

"No, no," I said laughing. "We're a few years away from making an offer to someone of your magnitude. Actually, we've got some people lined up — Ed Silver, Jack Simmons, Gwen Atkins."

I looked up for a sign of recognition of the names I had invented. I saw none. I was beginning to like Crystal Fontaine. I reached into my pocket and came up with the photo of Barbie Lewiston.

"I told Mr. Rockford that Miss Lewiston had been here twice for your advice," said Oshana.

I drank my ice water while I looked at them.

"I've heard she might be available, according to Dr. Lewiston. The part doesn't take a lot of acting talent. I need a fresh, young face who can say a few lines," I said, taking a long drink as she examined the photograph.

Crystal closed her eyes and shook her head as if for a dearly remembered departed relative.

"She looks good in the picture," I said, taking it back and pocketing it. "And if she looks half as good in person and can act even a little . . ."

"She looks even better in person," said Crystal. "Her skin is amazing. As for her acting . . ."

"You wouldn't know where I could find her?" I asked hopefully. "How to get in touch with her?"

"Andy Lewiston doesn't know?" Crystal asked, handing her empty glass to Mark, a few diminished cubes clinking as he gave her a refill. I said "No, thanks" when he offered me one.

"Nope," I said. "Barbie left him a note saying she was going off to work with someone in the industry her uncle had sent her to. She didn't give a name."

"You think it might be me?" Crystal said incredulously.

I shrugged.

"Mr. Rockford . . . ," she began and then shook her head and looked up at Mark, who understood and disappeared again.

I watched Crystal Fontaine's face as she considered what to do next.

"Come," Crystal said, getting up and motioning for me to follow.

We moved from the cozy living room into a cozy brightly colored den. Mark was there putting a videotape into a machine resting on top of a massive television set.

"As usual, Mark has correctly anticipated

what I was going to do," Crystal said as she sat on the sofa facing the screen and motioned for me to join her. I did. Mark started the tape.

INTRODUCING BARBIE LEWISTON was printed in orange against black on the screen.

I sat back. Mark stood off to the side, arms folded, looking at the screen. And there was Barbie. She had a bright smile, perfect soft yellow hair and a face every bit as pretty as her photograph. She was wearing a black dress worn just low enough to show a little breast. She was sitting on a high stool. The background behind her was solid white.

"Lighting is good," said Crystal. "Sound is adequate."

Barbie Lewiston, in a high voice with a slight Southern accent she tried to cover, announced that she was going to begin with Ophelia's mad scene from "the pen of the immortal Shakespeare."

I'll give her this. She knew the lines and looked innocent and sincere. Her monologue, however, was abysmal, not much different from a ten-year-old's reading the ingredients on the side of a box of Captain Crunch. Something approaching emotion would suddenly pop up, but it was the wrong emotion. At one point, Barbie put a fist to her eyes to indicate that she was weeping, but there was no illusion of reality to it. I turned to Crystal, who held up a hand to stop me. I looked at the screen again. Barbie got off her stool, threw her head back and did Scarlett O'Hara's lines when she was getting dressed by Hattie McDaniel. She mimed the corset business and allowed her Southern accent to come through. It was a better choice than Ophelia, but still amazingly bad, flat, emotionless. I was better than Barbie. Dennis Becker, my friend on the LAPD who usually looked as if he had just had an overdose of coffee acid, could outact Barbie, even playing Scarlett. And Angel would look almost credible compared to the Barbie who babbled away on screen.

"Enough?" asked Crystal.

"Enough," I said.

Mark turned off the tape.

"I met Barbie Lewiston twice," she said. "The first time she did a little mandatory gushing about how wonderful she thought I was in everything, especially *Life's Folly*, for which I probably should have received an Oscar nomination, and for *The Border of Life*, a disaster I'd like to forget. She had the tape with her. I looked at it with her watching my face. Fortunately, I am an actress, though Miss Lewiston is not. I showed noth-

ing but intense concentration while I considered what to tell this nice girl from someplace South that she should go home and
enter a program for dental assistants. I told
her I'd think about it and that I had found
her tape interesting. She left it with me to
show to anyone I might want to present her
to. She came back, by appointment, the
week after, when I had had time to work
out something to say. I liked her and I had
no intention of pissing off her uncle, who
might have to put a knife to me again sometime. I told her she had promise. I didn't
tell her what that promise was, that it was
assurance of total disaster as an actress. I
suggested that she go back home, work in
community theater, try out for local com-
mercials, get experience and come back in
two years. She said this was her only chance,
that if she went back to Little Rock, her
father would never support her talent in New
York or Los Angeles. I sympathized and told
her that all the greats had done community
theater, dinner-club theater. I have no idea
if anyone would even hire her to do those
murder mystery weekends in Arkansas, but
she didn't need Los Angeles to break her
heart. She'd be better off having that happen
at home. End of Barbie Lewiston story. I
gave her an autographed photograph and

told her to write to me often."

"May I see that tape?" I asked.

Crystal nodded at Mark, who had put the tape back in its box. He handed the box to me.

"Mind if I borrow this?" I asked.

"Keep it," Crystal said. "But you really don't want her after what you've seen."

"Maybe I can find a part for her with no dialogue," I said. "It might make Andy Lewiston happy enough to give me a discount on a new set of knees."

We were all standing now. Crystal offered her hand. I took it. She smiled. I liked her, but I had been wrong about people before.

Mark stepped forward and motioned me to follow him while Crystal moved to the cabinet of videotapes. I wondered what she was going to watch. Something she had been in? Or some hidden favorite like *King Kong* or *The List of Adrian Messenger*.

He ushered me to the front door and I turned to shake his hand.

"None of my business," he said, "but you're not looking for Barbie Lewiston to put her in a movie."

"CD-ROM," I corrected. "Interactive video."

Mark smiled.

"I think the girl is eighteen going on thirteen," he said. "If Dr. Lewiston hired you to find her, good luck, and let us know if we can give anymore help."

"You can speak for Miss Fontaine?"

"I can," he said.

I stepped out. He closed the door. I looked at the video box in my hand: "Presenting Barbie Lewiston." At the bottom of the white box on the back was the name of a video company and an address in Panorama City.

CHAPTER FOUR

There were faster ways to get to Panorama City, but I took Laurel through the canyon, recognizing almost every hill and marveling that anyone would continue to build massive houses on the sides of these earthquake- and landslide-prone hills. In the Valley, I turned left on Victory Boulevard past a huge shopping mall on my right and a somewhat smaller one on my left as I headed toward Van Nuys. There were still empty lots and little developments set back from the street buffered by tennis court–wide patches of half-dead grass.

For a while, Rocky and my mother had lived in one of those small development homes when they moved from Oklahoma, where I had been born. That was a few years after World War II. The houses were small, but Rocky was handy. When he wasn't on the road with a big rig, he was putting in a swimming pool, a sauna, adding rooms, remodeling the interior.

My mother . . . Well, that's a story for another time; but I went to grade school in that development in North Hollywood, one-story, sprawling, with a concrete playground. I took a quick detour into the development where we lived till I was about ten. Nothing had changed much. Same houses, even ours. School yard had been repaved after we left, but it was cracking again.

Lots of houses were for sale. The only people I saw were three old ladies on chairs under a covered eave on a small front porch. I smiled at them. They wondered if I was casing the place; maybe they'd go in and call the police before I made my next left turn.

I took Victory to Van Nuys Boulevard, which had once, when I was a kid, been considered the place to shop in the Valley. Van Nuys had also been the place to live if you could afford it. Movie actors on their way up had lived here, along with businesspeople who had made money back East manufacturing thumbtacks or billiard balls. Now a few television people on salary lived here on one of the dozens of side streets of pleasant houses on cul-de-sacs. The days of teens roaring down the street trying to pick each other up or pick fights was well beyond my time, and that was already becoming a thing of the past. The police had cracked down on cruising. It hadn't cut the practice, only slowed it down and moved it out. Instead of water balloons and middle fingers pointed up to go along with the sexual invitations — which would have turned off any normal human female — the cars now carried concealed weapons, including automatics. More than one car showed dents and bruises. More than one teen and one bystander had died. And the Valley was still considered safe by Los Angeles standards.

I passed the hospital where all the stars used to go and a few still did and found myself in Panorama City, an extension of Van Nuys with shops and mini-malls lined up for miles on both sides of the street. I turned left on Roscoe and then right on Sepulveda. Panorama Productions was in an office building a few doors down from the corner. It was in an old dirty-brick two-story. I parked, put my money in the meter and walked back to the building noticing a few thin earthquake cracks. The cracks in the brick had been filled in with something like gray putty.

The small tile lobby was clean and an elevator stood open waiting for me even though there were only two floors in what I discovered was, according to a tarnished plaque, the Worstor Office Complex. Panorama Productions was easy to find among the handful of mortgage brokers, dermatologists, lawyers, and marriage and family coun-

106

selors. Panorama Productions had the biggest sign, black on white tile, tasteful. They were on the second floor. My knees ordered me to take the elevator.

I discovered when I arrived that Panorama Productions took over most of the second floor of the Worstor Complex. I went through the glass door and found myself in a reception room complete with a receptionist — who was thin and pretty enough to be a client, but had probably settled, at least for the time being, into sitting behind the desk at Panorama Productions, hair tied back, wearing a dark suit, just enough makeup and a winning smile.

The chairs in the reception room lined up against the walls matched the cheerful decor of the room, bright yellows and enamel red, including the receptionist's desk. The sign on the desk said she was Jesie Edwards. We smiled at each other.

"I'd like to see whoever is in charge," I said.

"You want an audition tape?" she asked. "I can see you as very versatile, from kindly grandfathers who own small-town drugstores to gang bosses. Big demand for character actors now."

"That a fact?"

"It is," she said sincerely.

"I always thought of myself as the leading man type," I said.

"Well . . . ," she said. "It's certainly a possibility."

"The boss," I said pleasantly, handing her my R&R Industries card with the Houston address and "James Rockford, President" in the lower-left-hand corner.

"And you are . . . ?"

"James Rockford," I said.

"I'll see if Mr. Marcinovitch can see you," she said, rising and straightening her black skirt. "If you'll just have a seat."

She headed for an office in the corner. After she entered, I looked at some of the photographs on the wall in the reception area, all with stars, most with a handsome white-haired not-very-tall man almost always in a white suit and no tie. There were Burt Reynolds, Demi Moore and Bruce Willis, Charles Durning, Alfre Woodard . . . the walls were full. All the pictures were signed with things ranging from: "To Alex Marcinovitch" to "To Alex" to "My friend, Alex" to "To Alex, a real pro." I wasn't impressed. When stars appeared at benefits or openings, the Alex Marcinovitches of the world would show up with their own photographer with a Polaroid, hand the star a card saying they were a producer, and then put their arms around the star before they could consider saying no and hand them a pen. If the star didn't sign, the Alex Marcinovitches could fake their signature later when they blew up the photograph. Only an autograph dealer would be able to detect the forgery. Marcinovitch wore the same toothy grin in every photograph. He was among friends.

I was looking at a picture of O. J. Simpson signed: "O. J. Simpson, Peace." It showed O. J. in Buffalo Bills uniform carrying the ball on a run toward the goal line. Miss Jesie Edwards came out of the office and motioned for me to come forth. I did and she held the door open for me to enter. When I was inside the office, she closed the door gently and left me alone with friend and discoverer of stars Alex Marcinovitch, who had risen behind his desk, hand extended, even white teeth grinning in delight. He was wearing dark trousers and a short-sleeved shirt and a conservative old-school tie. He was even shorter than he looked in the photographs.

"Have a seat," he said, pointing to a little round table on the carpeted floor. The table was wood, polished, with three black lacquer-armed chairs around it.

I took a seat and Marcinovitch came out from behind his desk, after offering me coffee, which I politely refused. Marcinovitch had no photos on his office walls, just original art by probably unknown artists — mostly flowers and still lifes. He sat across from me and put his small hands on his knees, waiting.

"I run a growing computer software company in Texas," I said. "We're considering expanding into live-actor CD-ROM. In the last two days I've spoken to Carl Corbin and Crystal Fontaine. They both found my search for talent interesting and Miss Fontaine showed me an audition video you made of a young lady I might be interested in casting."

Marcinovitch nodded understandingly. I could have been a dirty old man or I might be the real thing or I might be both. He was going to be happy to help regardless of who I was. His waiting room wasn't crowded with would-be talent.

"Wasn't there an agent's name and number at the end of the tape?" he asked.

"None," I said.

"Usually they have us include that at no extra charge," he said. "Or they use a home answering machine number. Of course, under the circumstances, we will have to serve as something like a broker-agent for finding the young woman and putting you in touch with her."

"I'll pay a reasonable fee," I said.

Marcinovitch was in heaven. He was actually making a deal, not just turning on a video camera for mostly talentless people doomed to go back to Lakeland, Florida, or Bangor, Maine, or simply hang around forever waiting.

"Her name?" he asked.

"Barbie Lewiston," I said.

"Barbie Lewiston?" he asked, his lids coming down in thought.

"Crystal Fontaine gave me the tape," I said, pulling it from my pocket and placing it on the table before him.

"Crystal Fontaine?" he asked.

I nodded as he took a pair of half-glasses out of his pocket and read the label. He shook his head. I pulled Barbie Lewiston's laminated photo from my pocket and handed it to him. A bolt of electric surprise went through his body. He looked up at me. I smiled.

"You want this girl in a CD-ROM?"

"Probably opposite Dennis Hopper," I said seriously.

He was sure now. I was a dirty old man producer.

"I know she can't act," I said. "But she doesn't have any lines in the CD. She plays a mute, partially clad android. She'll be perfect."

Marcinovitch handed back the photo and shook his head in understanding before saying,

"She's got the desire, and maybe with professional help the girl can make it. Industrials, small television roles. I've been surprised by the success of some of my clients whose talents were about on a par with those of Miss . . ."

"Lewiston," I said. "Barbie Lewiston. Can you tell me where to find her or her agent?"

"Fifty-dollar fee," he said.

"Sounds reasonable," I answered.

He moved to the phone, picked it up, pushed a button and asked Miss Edwards to bring in the Barbie Lewiston file.

While we waited, Marcinovitch suggested that I might be interested in looking at tapes of some of his other, possibly more talented and just as beautiful talent.

I declined, saying Barbie Lewiston was just what I wanted.

No doubt now. I was a dirty old man, but one with money. Jesie — with one *s* — Edwards came in with the file without knocking, handed it to Marcinovitch who had come back around the table, and gave me a look that indicated that she had seen the Barbie Lewiston tape and could think of only one reason why I might be interested. She left, closing the door quietly. Marcinovitch sat down again and started to go through the thin file, taking more time than I was sure he needed. He was working for his fifty.

"Ah," he said. "Here."

He pointed at a sheet in front of him.

"Three numbers," he went on and then stopped and waited.

I reached into my wallet, took out a fifty and laid it on the table. The first two numbers he gave me were Andy Lewiston's home and office. The third number was interesting.

"Any names other than Barbie's go with that?" I asked.

"No," he said. "No agent, nothing. Just the phone number."

I wrote down the number and pocketed it, starting to get up with my hand out.

"You've been a great help, Mr. Marcinovitch."

He shook my hand and said,

"Say, listen. You got a minute or two, I can get the photographer from down the block to take our picture. I've got my suit in the closet."

"Sorry," I said. "Another time."

He followed me out of his office door.

"You know, there's a copy guard on that video," he said. "On all our videos. If you need more copies, just call us for rates."

I took the card he handed me and put it in my pocket.

Jesie Edwards was busy pretending to look for something on her computer, an early model Macintosh with a dot matrix printer next to it. Being this far from the action may have saved Alex Marcinovitch on rent but it didn't bring him the walk-in business of Hollywood.

"It might not be a bad idea for you to do an audition tape," he said. "You have a good face and manner. Ever thought about doing some acting?"

"Not as a profession," I said. "Miss Edwards already discussed the possibility with me. I'm intrigued, but . . . no thanks."

Alex shrugged and went back in his office when I left. I wondered what he did in there all day when there were no clients. He had no computer or typewriter and I didn't see any books. I had an image of him pacing the floor.

I headed for a drugstore across Sepulveda. I had a call to make.

An hour later I was knocking at the door to an apartment in Monterey Park just off

114

the Pasadena freeway. The building was a four-story, well kept, with lots of bushes and flowers around it.

My journey had begun with a phone call to the number given to me by Alex Marcinovitch. After five rings, an answering machine came on with a woman's voice brightly telling me "we" are unable to answer the phone. Leave a message. We'll get back. I was about to hang up when the same voice overrode the mechanical version and turned off the machine.

"Hello," said the woman with a hint of suspicion.

"Hello," I said. "My name is Rockford, James Rockford of R&R Enterprises. We make interactive CD-ROMs and I would like to talk to a Miss Lewiston about working with us on a project. I've seen her audition video . . ."

"She's not here," she said with some of the brightness gone.

"Well, when will she be back?" I asked. "I can call back. I'm from Houston, but I've got a lot of business here over the next few days."

"I don't know," she said. "Give me a number and I'll get it to her when I can."

I gave her my home number and started to ask another question, but she said, "I'm late, sorry," and hung up.

My next call was to Lieutenant Dennis Becker of the Los Angeles Police Department. I had to wait two minutes before Dennis came on.

"Becker," he said.

"Rockford," I said.

"No time to talk, Jim," he said. "I've got two high-profile murders, one with a big local business guy who decapitated his wife, another with a teenage kid from Watts who sprayed a convenience store with a Cobray automatic because they wouldn't sell him cigarettes. Store owner, Pakistani with six kids, took two in the face. Plus the usual. No offense, but . . ."

"Simple favor," I said. "Less than a minute."

"Jimbo, are you listening to me? I'm not even supposed to talk to you."

"I know that, Dennis, but this is life-and-death; a young girl's probably being pawed now by some movie type and I want to find her before it goes too far."

"Okay," Dennis said with a deep sigh. "You said it was quick."

"I'll give you a number. You give me an address."

"You've got an address finder at your place, Jim. It's in the second drawer."

"What were you doing in my . . . ? Forget it. I'm someplace where I can't get to it and I know you've got one on your computer. Do it. Fast. Then good-bye and I'll call you about the fishing trip we've been talking about."

About ten seconds later, I had the address.

"If I see any women's heads rolling down the freeway, I'll give you a call. I'll call you early next week."

I was wrong. I would be talking to Dennis long before next week, but I didn't know it at the time. I was, I thought, on a routine search-and-find job. No fuss, no problems. Locate the girl. Tell her uncle. Get my knees fixed.

The downstairs door of the apartment building had been a joke. I opened it with the foldout screwdriver on my Swiss Army knife. Why did the Swiss Army have the best pocketknives? They never fought anybody. It was a question to ponder some sleepless night. Right now I was knocking at the door of a Ms. Gail Chernowitz in Apartment 4E.

It may have taken me too long to get there. She may have been up and out. Maybe, however, she'd be home, or, better yet, Barbie herself would open the door. I knocked again. This time a woman's voice answered,

"Who is it?"

"Fire inspector," I said. "We're getting smoke on your circuit breakers. You've got a faulty appliance."

I didn't know what I was talking about. I found that was usually a safe course to take.

"Oh, shit," she said, and I could hear locks opening.

She was wearing a plaid skirt and a blue blouse. Her feet were bare and she held a brush in one hand. I had caught her in the act of brushing her long, very dark hair. She was somewhere in her late twenties, probably, darkly pretty with perfect ebony skin.

"Gail Chernowitz?" I asked.

"Yes," she said. "I'll tell you my life story some other time. I've got to get to work."

I stepped in and closed the door. She started across the small, neat and comfortable little living room toward a door I assumed was a bedroom.

"I'm not a fire inspector," I said, stopping her in her tracks.

She turned, stopped brushing and shook her head, her back to me.

"I should have known," she said. "How did you find me? No, forget it. I don't care."

She turned, determined, angry and frightened.

"You said you should have known?" I asked.

"Tell him I'm not coming back," she said firmly, pointing her hairbrush at me. "I don't care how big the check is you have in your pocket. I don't care if you're here to break my arm or cut my face. I'm not going back."

"I'm Rockford," I said. "I called about an hour ago. R&R Industries. I'm not looking for you. I'm looking for Barbie Lewiston."

There was a purse on a table near the bedroom. She threw the brush on the sofa, went to the purse and came up with a small revolver.

"I'm just looking for Barbie Lewiston," I repeated.

"And I'm looking for a new life," she said. "I'm not going back to him."

"Who?"

Something in my face must have shown honest confusion. She tilted her head to the side.

"You're not from Vegas?" she said.

"No," I said. "I don't go to Vegas; I don't gamble. I'm not against it. I'm just too weak to stop once I get started."

I was smiling the smile of the honest Texan.

"Bloom didn't send you?" she asked.

"Bloom?"

"Forget it," she said. "Why are you going through all this trouble to find Barbie? I told

119

you on the phone I'd give her your message."

"She's living here?"

"Moved out," she said, still holding the gun leveled at my chest. "She was only here a couple of days. We met when she came into the restaurant where I work. She had a chicken breast sandwich and we talked. She came back for a couple of days and said she was living with some relative but needed someplace to live on her own. I like Barbie. I took her in for half the rent, which I can use, and she slept on the foldout."

"Then?"

"She was gone," said Gail with a shrug. "Left a note saying — What's the difference? It's none of your business."

"I don't know a Bloom," I said. "But I'm not with R&R Industries either. I'm a private investigator. I've been hired by Barbie's uncle to find her and make sure she's okay. My name's Jim Rockford. I'm in the phone book. If you want to check on me, I'll give you the number at LAPD where Lieutenant Becker will sigh deeply and tell you I'm all right. Now, will you please put down the gun. Guns make me nervous. I'm in all this because an unpleasant kid shot me in the knee. I don't need any more holes, especially from pretty, frightened young women."

"Hell," she said, putting the gun back in her purse. "If you're from Bloom and you found me here, you or someone else will find me again."

She went back to brushing her hair, but her hand was shaking ever so slightly.

"Barbie left a note?"

Gail nodded.

"Can I see it?"

"I don't save notes," Gail said. "It said someone in the business with connections was interested in guiding her career. And that she'd be in touch. She left me enough cash for two months' rent. I don't know where she went or who with and I'll be surprised if she doesn't call me. We got to be pretty good friends."

"Mind if I sit?" I said.

She shrugged. I picked a reasonably straight-backed chair with arms and sat watching her brush her hair. It brought back memories of someone else a long time ago.

"She talk about this show business angel?" I asked.

"A little. It's someone who's been around a long time. Someone with a lot of money. I got the feeling she'd known whoever it was for a while before I met her. She talked about this guy having invested in movies and having big connections."

"Guy?" I asked.

She was almost finished with her hair. She shrugged again.

"I think she said 'guy,' but it could have been a woman. Tell you the truth, I didn't pay a whole lot of attention. I had other things on my mind and I gave up listening after she paid no attention to my warning. Mister, if someone backs Barbie's career, they've only got one or two things on their mind, and none of them is her career. Barbie can't act."

"I know," I said. "I saw her video."

"Pathetic," she said, looking around the room and spotting her shoes. "But I like the girl. It was good to have someone around to talk to."

I took out my card, my real card, and handed it to her.

"She could be in trouble," I said. "We agree. If she calls, let me know, and if you can get any names or an address or phone number out of her, I'll get her uncle to hand you a check."

"I can use it," she said, slipping into her shoes. "I'm waitressing. Staying away from the places the dealers go. I don't want to take a chance on being spotted by someone who knows Bloom. Can you beat it? I'm a college graduate. Queen of homecoming.

Young Miss Ohio. No trouble getting an agent. Did an album, got a gig in Las Vegas and boom, Bloom. Now I'm hiding out."

"Gail Chernowitz," I said.

"Neither Gail nor Chernowitz," she said. "Now, if you'll excuse me, I've got to go stand on my feet for eight hours taking abuse from customers who leave small tips. But hey, it's better than Bloom."

I got up.

"Barbie leave anything here?" I asked.

"A carry-on," Gail said, standing straight. She was a beauty. Maybe I'd come back sometime and discuss what we could do about Mr. Bloom in Las Vegas. "In the closet."

She had nodded toward a door. I moved to it, opened it and there was a blue carry-on under the clothes. The closet was far from full.

I reached over and took out the bag. It looked empty. I checked every pocket and almost missed the movie ticket stub. I was about to throw it away, but I turned it over first. I was moving fast. Gail had to go and I knew she had no plans to leave me here alone.

On the back of the ticket stub in what looked like a woman's writing was: "Meet H, Patio Club, Tuesday, 6 P.M."

123

Gail was at the door. I read her the note on the back of the stub.

"Hers," she said. "I don't know what it means or what Tuesday she's talking about. You're the detective. Go out and detect. And find that girl. She's eighteen, no experience with the kind of people you can get involved with out here. And since she has the face and body of a *Penthouse* special, they'll find her."

I pocketed the stub, went past her through the open door and asked if I could give her a ride. She said no, and I figured she didn't want me to know where she worked. I think she trusted me around the edges, but Bloom might be a heavy hitter, and if he came down on me I might tell what I knew and the less I knew, the better. I liked her.

Next stop, the Patio Club.

The Patio Club was familiar to me. It was the kind of place where deals were made at private little tables in a room full of flowers. It was on Olive, not far off the Golden State freeway. The Patio Club was in easy striking distance of Disney Studios and NBC and a not unreasonable distance from Universal. The area was dotted with independent television and film production company offices, upscale antique shops, boutiques, designer shops, ethnic and nouveau restaurants. A tasteful men's clothing shop and an upscale toy shop flanked the Patio Club.

I got there at six, walked in with confidence and told the pretty Asian girl in a happy yellow dress who greeted me at the podium that I was meeting some people at six. She asked me their name and I said with a knowing whisper that I didn't know what name he had used.

"He likes to keep a very low profile," I said, still whispering. "You understand."

"Perfectly," she said, looking at her reservation book. "That was for how many people?"

"I don't know," I said with a shrug. "He might want to meet me alone or with one or more of his people at the studio. Look, I'll just sit at the bar where I can see him come in."

"All right," she said, her problem solved.

I moved past her into a dark, soberly wooded and leather-sided bar with three small tables and a bar with a dozen stools with wood backs.

There was only one other customer in the place, a heavy-set guy with what remained of his cornsilk hair combed back. He wore a sport jacket not much different from mine and a look of sadness he directed at the martini in front of him. I had the feeling it wasn't his first martini of the afternoon.

The bartender, young with a little mustache, hoping to be the next Kevin Kline or Patrick Bergin, stepped in front of me with a smile.

The bartender wore dark slacks, a white shirt and a red bow tie. He said nothing, just stood looking helpful.

"Best draft beer you've got," I said.

He nodded and strode off down the bar.

The man with the martini looked at me and said in a voice that told me he needed a designated driver, "Six years, two months and two weeks. You know what that comes to in days?"

"No," I said.

"Neither do I," he admitted, "but a long time in this business. One day I'm a vice president and then this morning I walk in and get told that the president and owner sold the company and the new owners want their own people. Six years, two months and ten days."

"Two weeks," I corrected.

"I ought to know how long I worked for that bastard," he said.

"Sorry," I said as the bartender returned with a coaster and a good-sized glass of amber beer without too much foam.

"Nod if you need anything," he said and

made himself scarce.

"You think that's fair?" the drunken ex–vice president said.

"You're in the wrong town if you want 'fair,' " I said with a little head shake and as much sympathy as I could come up with.

"You're right," said the ex-VP. "I should have figured, had plans. I'm fifty. They come after you when you've got a job, but when you haven't got one they think you're not worth going for. You know what I mean?"

"Yep," I said, deciding to go into my Gary Cooper mode as I took small sips from my beer. The beer was fine and the time was now two minutes after six.

I looked past the bar, through the door into the restaurant section. In contrast to the bar, it was bright, colorful, with a glass roof. There were booths with fresh flowers near them if you wanted privacy and tables where you could sit if you were somebody recognizable who wanted to be recognized but didn't want it to show. There were a few people at tables. I couldn't see the whole interior. The restaurant was small, but what they lacked in size they more than made up in price. I ought to know. I was left holding a dinner bill for four by a client the last time I was here. I billed him for it after I did the job and he compromised without discussion by paying me three-quarters of the bill. I assumed he felt the last quarter was my responsibility.

Six-fifteen came and went. The drunken man stayed. I was on my second beer. It looked like I had the wrong Tuesday at six. I pulled out my photo of Barbie Lewiston and placed it on the counter where it was definitely dry and waved the bartender over.

"Ever see this girl before?" I asked.

He looked at me with a tinge of suspicion.

"I don't know," he said.

"I'm a CD-ROM producer," I said, giving him my R&R card. "Her agent said she'd be here today, but I might have had my days mixed up."

He looked at the card and said,

"You looking for actors, too?"

"Could be," I said with a Texas grin. "Could be."

It was his turn to go into his wallet and pull out a card that told me he was Tommy Kelk and listed both his home number and that of his agent.

"Thanks," I said.

"You want a photo to go with that?" he asked, trying not to sound too hopeful.

"Well . . . ," I said, not wanting to get the kid's hopes up, but not wanting to break cover. "That would be nice."

"Got one in the back. Wait."

I watched the door. A few people had come in and gone straight to the restaurant. None of them was Barbie or anyone I recognized, with the possible exception of a woman in dark glasses who might have been Joan Rivers.

"You want some advice?" asked the guy at the bar, turning back to me, a fresh martini in front of him.

"Sure," I said, finishing my second beer.

"Stay away from the television business. That's my advice. Sell illegal guns, shoes, denture cream, property in Lodi, rubber life rafts. Work in a factory with illegal immigrants on both sides of you who can't speak English. McDonald's is always looking for help. Maybe that's what I'll do — apply for a job with McDonald's as a manager. Shit, they'll probably tell me I'm too old."

I shrugged and said,

"I'll stay out of the television production business."

He nodded as if I had made a wise decision. Then he began working on his new martini with a look of accomplishment on his face. Kelk the bartender who wanted to act returned with an envelope.

"Five-by-seven and an eight-by-ten," he said, handing it to me. "Complete credits on the back of the eight-by-ten."

"Thanks," I said, taking the envelope.

"Kid," the drunken man said. "Take the envelope back. Take your card back. Stay behind that counter. The business will eat your heart out. Believe me."

"I'll take the chance," the bartender said gently.

"On the other hand," the drunken man said, "you can make a lot of money fast."

"The girl?" I asked Tommy again.

This time he looked carefully, picking the photo up.

"Yeah," he said. "I think I've seen her in here, maybe last week. Can't be sure. You know a lot of good-looking young girls come in here."

"Was she with anyone?"

"I wish I could remember, Mr. Rockford, but I can't be sure. Sorry."

Tommy was a smart barkeep. He had looked at my card and remembered my name.

The man with the martini staggered over to where I was sitting, trying to hold onto his dignity and his drink.

"Let's see," he said.

I showed him the photograph but didn't hand it to him. He managed to focus and said,

"Barbie . . . Barbie Lewis, Lester, Stone. Lewiston. Barbie Lewiston," he said with confidence. "Nice kid. Can't act."

"How do you know her?" I asked.

He laughed and looked at the bartender as if he knew the joke. The bartender gave him a polite smile.

"My ex-boss, my ex-friend, my ex-employer of six years, God knows how many TV pilots and four made-for-televisions," he said.

"Who are we talking about?" I asked.

"Jack Stuart Hill," he said. "Former stud daytime serial actor and then television production company with me at his right hand and a string of Barbie Stones —"

"Lewiston," the bartender corrected.

The drunk nodded and raised his free hand to show that he stood corrected.

"A string of Barbie Lewistons on his left," the drunk went on. "And when I say string, I mean string. String 'em along. String 'em up. String down their dresses. All young. Barbie Lewiston doesn't have a chance in a hot dog factory of ever getting a shot. She can't act. I can outact her. The next bag lady you run into can outact her."

"But they don't look like her," I said.

"Now you got it," he said, winking at me.

"Where can I find Jack Stuart Hill?" I asked.

"This guy's funny," the drunk told the bartender. "I told you. He just dropped me this morning. He's gone. The new owners might know, but I wouldn't count on that, either."

"New owners?" I asked. "You've got a name and an address?"

"Turn around," he said.

I hesitated for a second or two and then turned around.

"What do you see?"

"The inside of a bar and the entrance," I said.

"Look farther. That's what I should have done."

I looked through the window of the entrance door to a building across the street. The building was one-story, not very big. It had a very modest sign over the door, but I couldn't read it from where I sat.

"It says Jack Stuart Hill Productions," the drunk said.

I pulled out a twenty and laid it on the counter.

The drunk was weaving back to his seat mumbling.

"I don't think he can handle another round," I said softly to the bartender. "Keep the change and see if you can get someone to pick him up or get him a taxi."

"You've got it, Mr. Rockford," he said.

"You got a wife, pal?" I asked the drunk, who was back at his former stool.

"Wife, three kids — one in college, other two in private schools," the drunk said. "Wife'll . . . When she finds out, I don't know what she'll do."

"Thanks," I said, moving back to the reservation podium.

"Looks like either Mr. Hill or I got the day wrong," I told the pretty Asian girl in the yellow dress.

She looked a little puzzled.

"Mr. Hill always makes his reservations in his own name," she said.

"What do I know?" I said with a shrug, my hands in my pockets. "I figured someone as famous as he is . . . Say, could you tell me if he had a reservation last Tuesday at six, or the Tuesday before that, or next Tuesday?"

She looked at me for a moment trying to decide who or what I might be.

"Please," I said. "I've got to know if I've missed an appointment with Mr. Hill. It was hard enough to get it in the first place and if I have to apologize . . ."

Since there was no one in line behind me, she said, "Okay," and checked the next week. Nothing was scheduled in at six. She checked the last week and found it right away. "Booth for two. Six o'clock. Mr. Hill."

"Oh God," I said with a sigh, looking at the wall. "Thanks. Thanks very much."

I went out in a mournful slouch and kept it till I was out of sight of the entrance to the Patio Club. I was holding the bartender's photo and résumé in my hand. I crossed Olive near the corner during a traffic break and walked to the former Jack Stuart Hill Productions office.

There was a girl at the reception desk. Pretty, blond, not quite a Barbie Lewiston clone but enough alike to show Jack Stuart Hill's taste.

"My name is Rockford," I said, handing her a card. "I represent an actor Mr. Hill is interested in. He told me to come in at six-thirty to meet."

"I'm so sorry," she said, sounding sorry, "but Mr. Hill is gone. He sold the studio yesterday. The new people fired just about everyone but me and Mr. Hill's personal secretary. The new owners are in the conference room. Been in there all day. Had me get dinner delivered."

"How can I find Mr. Hill?" I asked.

She shrugged, but there was something in the shrug that let me know she at least had an idea.

"Listen," I said. "It's really important to my client. This is his first big break and mine, to tell the truth."

She bit her quite red lower lip and thought for a second before coming up with, "What the hell? I don't work for him anymore, and he never got me anything but a walk-on in a couple of pilots no one picked up."

I got the feeling Jack Stuart Hill got more than a couple of walk-ons from the girl. She didn't have to look in her Rolodex. She just gave me the address in Sherman Oaks. "Mr. . . ."

"Rockford," I said.

"Don't trust him," she said. "He'll lead you down the stone path and throw you to the armadillos."

I was writing the address on the envelope with Tommy Kelk's life and hopes inside.

"I'll remember that," I said. "Thanks."

Someone came out of the door marked CONFERENCE ROOM. I didn't stay around to see who it was.

I was tired. It was late. I headed home.

CHAPTER FIVE

When I got back to my trailer, the last of the surf riders were packing up and putting their boards atop their cars — all of which were newer and in better shape than mine — and heading away from the sunset. I had lost my taste for the surfers a couple of years back during the Rodney King fires. I'd come home one night in time to see a rubber raft setting out to sea with two men, my answering machine and my television set. I thought I recognized the two as daytime surfers, but I was never quite sure.

I unhooked the back of Rocky's truck and sat on the rear, watching the sun go down. I used to keep a couple of beach chairs on the small wooden deck of my trailer, but someone had stolen them. I didn't feel like going in and facing my phone messages and lugging out a chair. I could have used a beer. One arrived as if delivered by a genie.

"Jimmy," said Angel, handing me a beer from my own refrigerator and jumping up to sit next to me, another beer in his hand.

"Thanks, Angel," I said.

"Saw you coming down the road. You got Rocky's truck back."

"Two hundred dollars added to what you owe me. Those goons were going to bust me up, Angel."

"They came here?"

"They came here."

The sun was almost gone now.

"Makes you wish you could —" he began and then got one of his great ideas. "What if we videotaped a sunset and I get my cousin Bado to —"

"Bado?" I asked, taking a sip.

"Not his real name, Jimmy. And that's not the point. We tape moons going down behind mountains, suns coming up over the fields of corn, storms, snow drifts. And here's the beauty part: We sell it to people who never get to see these things. You know, $19.95 on TV, a 900 number, voice-over by that friend of yours . . ."

"Sounds like a great idea, Angel," I said as the sun almost disappeared.

The surfers were gone. Only the lights from the other two trailers were on. The sky was full of stars, more than most people ever see. I knew that farther up the coast, before you hit San Francisco, there were places you could see so many stars that even a moonless sky lit up your face.

"You've gone dreamy on me, Jimmy," Angel said.

"I'm here, Angel," I said. "Did you find the cat?"

"No, but I got a lead or two," Angel said enthusiastically, turning to face me. The setting sun held nothing but fiscal possibilities for Angel. "But Jimmy, I put on my best suit — you know the one, the bright green one — trimmed my beard. See, take a look. Did it myself. Not a bad job."

"Where are we going with this, Angel?"

"A little patience here, Jimmy. You know I have my own ways of getting information out. Bad news I already told you. I don't have your cat yet. And I had to get some business cards made up by my cousin Paco."

"That his real name?" I asked.

"Real as the cracking concrete all around us," he said. "Business cards say I'm Angelo Martini of Feline Finesse. I put your number on it and said you were the Rockford Answering Service when I gave out the cards."

I was too tired to strangle Angel. I didn't even look at him.

This, Angel knew, was when I had to be watched carefully in case he had to run.

"Look, Jimmy, I tried just walking up to doors and knocking," he said. "You think it's easy to get inside these ritzy Beverly Hills places? Well, it isn't. And you can't just say, 'Hi, my name is Angel Martin. You seen a funny-looking orange cat with a pushed-in face around here?' You just don't get respect. You know who actually opened the door himself at one of the places I went?"

"Tom Cruise," I guessed.

"No, but close. Tom Hanks. At least I think it was Tom Hanks. Looked a lot like him."

"Get to the point, Angel," I said, looking at my now-empty bottle.

"Well, to get the cards, I had to tell Paco it was a rush job, make 'em while I wait. I had him send you the bill. I got to be honest with you, Jimmy. I got a great deal from Paco, but the cards aren't cheap."

"You're paying for them, Angel," I said.

"Now, Jimmy, that's not fair. I'm working for you."

"Every purchase you make, if any, you get approved by me. Pretty soon you're going to be so deeply in debt to me that I'll be standing over your grave while the priest says, 'Here lies Angelo Evelyn Martinez, drowned in a cesspool of debts.' "

I got down off the back of Rocky's truck and motioned for Angel to do the same. He did. I knew he had something more to say. Keep the best or worst for last, but Angel was smiling and looking around to be sure no one would overhear us in a nearly abandoned parking lot in Malibu.

"There I was, going door to door, you see, handing out my cards all afternoon, using a slight Italian accent and telling people one of my clients in the neighborhood had lost her precious Self cat. No one had seen it, but people, movie stars, producers, writers and some people whose money comes from who-knows-where, were interested in my services as a groomer of cats. The idea of a place that dealt only in grooming cats got to them. Jimmy, I got four orders on the spot to groom felines of the rich and famous. Can you beat that?"

"Easy," I said. "You're supposed to be finding Olivia Carstairs's cat and paying me back."

"I'm still looking," Angel said, following me into the trailer. "I'll find it, but you know what these people are willing to pay to have their pet and pedigreed cats groomed by Angelo Martini of Rome?"

"No."

"Lots," said Angel. "I'm goin' back tomorrow with a tasteful truck to be purchased within three days from my friend Alex Thurston — remember him from cell block six?"

"No," I said, settling into the chair behind

140

my desk after dropping my empty into the recycle box under the sink. "But if you charge that to me, so help me . . ."

"No," shouted Angel. "Contingency. I pay Alex back in three days from the money I make grooming the cats. This business can grow, Jimmy. Grow fast. I'll have you paid back in a week. And then Feline Finesse starts expanding. You can come in with me."

"Thanks, Angel, but no thanks. I just want Olivia Carstairs's Self cat. Now, I'm tired. I want to watch a football game or something on television, maybe read one of the magazines that have been piling up in the box in my bedroom and go to sleep."

"Making a mistake, Jimmy," Angel said, shaking his head. "One will tell two others. Pretty soon this whole town'll be sending their cats to Angelo Martini's."

"What do you know about grooming cats?" I asked.

Angel had parked on my sofa, still holding his empty beer bottle. He had one leg folded over the other and his arms spread out as if we were about to start a nice long discussion of the situation.

"Not a thing," Angel admitted, "but Paco has a friend named Julio or Raul who has a pet shop on the East Side, nothing fancy, neighborhood where you have to pull the bars down, set the alarms, use a big lock and set up a system to electrocute anyone who makes his way past all that. Julio'll be happy to groom the cats. He's great. Best of all he's fast and cheap. I tell the clients I only do two cats a day so they get their cats back the next day. Julio is an artist. He'll give the cats a bath, clean their teeth, brush and maybe trim their hair, and spray them so they smell good. And listen to this. Great idea even if I have to say so myself. We take straight-from-the-shelf supermarket cat food, pour it into big fancy bags and tell the clients it's a diet specially designed for their particular cat. More bucks. Can't lose."

"I want my money and I want that Self cat," I said. "Even if you find the cat, you owe me the two hundred I had to pay the goons. That wasn't part of the deal."

Angel smiled.

"Jimmy," he said, leaning forward and pointing the empty beer bottle at me. "I'm sitting on a gold mine here and it's all because of you. I don't forget my friends. I'm giving you a chance to get into this thing with me."

"No," I said. "It's the same deal you offered me with the Bibles by mail personally signed by the Reverend Andrew Martin of the First Church of the Holy Scriptures; the same deal you tried to get me in on when you wanted to break storefront windows and be on the spot to board them up for a price; the same deal —"

"Enough," Angel said, holding his hand and beer bottle up with as much dignity as he could muster. "This is a legitimate deal, not a scam. You don't want in, you don't want in."

"I want you looking for that cat tomorrow," I said.

"Every waking hour," he said, standing. "You want another beer?"

"No," I said.

"You want to go to Angelo's for a pizza, some darts? Maybe Jean and her friend . . ."

"Carol," I said before I could stop myself.

"Right, Carol. Jean and Carol might be there, getting off work in an hour or so," said Angel, leaning over my desk.

"I'm tempted, Angel," I said, "but my knees say no. They've got a lot of walking to do tomorrow. I'm tired. I'm cranky. I probably have a half-dozen calls on the machine for Angelo Martini's Feline Friends service."

"Feline Finesse," Angel corrected, opening the cabinet under the sink and depositing his empty bottle.

143

"I stand corrected. You go to Angelo's," I said.

"Money hasn't started rolling in on the cat service, Jimmy. I'm bust wide open till the stars, producers and writers of Beverly Hills pay their bills."

He was standing by the sink looking as if he were going to cry. From the confidence of a Greek god to the self-pity of mass murderer in seconds. I dug out a twenty and handed it to Angel.

Angel was beaming again.

"Add it to the bill, Jimmy," he said.

"I will, Angel," I said.

"I'll report tomorrow," he promised, moving to the door. "And I promise: No moves on Carol, just Jean."

"You have my permission to move on Carol," I said.

"No one ever had a friend like you, Jimmy," he said.

"Or like you Angel."

He was gone. A beat later his rental car gagged into something resembling life and headed out of the lot toward Angelo's.

My mail was on the desk. Angel had probably put it there when he came in. I was sure he had checked each piece to see who it was from and what might be in it. As it turned out, there was nothing to be overjoyed about. Mostly bills, including a new one from the homeowners association. There was also a letter from a former client who was now married and lived in Appleton, Wisconsin, with her lawyer husband who didn't know she had spent nearly five years as a high-class hooker. She had a kid now, a boy named Joseph. That was Rocky's name. She had called when Rocky died. She'd heard from a friend who had also gotten off the game.

I put the letter down. Rockfords don't cry. Not much. I looked at Rocky's smiling face in the photograph on my desk, pulled it in and said,

"You're a godfather, Dad."

Then I turned on my answering machine. It was loaded with calls. Five were for Angelo Martini. I wrote the messages and phone numbers on a yellow pad. I thought voice number three for Angel sounded suspiciously like Tom Selleck. There was a call from Dr. Andrew Lewiston asking if I had found Barbie yet and what I was doing. There were three calls from bill collectors; one was a machine telling my machine to stay on the line till a representative could come on the line with an important message. My machine hung up. I patted it gently. The last call was from Moira Green, born Moira

Greenberg, executive secretary extraordinaire. I had once almost asked her to marry me. She stopped me. Now she wanted to know if I wanted to get together for dinner, lunch or just a drink. She had been promoted, gotten her boss's job. She wanted to celebrate. She wanted to celebrate with me. When the messages were over, I sat drumming my left hand on the desk. I checked my watch. It wasn't all that late. I called Moira and got her answering machine, which said simply, in a businesslike voice: "This is Moira. Please leave your message."

I half expected her to pick up the phone when she heard my voice, but she didn't. She was either in the shower or out. I hung up, took my own shower, put on my pajamas and robe and watched *Drums Along the Mohawk* for the twelfth time on the old movie channel.

When it was over and Moira had not called back, I had a bowl of Captain Crunch with milk and went to bed.

CHAPTER SIX

It looked like a typical day on Cove Road. The sun was shining. The gulls were screeching. I had made a pot of fresh hazelnut coffee from beans I had ground myself, and I dropped two frozen blueberry waffles in the toaster. They popped out when I had my pants on and was out picking up my paper. I had paid my *L.A. Times* delivery bill for the entire year. You'd think it was the only thing I could count on, but about three times a week the paper wasn't there. It had been stolen. This time it was there, but Rocky's truck wasn't. Wearing no shoes, a T-shirt, and a pair of trousers, carrying a cup of hazelnut coffee and a newspaper, I walked over to the wreck that Angel had rented the day before. There was a note under the windshield wiper:

Jimmy:
I can't take this piece of junk around the neighborhoods you've got me going. Besides, I need Rocky's truck for a day or two to haul the cats I'm grooming till my cousin gets the Feline Finesse van

painted. I'm sure you won't mind. First priority — Self cat.

— Angel

The note was printed, legible. Angel had not scrawled it in the darkness of my parking lot the night before. He had come prepared. He had also conned me. I should have known. I taught it to him. He had started his rental clunk the night before so I could hear him leave, had gone about fifty feet, turned around, turned off the engine and glided back in relative silence as close to Rocky's truck as he could get. He knew I was keeping the truck in better shape than my car. I hadn't even noticed the truck's starting.

I tucked the note under my arm along with the newspaper and gulped down some hot coffee for two reasons: First, to burn the roof of my mouth in punishment for my stupidity and, second, to urge me into original ideas for what I might do to Angel when I found him.

I went back to the trailer, ate my waffles like cookies, finished my coffee and got dressed.

It was a bad start to the day. It quickly got a lot worse.

The ride to Sherman Oaks wasn't bad. I

had set the alarm and gotten up very early, with the sun. There was traffic. It was moderately heavy, but I got to Ventura Boulevard a little after six in the morning. I drove past Studio City and all the tightly packed shops, which wouldn't open for hours. There was almost no one on the streets. A few cars. A few people eating breakfast at the few places open for breakfast this early. A few of the wandering homeless who the Sherman Oaks police would round up in the next few hours and deport to Encino or Tarzana, where they would be treated to a cup of coffee, a kind word and advice to get over the hills and somewhere along Hollywood Boulevard, where they could step on the stars engraved with the names of the past and present great, most of whom had been great for no more than a year or two. One guy with his mind hiding out somewhere in northern Utah had told me with pride that he had slept on Marilyn Monroe. The police had peeled him off the sidewalk when dawn came, but he was blissful, and I had given him three bucks for pointing out someone I was looking for.

But now I was in Sherman Oaks, respectable, close enough to the studios, exclusive enough if you went down one of the streets that dead-ended at the hills. That was what I did. I found the street. A woman in a

Japanese kimono was walking a little dog. The woman, whose hair was pulled back and could have been any age, had her eyes half-closed while the little pooch carefully considered upon what bank of grass to make a deposit. The woman carried the mandatory pooper-scooper. She might or might not use it, depending on whether she thought she might get caught.

I had been listening to music on the radio: golden oldies, the Beatles, Rolling Stones, Frankie Avalon, the Supremes. For me the real oldies went back to before the fifties, back to about 1910. Normally I'd listen to some soothing-voiced morning radio talk show host with a deep voice, a British accent or the soothing voice of a sexy woman.

This time I listened to golden oldies, thought about what I would do to Angel and tried to ignore the pain in my knees.

I found John Stuart Hill's house on a cul-de-sac, set far back from the street, where no cars were parked. The houses on this street were surrounded by walls of well-trimmed shrubs about six feet high to protect the residents from having to see each other. The rear of Hill's house was supposed to be protected by the hill it nestled against, but like other houses against the hills in the valley, the last big quake had brought down a slide of dirt. If there was a back door to Jack Stuart Hill's house, there was no getting out through it till a team of men with shovels and a big empty truck found the time to do the job. I parked, looked at the house. It was white. It was wood. It was two stories and probably had four bedrooms. There was a pool and a cabana to the right of the house. The pool and cabana were surrounded by an aluminum picket fence. The hill had slid almost, but not quite, to the pool.

I walked up to the driveway, my R&R spiel ready.

I was about five feet away when I noticed that the door was open — not much, three or four inches. People didn't leave their doors unlocked all night in Sherman Oaks or anyplace else within fifty miles of the city. Maybe people didn't leave their doors un-locked all night anywhere in the United States anymore. But they certainly didn't leave their doors open.

There could be many reasons. I didn't explore them. I moved to the door and pressed the bell to the left of the doorway. With the door open, I could clearly hear the chimes that played a few notes of "Lara's Theme" from *Dr. Zhivago*. No one came. I tried the knocker on the door. It was old, brass, polished and clanged against a small square of metal embedded in the door. It was loud. My knock also pushed the door open another foot or more, which was one of my intentions. My other intention was to turn around, go back to my car and get away from Sherman Oaks.

But Barbie Lewiston and who knew what or who else might be inside. I took my chances and went in. The nice thing about being a private detective is that I don't need to get search warrants. The police do. Of course, private investigators could also be arrested for breaking and entering. I wasn't sure what the penalty was for simply entering. I'd have to ask Beth, my lawyer, the next time I talked to her, which I figured might be soon.

The lights were all on. The hallway lights. Lights coming from every room down the hall and the wide, bright and very large living room covered in handmade Mexican tiles. The living room, like the rest of the house as I discovered, was decorated in a kind of hacienda style. The living room overlooked the pool and the hill that might shake loose with the next quake or heavy rain.

But this, I was sure, did not bother John Stuart Hill. I found him on the landing at the top of the stairs after looking through the downstairs rooms, announcing myself with a hearty "Hi" before entering each one. They all looked relatively clean and normal except for the lights all being on after sunrise.

After looking around downstairs, I headed up and found Hill.

Hill was wearing an expensive purple silk robe, but with two bullet holes in it I doubted if it would now pull in two bucks at the nearest Goodwill store. He was on his back. A third bullet had gone in just above his nose. He looked surprised. Who wouldn't be? I put his final age at about fifty. His hair was dyed black and his face was a kind of good-looking tough. I was sure I had seen him as a minor actor in movies or television years ago. Under his silk robe was a bare chest with modest tufts of white hair. In the pocket of his robe was a wallet. There was blood, a lot of blood, on the expensive tile on the landing. Some had traveled far along the landing in rivulets that ran like bloody rivers between the tiles. The blood was sticky but already drying or dry. I avoided stepping in it, wished I had brought my gun from the cookie jar back in my trailer. I looked through the wallet. ID, driver's license with photo, business cards, photographs of young girls with Hill's arm around their willing shoulders and waists, and $570 in cash. I put the wallet back and looked around the upstairs rooms, avoiding the blood.

I was using a handkerchief now and trying to remember what I had touched downstairs that had to be wiped. The bathroom was clean except for a towel that had been aimed at a hamper but missed. The cabinet had a few over-the-counter drugs and a few prescriptions, all for Hill, nothing abusive. They did tell me that he had high blood pressure, a recent infection, and something requiring a strong painkiller. I considered taking a couple of the painkillers for my knee, but I had a few left from the ones Lewiston had given me.

The "bingo" came in two rooms. The first room was at the end of the upstairs hall. The room on the left was open. There were display cases along the walls with museum-style lighting. The cases were empty, but on the floor behind the door I found something familiar: a little blue bottle not unlike the green bottle I had recovered for Dwight Cameron. I left it on the floor but knelt to look at it. It was definitely one of those Chinese bottles painted from the inside and probably dropped by whoever had been here and shot Hill. My guess was that the cases had been filled with bottles or other museum-quality items. I checked Hill's bedroom. His bed had not been slept in, but the covers had been pulled down. Two other upstairs bedrooms looked as if they hadn't been used for a while. The fourth bedroom, the second "bingo" made me sit down on the bed and seriously consider going for Hill's pain pills.

Someone had been here. There was the smell of a woman in the air. The bed had been slept in. The dresser drawers were open as if someone had gotten out of there fast, so fast that they had left a few things, like a pair of blue nylon panties with the initials "B.L." neatly sewn in. The initials were white. The panties were on the floor next to the bed. There were other signs of Barbie Lewiston, including a small bottle of Xanax prescribed by Dr. Andrew Lewiston for Barbie Lewiston. The bottle had probably rolled off the bed when Barbie packed and ran.

There was another possibility: Someone had purposely left the panties and the telltale bottle to point directly at Barbie. I placed the panties and the Xanax bottle on the bed, looked at them for a while and put them back where I'd found them. I'd been hired to find Barbie Lewiston, not to cover up a murder she might have committed.

I stood for a second thinking. I had

searched the house, even the kitchen, including the refrigerator, which had a bottle of very good champagne chilling. Then I moved. Into the hall, avoiding the blood, down the stairs, wiping everything I had touched, which might well mean I was also wiping away the killer's prints. There were surfaces I had touched that I didn't bother with because I knew the fingerprint guys couldn't get prints off of rough surfaces, like the white rocks around the fireplace in Hill's den.

I left the door open as I had found it, wondered whether the woman in the kimono walking her dog had seen me. There was no sign of her or anyone else as I got off the street. I got in my car and headed to Ventura, deciding which call to make first.

I found a space not too far from an outdoor telephone, checked my change, parked, but didn't get out of the car.

I had decided to call Dennis Becker, probably my oldest and best friend even though he was a member of the LAPD. The trick was that the police had new technologies that made it difficult to remain anonymous. If I called, the call might be recorded. I could use a fake accent, but a voice match could be made if it came down to that. The safest thing was to simply drive to Dennis's office, which I did.

Dennis has been losing his hair at the rate of about a quarter of an inch per year for the last decade. He showed signs of his age, but so did I. He still sat at the same desk he always had and looked up, not particularly happy to see me.

"I've already got a busy day, Jim," he said, putting down a phone.

I stood before him as he answered another call and took notes. When he hung up that one, I could see by the lit-up button on his phone that he had another call.

"I've got no time for coffee. I've got no time for lunch. I plan to run into the john later so I can douse my head and take time to breathe. People are killing each other out there. Kids. It's easy to catch 'em, hard to hold 'em. That's my story for the day. Maybe you can come to the house on Sunday. We're having a barbecue. Bring a date if you want."

"Sounds good to me," I said with a smile.

"Now you say, 'Good-bye, Dennis. What time do you want me on Sunday?' "

He started to reach for the phone.

"I've got a murder for you, Dennis," I said. "One with complications."

Dennis sighed, ran a thick hand over the top of his head and bit his lower lip. He looked around the office. People were scurrying, typing reports. The door to Captain Diehl's office was mercifully closed. Diehl didn't like me and he didn't like the fact that Dennis and I were friends. Every favor Dennis did for me was done at the risk of Diehl's finding out and dropping Dennis back to sergeant with the accompanying decrease in salary.

"Report it downstairs," he said.

"This one can make you look good, Dennis," I said, leaning forward. "Private informant tells you a big TV and movie producer has been murdered. You investigate."

"Why are you being so nice to me, Jim?" he asked with reasonable skepticism.

"I have a client," I said.

"Who might be the killer?"

"No, but I might be able to turn up some evidence that can help. Client pays the charges."

Dennis looked at his phone. All three lines were lit up.

"So, where is the body?" he asked with a sigh as deep as the Grand Canyon.

I told him.

"Why didn't you call the Sherman Oaks police?" he asked.

"We're pals," I said. "Besides, you can

keep my name out of it. I'm the private informant."

I gave him the address, the name of the victim, and said I'd found the door open and the body on the landing when I came to talk to Hill about my client's case.

"What's your client's case, Jim?" Dennis asked, searching in his desk drawers, probably for a bottle of anything resembling aspirin. He came up with a bottle and a file. He dropped the file on the desk in front of me.

"You know what's in this file?" he said, lowering his voice and looking at Captain Diehl's door. "It's a bunch of one-page reports of murders and suicides you have discovered and reported over the last decade. I don't know how many you didn't report. Diehl asked for this report more than two months ago. I've managed to stall him. My guess is he plans to go after your PI license."

"I don't think he can," I said.

"I don't either," said Dennis, "but he can put you in front of a review board that'll ask you tough questions about your past and your methods. Who knows what recommendation they'll come up with? A recommendation that will go to the license bureau and be reviewed again by the chief of police, who rubber-stamps the bureau. It won't be fun."

"I can handle it," I assured him, feeling anything but assured.

I'd worry about it later.

"Dennis. I'm giving you a corpse. You give me a few days."

"A few days? Like two, three, six?"

"Let's say three," I said. "To find my client and maybe some ideas about who the killer might be."

"Let's say good-bye," he said.

"Offer still open for Sunday?"

"Still open," Dennis said. "Now go. I'll call you later."

He picked up the phone, an open line. I figured he was calling the police in Sherman Oaks. I left and headed for the nearest public phone.

"Dr. Lewiston is in surgery this morning," Nurse Janet Caples said when I got her on the phone.

"It's important," I said. "About Barbie. Very important."

"If you give me a number, I can have him call you as soon as possible," she said.

"As soon as possible may be too late," I said.

She hesitated for a decade or two and gave me a number. I thanked her, hung up and called the number.

"Surgical," a woman's voice said.

"Dr. Lewiston," I said. "Tell him Jim Rockford has to talk to him. He'll want to take the call."

"Dr. Lewiston is just coming out of surgery and then he has another operation in twenty minutes," said the woman.

"That's interesting, and I know that's how he makes his more than adequate living, but I think he'll want to take a second or two out of his busy schedule to talk to me."

"I'll tell him you wish to speak to him, Mr. Rockford."

The line didn't go dead and then Tony Bennett came on singing "All the Way." Bennett was about halfway through the song when Lewiston came on.

"You found her?" he asked.

"Not exactly," I said. "But I know where she was last night. There was no Jack Stuart Hill on the list of show business people you had done surgery on and sent Barbie to see."

"Jack Stuart Hill?" Lewiston said. "He wasn't on the list because he has never been a patient of mine and I didn't send Barbie to see him."

"But you know who he is?" I said.

"Yes, former actor, small-time producer, son of a bitch and a collector."

"Collector?"

"Bottles, like Dwight who sent you to me.

Like me. Hill has an excellent collection. Claims it's the best in the world. I've seen it. It's good, but I don't think he appreciates it in the best sense. To him the bottles are just a good investment for which he wants an extortionate price. What has Jack Stuart Hill got to do with this?"

"He's dead," I said. "There's good reason to think Barbie was at his house last night and maybe more nights. There's even good reason to think she might have killed him."

"Rockford," he said wearily. "I've been up since four this morning. I've already done two knee replacements and a very complicated piece of wrist surgery. Did you know that Thomas Jefferson broke his wrist jumping over a fountain in Paris in a dash to get to his mistress? Did you know that his wrist mended at a slightly odd angle causing his handwriting to change and diminishing the output of his considerable creative ability?"

"I didn't know that," I admitted.

"Had I been Jefferson's surgeon, I could have repaired that wrist and restored it to its former state and a life of pain-free ability to write, draw. In short, I could have increased that body of creative work he left to the world."

"That would have been a great contribution to the world," I said.

"I have prolonged and restored the careers of athletes, actors, writers, producers, musicians — most of whose work I deplore — and politicians — a few of whose principles I have actually agreed with. Do you see where I am going with this, Rockford?"

"Find Barbie, protect her, protect you and get my knee surgery," I said.

"Simple as that," he said. "Barbie wouldn't intentionally step on an ant, let alone shoot a lowly lecherous producer."

"Last thing, Doc," I said. "Someone not only shot Hill but stole his bottle collection."

The silence was long.

"You know if Hill owns a boat?" I asked to keep things moving.

"Boat?" he asked, sounding far away. "I think so."

"Do you know the name of the boat?" I asked.

"Name? I was only on it once to pick up a bottle I'd purchased from him for far more than its market value. I think it was docked in Santa Monica. Why?"

"Remember the name of the boat?" I asked.

"Name. No. Wait. *Queen Mab*. No . . ."

"*Princess Louise*?" I suggested.

"That sounds right," he said. "*Princess Louise*."

"Thanks," I said. "Last question. Did Barbie ever meet Hill?"

"Let me think," he said. "Yes, once a few weeks ago. Hill said he wanted to buy a few items in my collection. Barbie was at home. I told Hill I wasn't interested at the price he was offering."

"Did Barbie speak to him alone when he came?"

"I don't know," he said. "I may have taken a call from the office or hospital. They may have been alone briefly."

"Thanks, Doc," I said. "I'll get back to you."

"Find her," he said. "If she's involved in any . . . Please find Barbie."

"I'll find her," I said confidently, with a confidence I didn't feel.

I hung up, confused. One way to pull it together was that John Stuart Hill was the buyer in the rain the other night, the one with the hooded raincoat who got off the *Princess Louise*. It made sense. He had hired Hanson to steal the bottle. He never got the bottle. I brought it back to Dwight Cameron. Now Dr. Andy Lewiston's niece, who I've been hired to find, winds up with Hill, who winds up dead, his bottles gone. I didn't know how many fanatic Chinese bottle collectors there were out there. I should have asked Lewiston, who might be able to give me an educated guess.

Another possibility existed. Hill got rough and romantic and Barbie got frightened and shot him and took off with the bottles, thinking she could sell them and knowing from her uncle that they were worth a great deal. I didn't like that possibility.

Third possibility. A thief comes, orders Hill to give up his bottles. Hill refuses. Bang. Bang. Bang. Barbie hides upstairs. Thief takes the bottles. Barbie finds the body, packs and runs, leaving her panties behind. But all the lights had been on at Hill's, suggesting that he had been killed the night before and that he had not gone to bed yet. Any thief would see the lights, listen for voices unless he was really high and desperate. If he came for the bottles, he would probably know where they were and could have broken in when Hill went to sleep. Chances were good that he could get away with the collection without waking Hill.

Fourth possibility. Someone had been hired to kill Hill and take the bottles. Whoever had done the killing hadn't bothered to check Hill's wallet or take anything else of value as far as I could tell. I had spotted some expensive rings in Hill's bedroom inside a little wooden box. The killer hadn't searched the room.

One could go mad considering the possibilities or one could do something. I drove to Santa Monica, put on my sunglasses, took off my jacket, got my semiwrinkled blue zipper jacket from the trunk and put on my Greek fisherman's hat. I hoped I would pass for a wealthy boat owner who was as stupid as he was rich.

Some of the slips were empty. Most still held their boats gently rocking as the small waves came in. It was a good day for boating. I adjusted my cap and started down the long dock. I nodded at a few people lunching on their decks. They nodded back. I touched my cap to a not-too-young but very well-built woman in jeans and a man's denim shirt designed to show her more than adequate bosoms. She also wore sunglasses and let her long golden hair blow behind her. She didn't seem to notice me and sneakered her way to land.

It looked like the police had not yet learned of the existence of the *Princess Louise.* It might take them hours. It might take them days. Depending on their investigation, it might never take place at all. There seemed to be no one aboard the boats to the right and left of the *Princess Louise.* My leg wouldn't let me hop onto the deck, but I got on with some pomp, suggesting I was in no hurry if anyone was watching.

I took off my sunglasses and peered through the window of the *Louise*'s cabin. It was moving toward midday. It should have been bright inside. I couldn't see anything and then I realized that black shades had been pulled down from inside the cabin.

I moved to the door, tried it. It was locked. I moved to the rear hatch, tried that. It wasn't locked. I opened it and with more than a little pain and awkwardness I climbed down the short ladder and closed the hatch behind me.

I wasn't sure what I was looking for — an address book, something written, letters, maybe even the missing bottles or Barbie cowering in a corner.

What I found when I entered the cabin was darkness with a few slits of light coming through the black shades. I was about to start groping the walls for a switch when someone beat me to it.

The someone was familiar. His name was Hanson. He had a large gun in his right hand and it was aimed at me.

"Told you I'd be back for you," he said with a grin that showed natural, well-polished teeth. He brushed back his straight yellow hair and motioned for me to sit. I did on a thin pillow that ran across a built-in bench below the windows. "Got here no more than a minute or two before you. I've had a busy morning."

He was wearing jeans, deck shoes and a white pullover Polo. I liked the Polo. Normally, I would ask where he got it.

"How did you know I'd be here?" I said.

"Didn't," he said with a grin. "Got lucky. I came to find the guy I was supposed to give the box to, the one you took from me."

"The one you took from Dwight Cameron," I added. "Why did you want to find the guy?"

"Make a deal," he said, staying as far from me as he could in the small space. "He'd tell me where to get more little bottles. I'd get them. He'd pay."

"He's dead," I said.

"Dead? Who?"

"The guy you came to make a deal with."

Hanson mulled this over and definitely looked sorry for himself.

"But I got lucky," he finally said. "I got you."

"Don't you want to know who the guy was or how he died?" I asked, carefully taking off my Greek fisherman's cap and placing it on the pillow next to me.

"No, I don't care if he had a heart attack

or blew his brains out," said Hanson. "He's gone. That is, if you're tellin' the truth."

"He was shot. With a gun like yours. I'd say you might be in big trouble."

Hanson tried to smile.

"That's nuts," he said. "I don't even know the guy. But I do know you."

"Hanson," I said wearily. "The other night I'd say we came out about even in pain. My chin and leg. Your face and stomach. If we really explore the event, I probably got the worst of it."

"But you took the bottle and I walked away with my whammy between my legs."

"Whammy?" I said.

"I don't use bad words," Hanson said seriously. "Afraid I'll use one in front of my Aunt Jackie."

"You shoot Hill?" I asked casually.

"Hill? Who the hell is — Oh. Why would I shoot him?"

"To get his bottles and find someone else to sell them to," I said exasperated and trying not to show it. "How did Hill hire you if you didn't know his name?"

"I didn't even know where the hell he lived," Hanson said. "All I knew was this boat. I figured I'd search the boat, maybe find out where he lived, pay him a visit if he didn't show up. I met him in a bar, same as I met you when you said your name was Carson. Only he didn't give me a name, just said someone had recommended me for a job. We talked. I was careful. He gave me $500 in cash in an envelope, told me what he wanted and where to find it. Then he told me to meet him on the dock the other night. I saw him get off the boat. It was raining, but I've got good eyes — twenty-twenty, runs in the family."

"Some people have all the luck," I said.

"Not me," he said. "I could have just skipped with his $500. But I did the job."

"Guy who hired you," I said. "About fifty, well built, black hair, good-looking?"

"Yeah," Hanson said. "What's your point?"

"Just checking. Mind if I ask one or two more questions?"

"Not gonna save you from a bullet in the gut," he said.

I shrugged and asked,

"You ever kill anybody?"

"What's the difference?"

"You haven't," I said, trying to look relaxed. "I have. It's messy and it stays with you even if you get away with it. We've both known cons who were sent up for some felony but the cops didn't know they had put someone away with a gun or a knife or

170

pushed them off a roof."

"What's your point?" Hanson said nervously.

"You kill me and you'll wake up in the middle of the night with a dream you'll have over and over of me covered with blood and coming for you."

Hanson laughed, but it wasn't as confident as he wanted it to sound.

"I'll shoot you in both knees," he said.

"I'll recover. Maybe a year. Maybe longer. Then I'll come for you."

"Then," he said, "I guess I'll have to kill you like I planned."

Suddenly there were footsteps on the dock and someone stopped right in front of the *Princess Louise*. It was two people arguing. One a man. The other a woman. I had the feeling that the woman was the one I had touched my cap to a few minutes earlier.

"Listen, Amanda," the man said with some kind of Eastern European accent, "I can't afford a bigger ship right now. When we get the contracts, sign them and get the first check, we can talk about trading the *Tangerine* in for a bigger model."

"I don't believe you," she said venomously.

I stood up and took a step toward Hanson, who looked surprised at my move. He didn't shoot. I knew at least one good reason why. The two people on the dock would hear the shots and with whatever was left in me I'd shout "murder" and Hanson's name.

"Put it all together," I said. "Shoot me and you've got more trouble than your vengeance is worth. Now, pull the trigger or put the gun away, because I'm going through that door."

I moved to the door figuring I had a fifty-fifty chance of making it. I didn't know Hanson well enough to be sure how stupid or even crazy he might be.

"Yourself, yourself, yourself. That's all you think about," the woman on the dock shouted.

I was halfway through the door when the man on the dock shouted back at the woman, "Enough. Enough. If I want this, this heartache, I can get it from my wife."

I didn't look at Hanson as I completed my exit and closed the door.

Being alive felt good. The arguing couple on the deck continued. It was the woman I had seen earlier. The man was short and wore a white deck cap. He was dressed for a morning cruise, which it looked like he might not get. When he turned to me, I could see that he had a perfect and flowing handlebar mustache.

Both of them noticed me and stopped their argument, waiting for me to leave. I climbed on the dock, realized I had left my Greek fisherman's hat on the *Princess Louise* when I reached up to touch the brim. I could hear the door of the *Louise*'s cabin open behind me. I didn't look back. I moved beyond the feuding couple, doing my best to keep from limping toward land.

Hanson caught up with me when I felt the ground under my feet. It was dry now, not a field of mud like it had been when Hanson and I had tumbled in it.

"Rockford," he said.

I stopped.

"You remembered my name," I said.

"Someone told me. What's the difference?" he asked. "How about working out a deal here?"

He was talking softly now. Definitely intruding on my space. First he plans to murder me. Then he wants to enter a partnership with me.

"Deal?"

"Yeah," he said. "You tell me the scam and I tell you what I know and we take it to whoever killed this Hill guy."

I looked at him. He meant it.

"What've you got?" I asked.

"Nope," he said. "I tell you what I know

after you tell me what you know."

"Nope," I said.

"I got an idea about who might have killed Hill," he said.

"I'm on a case," I said. "I'm trying to find a missing person. Unless I turn out to be a suspect, I'm not interested in who killed Hill. And I'm definitely not gonna be your partner and blackmail a murderer. I could use more money, but not badly enough to risk going back in the joint. I'll work a good con on a case, don't get me wrong. But covering for a murderer? Felony. Maybe accessory after the fact. Maybe lots of things."

"You know where I live," he said.

"I know where you live," I said.

"You change your mind, be at my place at nine tonight."

He started to walk away and then he turned and pointed a finger at me, saying, "You ought to be thanking me for not blowing you away."

"Thank you, Hanson. If there's ever a time I can refrain from killing you, I'll do the same."

He looked puzzled, nodded and walked toward the road.

I went back to the *Princess Louise*. The arguing couple was gone. Now the cabin door was open. I got my Greek fisherman's cap, put it on and searched the drawers and cabinets, looked under the beds and came up with some books about Chinese bottles. The pictures of about a third of the bottles had little check marks next to them. I couldn't figure out whether they meant he had them or they were ones he wanted.

In the back of one of the books was a typed page with a list of names. Andy Lewiston was on the list. So were seven others. Only one was circled: Dwight Cameron, who had hired me to recover his precious green bottle.

I had another list, the one that Andy Lewiston had given me of patients in show business he had sent Barbie to. I checked the lists against each other. One name appeared on both: Carl Corbin. So Corbin was a Chinese bottle collector, too. The bottle connection might have been the reason he had gone to Andy Lewiston for his new knees. They probably knew and traded with each other. But what would Corbin, who had told me he was openly gay, want with Barbie Lewiston? I pocketed the list.

I stopped at a restaurant about a half-mile down. It was a run-down seafood place. The shrimp were great and the abalone just about the best I'd ever had. In spite of bad knees and confusion and a near-death experience, a good meal made me feel glad to be alive.

I stopped at Dwight Cameron's house. The man who answered the door had a British accent and told me that Mr. Cameron was out for the day. I had already given Cameron one of my cards. I gave another one to the British guy and asked him to have Mr. Cameron call me as soon as he could.

Then I headed home with the idea of spending a few hours fishing and thinking. Such was not to be.

CHAPTER SEVEN

When I hit the Cove, I saw Angel parked at the side of the road in a white van. There was a picture of a pink cat on the side, and writing in a fine black script indicated this was the vehicle of Feline Finesse. I pulled up next to him and read the printed letters under the larger ones in black script. The proprietor of Feline Finesse was Angelo Martini, Esq.

"Classy, huh, Jim?" he asked when I stopped reading.

"Classy, Angel," I said.

"No phone number. No address. Class," he said.

"Angel, give me three good reasons why I shouldn't haul you out of that truck and throw you in front of the next eighteen-wheeler that comes by."

"Okay, Jimmy," he said, leaning out of the window. "One, Rocky's truck is back in front of your place. Washed and fully gassed. Number two, I've got the cat we've been looking for, the Self. Found him in an animal shelter. He's in the back of the van. Number Three, here's the $600 I owe you."

I got out of my car watching out for traffic and motioned to Angel to do the same. He did. We moved to the rear of the van. He opened it and grinned, pointing to a cat in a cage.

"Angel," I said. "That is not a Self. It's just an orange tabby. It looks nothing like the pictures I gave you."

"She might not notice," he said.

"Angel, find the right cat."

"Jimmy, forget about the cat. Business is booming. I'm making a mint. Raul can't keep up with the cats of the rich and famous I bring in. In a week or two, I'll pay you whatever that Olivia Carstairs promised to find her cat."

"Douglas," I said. "His name is Douglas. And it's not a question of money . . . Well, not altogether. Find that cat."

"Okay, Jimmy. Okay," Angel said. "Don't have a conniption."

I started back to my car, turned and said,

"If you ever touch Rocky's truck without my permission again, they'll be searching for your pieces for the next century."

"Gratitude," he said, shaking his head and closing the door on the cat. "Remember, you asked for three reasons."

"I'm listening."

"There are two cops parked in the lot,

unmarked car, far enough away to see you walk into your trailer, well enough hidden by a really neat Lexus so you wouldn't look their way."

"You're sure?"

"I recognize one of them," Angel said. "Name's Corprelli. Mean bastard. In my business ventures, it pays to look around before you get out of your car. You never know who's lurking."

"Okay, Angel," I said. "We're even. Now find Mrs. C's cat."

I could drive away and think or I could go home and see what moves if any the parked cops made. That's assuming Angel was telling the truth. I decided to go home and face whatever might be there.

I never got to the door. I parked about fifteen feet away from the trailer, got out and headed for the small deck I'd built that led to the door. The car Angel had described had moved slowly from its place of hiding and had made a narrow arch heading toward me. I had one hand on my railing when the car parked close to the trailer and between me and my car. Two men got out. Angel was right. They were both cops.

"Rockford?" one of them asked, one who had been around a while. He had a sour look on his face, a small gut and a hand strategically and casually placed so he could go for the weapon under his jacket. The other guy was younger, slimmer, trying to look hard and failing.

"Corprelli?" I returned.

The cop with the sour look turned even more sour wondering how I knew his name.

"You own a handgun?" he asked.

"Yeah," I said. "A .38. Fully licensed."

"You carrying?"

He reached into his pocket and came out with a plastic bag inside of which was a gun that looked suspiciously like the one I thought was inside in the cookie jar.

"This yours?" Corprelli asked flatly.

"I'd have to take a closer look," I said, "and check to see if my gun is still in the trailer."

"We found it in the cookie jar," Corprelli said.

"You found — Do you have a warrant?"

The young cop reached into his inner jacket pocket and came out with a couple of pages of paper stapled together.

"What's going on?" I asked.

"We are arresting you on suspicion of murder," said Corprelli.

I stood stunned while he Mirandized me.

"Please come with us, Mr. Rockford," the

younger one said.

"Who am I supposed to have killed?" I asked, coming back down the steps.

"John Stuart Hill," said Corprelli, nodding for me to put my hands behind my back, knowing I knew the routine. The young one cuffed me and opened the back door of their unmarked car. I got in. He motioned me to the far corner and got in after me. Corprelli drove.

"Why'd you do it?" Corprelli asked casually as we drove down the highway heading for LA.

"I've been arrested for murder," I said. "I don't say any more till I talk to my lawyer."

"You wanna talk baseball?"

"Not particularly," I said.

"Suit yourself," he said.

I looked at the young cop in the back with me. I was John Gotti or O. J. Simpson. I might lunge at him with my teeth or open the door with my mouth and jump into traffic. I was a man to be watched. I shut up and looked out the window trying to figure out what had happened. They must have already run ballistics or I wouldn't have been arrested for murder, and a warrant probably wouldn't have been issued. Someone must have pointed a finger at me, probably with an anonymous phone call. I wasn't sure about the *why*. Maybe I wasn't sure about anything.

We hit headquarters and the two cops ushered me through, one on each side, past those waiting in the lobby, including four guys in spangled mariachi costumes complete with sombreros.

"In here," said Corprelli, reaching behind me to remove the cuffs.

The young cop opened the door for me and I walked in. Then the door closed. The cops didn't follow me. I'd been in this room before. It was used for taking statements, talking to witnesses and suspects, and once in a while holding small line-ups. There was a one-way window along the wall to my left. I wondered who was behind it; probably Captain Diehl.

I knew where Dennis Becker was: seated across the table in the middle of the room, his tie loose, his look definitely uncomfortable.

"Have a seat, Jim," he said, his eyes glancing slightly toward the mirror just in case I didn't know it was there.

I indicated with a blink that I knew. Dennis sighed deeply and started with,

"Want some coffee?"

"No thanks," I said. "I want to know what happened and I want my lawyer."

There was a phone on the table. Dennis pointed to it. I called Beth Davenport. No answer. Before Dennis could say anything, I called her beeper and said, "Beth. Jim Rockford. I've been arrested on suspicion of murder. I'm at police headquarters. I've told them I'm saying nothing till you get here. So get here fast."

I hung up and faced Dennis.

"All I'm saying without my lawyer," I said, "is I didn't kill John Stuart Hill."

"You knew him?" Dennis asked.

I folded my arms and said nothing.

Dennis looked down at a typed report in front of him.

"You don't mind if I talk?" he asked.

"I don't mind," I said. "But you'll have to repeat it all for my attorney, unless you're just going to read that report and give her a complete copy."

"She'll get a copy," Dennis said, looking at me with what I took for sympathy. "I'll summarize."

"Sometime early last night, someone entered the home of John Stuart Hill in Sherman Oaks. Hill was shot three times. In the morning, we were notified that something was wrong at the Hill house."

Dennis had been informed by me, but he didn't say that. I'm sure the report didn't say that. He was doing his best to protect me, but I could see by the few drops of sweat on his brow that it was going to be tough.

"We went to the Hill house," he said. "Found the body. Someone had tossed the place, taken the television, probably any jewelry he had. Place was a mess. Hill's wallet was next to his body. Credit cards were there. No cash. Hour later we get another call suggesting that we check your weapon."

"And you knew where I kept it," I said.

"Yeah," Dennis admitted uncomfortably.

I had lots of questions I couldn't ask with people on the other side of that mirror. The top one Dennis couldn't answer: Why had someone set me up for Hill's murder? Why me? Lots of other questions. After I had found the body and left Hill's house, someone had come, torn the place up, taken Hill's money and left before the cops got there. All of which suggested that someone was watching when I went through Hill's open door, someone with my gun in his pocket, the one he — or she — had used to kill Hill. And what about Barbie? Dennis hadn't said anything about the prescription bottle or Barbie's initialed panties. Maybe he was saving it for later. I wanted to ask Dennis about the empty case where Hill had kept his very expensive collection of Chinese bottles. But

I said nothing. Dennis looked at me.

"I'll take that coffee now, Lieutenant Becker," I said.

Dennis nodded, picked up the report in front of him, moved around the table, touched my arm in support as he passed so the people behind the mirror couldn't see it, and disappeared through the door.

Beth arrived less than ten minutes later with Dennis and a man I didn't recognize. Beth wasn't breathing hard. Her dark blonde hair was in place and she was wearing her absolutely no-nonsense green suit with the white frilly blouse buttoned up to the neck. She put her briefcase down, straightened her skirt and sat next to me.

"How did you get here so fast?" I asked.

"I was in the building with another client," she said. "Fate appears to be on our side, at least for the moment."

Dennis sat across from us alongside the man who put his briefcase on the table. He was about thirty, thin, neat blue suit beginning to show signs of wear. He had a full head of dark hair combed neatly back. I wondered if that hair came down at night. He also wore granny glasses, which he looked over, as I discovered, when he wanted to show that he didn't believe you.

"This is Assistant District Attorney Flaherty, James Flaherty," Dennis said. "I am officially informing you that this conversation is being taped."

"We may have some objection to that," Beth said, not opening her briefcase.

"You really have no choice," said Flaherty with a smile. He should have been playing an extra in a college comedy.

"But we have the choice of not allowing such a tape into evidence if we do raise an objection," she said. "My client, I assume, was informed only a short time ago that he was a suspect in this crime."

"About ten minutes ago," said Dennis.

"He is under stress," she said. "And I think the law would agree that assuming his innocence, it will take him a little time to get over the shock."

"We have the right to interview him now," Flaherty said. "And we intend to exercise that right."

"And I have the right to confer privately with my client and to see a copy of the warrant and the report filed before he answers any more questions. So, either Mr. Rockford and I go somewhere where he can confer with complete privacy or I will advise him at this time to answer no more questions. You may ask. My guess is in his present state he will not be able to answer."

The young lawyer looked at Dennis, who shrugged, and then looked at me and Beth over his granny glasses.

"I'll be right back," he said.

We all knew where he was going. Dennis, Beth and I didn't say a word. Flaherty was back in about two minutes saying that Lieutenant Becker would take us somewhere where we could confer briefly before the questions began. This was acceptable to Beth, who stood with her briefcase. Dennis also stood. Flaherty sat, opening his briefcase and removing a Thermos.

Dennis led us down a corridor and into a private visitor's room.

"It's not bugged," Dennis said. "You have my word."

"I'd rather be somewhere out of this building where we didn't have to take the word of an officer," Beth said. "Sorry, Dennis."

"I understand," he said. "This is awkward for me, too, and I'm gonna have to ask Jim some questions I'd rather not ask. I'll have an officer waiting outside. When you're finished, he'll take you back to the other room for the questions."

Dennis left, closing the door.

This was a duplicate of the other room, but without the mirror. That didn't mean it wasn't bugged or that a video recorder wasn't somewhere, but now we were into the lawyer/client relationship. They couldn't use anything they might get, and they were eligible for a lawsuit if we could prove that they had listened or taped. I plopped into a chair. Beth put on her glasses, sat, read the copy of the report and warrant that Dennis had given her, and then stood. There were many reasons I had considered asking Beth to marry me in the past. I had never quite done it and I had the feeling that there would be a reluctant "no" at the end of my question. We remain friends, and she gives me a decent rate for representing me. She likes being paid on time, but there were times when I was really down that she worked for nothing.

"Tell the story, Jim," she said. "Your way, start to finish. I won't interrupt unless I have to. Don't hold anything back."

I told her. I went all the way back to the green bottle and my run-in with Hanson that first night and today. I told her about Barbie Lewiston and her uncle, my client. I told her I preferred to keep her name out of it for the time being. Beth interrupted to say that might not be possible. I nodded and went on, going through every step of how I found Hill, went through the house, found the empty bottle display case, Barbie's underwear and found myself arrested for Hill's murder.

"So, simply, whoever killed Hill set you up for murder. But the killer couldn't be sure if or when you would go to Hill's."

"Then our killer, who called in to helpfully tell the police I had put three bullets in Hill, would have called anyway, and I would have been picked up without even knowing the murder had been committed and with my gun."

Beth paced the floor, arms folded, glasses back in her pocket. She paused at the barred window, looked out, came to a decision and said,

"Okay, let's see if we can get you out of here." She reached for her briefcase. "Answer all of their questions as briefly as possible. If you can do a 'yes' or 'no,' do it. If one of us is in doubt we'll try to whisper. Pause before you answer each question to give yourself a chance to think and me a chance to decide if I want to discuss the answer."

"How many times have we had to go through that speech over the last decade," I said wearily.

"I don't know," she said. "Six, seven, maybe more."

She moved around the table, touched my

hand and kissed my cheek. She smelled good. I considered proposing on the spot, but I didn't consider it seriously.

Then we were walked back to the mirrored room and the seated Dennis, who had his head in his hands, but sat up quickly. Flaherty's Thermos had disappeared back into the briefcase.

"We ready?" Dennis asked.

"We're ready," Beth said.

BECKER: James Rockford, you are charged with the murder of John Stuart Hill. Why did you shoot him?

ME: I didn't.

BECKER: We have your weapon, with which the crime was committed. We found it in your home after the murder.

BETH: You had a search warrant?

FLAHERTY: Absolutely.

ME: Was it a man or woman who called and said I killed Hill?

BECKER: We ask the questions. You answer the questions.

ME: Isn't it more than possible that whoever called set me up? How did they know it was my gun?

BECKER: We're not here for you to ask us questions.

BETH: We want Mr. Rockford's questions

in the record, answered or not.

Becker looked at Flaherty who said, "Okay, but on condition that he answer questions put to him." Beth nodded her agreement. It was between the two lawyers. Dennis and I just looked at each other uncomfortably.

BECKER: Where were you last night between the hours of 10 P.M. and 6 A.M.?
ME: That's the time of death?
FLAHERTY: That's not responsive.
ME: Home. I had a busy day and I've got bad knees. I laid back and watched an old movie. You want to know what it was?
BECKER: You could have checked the television listings and found things you'd seen before. Bottom line is no one can confirm you were at home during those hours last night and early this morning.
ME: Is that a question?
BECKER: Yes.
ME: Last night, the night before. There was one night a friend, male, slept on my couch.
BECKER: How did you know John Stuart Hill?
ME: I never met the man.
BECKER: (*hesitating and then plunging*

ahead) But you saw his body. You so informed me.

ME: I went to see him because he was a lead in a case I'm on. I came to see you immediately after.

BECKER: You told me that the house was spic-and-span when you left it.

ME: It was. I looked around, thought the killer might still be there.

BECKER: And being a good citizen, you were going up against him without a weapon?

ME: Something like that.

BECKER: By the time a police team arrived at Hill's house, the place was a mess, turned over, things broken. You didn't do that?

ME: My guess is that whoever took my gun and shot Hill was outside, saw me coming and going, went in and —

BECKER: What? Turned the place over for the pure joy of doing it? Or was he or she supposedly looking for something?

ME: I don't know. I told you when we talked before — Hill was a collector of rare Chinese bottles. There was a room upstairs with locked display cabinets. My guess is that whoever killed Hill was after the bottles. The cases were empty.

BECKER: Then what was the killer looking for?

ME: I don't know.

BECKER: Can you account for the fact that when the police arrived at Hill's house the display cabinets you're talking about were filled with bottles?

ME: When I left, the display case was empty.

FLAHERTY: So, whoever killed Mr. Hill, assuming it wasn't you, took the bottles, left a clean house and after you left trashed the house and put the bottles back.

Beth touched me. I leaned over. She whispered in my ear. I nodded.

ME: That's one possibility. There are others that are far more plausible.

FLAHERTY: Would you like to give us one or two?

ME: Well, they . . .

BECKER: More than one?

ME: Okay, maybe "he." He was there to rob Hill, steal something valuable. He made too much noise. Hill caught him. The thief shot him.

BECKER: With your gun.

ME: Thief shot him, panicked, ran, came back later and took what he wanted after I left.

FLAHERTY: And returned the bottle collection? Were all the lights on when you entered the Hill house?

ME: Yes.

BECKER: How much cash are you carrying?

BETH: That's not a relevant question, Lieutenant.

BECKER: Hill always carried a wad of money in his wallet. His wallet was empty a few feet from the body. You didn't notice?

ME: I didn't see his wallet near the body.

Which was, in fact, the truth. Then it dawned on me. I had been stupid. I whispered to Beth, who sighed and whispered back. I had forgotten to wipe my fingerprints from the wallet.

ME: I checked his wallet. It was in his robe pocket. I wanted to see if it was Hill. I had never met the man.

BECKER: Did you notice if there was cash in his wallet?

ME: Yes, a little over seven hundred dollars.

BECKER: You want to tell us how much cash you're carrying? We didn't find any in your trailer.

ME: Six hundred dollars and change.

BECKER: Which you got where?

ME: From a friend I'd loaned it to.

FLAHERTY: Friend's name?

ME: Angel Martin.

BECKER: A repeat offender. Primarily confidence scams. His list of arrests is pages long. Rockford, your friend lies for a living. No court is going to believe him.

FLAHERTY: Mr. Hill is reported by his maid to have a valuable collection of jewelry, primarily men's rings. The police couldn't find them, but they found an open and empty ivory inlaid box in his bedroom.

BETH: Were there any fingerprints on the murder weapon?

BECKER: Wiped clean.

BETH: So, if I understand what you are both saying, my client committed a murder with his own gun, tore the murder scene apart, stole the victim's wallet and jewelry collection, immediately went to Lieutenant Becker to report the crime, said no one had torn up the house, and reported that a possibly very valuable collection of rare bottles had been stolen when, in fact, he had left them in their cases? And then he put the murder weapon back in his home where it could easily be found?

FLAHERTY: Mr. Rockford's list of convictions is short and his list of arrests long. Panic and a limited intelligence could easily account for these discrepancies both in his answers and his actions.

BETH: I assume that comment was for the record. My client was convicted once, went to prison, and received a full pardon. My client is in a sensitive profession. He sometimes gets involved in finding criminals, often dangerous ones. Occasionally his investigations will lead to his becoming a suspect, as in the present case. In each past case for which he was arrested, the real perpetrator was located, arrested and tried unless they plea-bargained, committed suicide or shot it out with the police and were killed.

FLAHERTY: Excuse me. I didn't realize I was dealing with a saint. You've never committed a crime, Mr. Rockford? Breaking and entering?

ME: Hill's door was open more than a crack.

FLAHERTY: No crimes?

ME: Before I did time I was a confidence man. No convictions. When I got out, I went straight. Legal. I've kept the police informed, usually through Lieutenant Becker, of any of my activities that might involve breakage of the law and I think the lieutenant and even his captain will have to admit that I've helped them on more than one occasion.

BECKER: That's true, but we're talking

about John Stuart Hill's murder now.

ME: Unless my memory is off, and the tape can check, Mr. Flaherty started the discussion of my so-called criminal past.

FLAHERTY: Among the items taken from your possession when you were charged was a small vial of unidentified pills.

ME: Pain pills from my physician. I'll give you his name if you need it, but you can check with your lab.

FLAHERTY: You also had a sheet of paper in your pocket, a sheet of paper with a number of names, one of which was Hill's, another of which was circled. Who are these people?

I looked at Beth and she nodded.

ME: Collectors of Chinese bottles like the ones stolen from Hill's house.

FLAHERTY (*with a weary sigh*): There appear to be no missing bottles from the victim's collection. Where did you get this list and what were you doing with it?

ME: I can't give that information. Client privilege.

FLAHERTY: A judge can order you to tell him or a jury.

ME: Maybe when a judge does I'll answer.

BETH: Anything else, gentlemen?

FLAHERTY: Not now. Mr. Rockford has been officially charged with murder. We appear on the docket tomorrow morning at eight A.M. to argue bail unless you have any objection and need more time, which the state and county will be happy to supply while holding Mr. Rockford.

BETH: Tomorrow morning at eight. I assume my client will be kept in the lockup at the courthouse tonight.

BECKER: Yes.

We all got up. Dennis looked the worst of the quartet. His shoulders were down. He didn't look me in the eye. Beth asked to talk to me briefly in private once more. Flaherty nodded agreement. He really had no choice.

Out in the hall, down which Flaherty fled after checking his watch, Dennis touched my arm and said, "I'm sorry, Jimmy. I had to do my job."

"I know, Dennis," I said. "Are we still on for Sunday barbecue?"

"If you're not otherwise detained," he said with a touch of a smile. "You and your attorney."

"I don't think my coming would be a good idea, Dennis," Beth said. "Unless we have all this wrapped up by then."

"I'll get you a one-man cell," Dennis said.

"Thanks," I said and Dennis turned and headed for the door to the room on the other side of the mirror.

The big uniformed cop was there to escort us to the same room Beth and I had talked in before.

I sat confused. Beth paced, ideas going through her head. Possibilities.

"They said nothing about the girl's pill bottle and panties," she said.

"Doesn't mean they don't have them and aren't looking for her," I said.

"I think they would have asked you about her in some way if they had found them," she said. "They would have said something, asked if you recognized the name, something."

"You think someone tore the place apart to find traces of Barbie Lewiston and cover for her?" I asked.

"It's possible," she said. "Maybe she or a friend of hers came back, found the pills and panties and, while they were at it, took the jewelry and cash."

"My gun?" I asked.

"Give me time to work on that one," she said.

"Or get me time to work on it," I said.

"Flaherty may have a little surprise in the morning," she said. "I know the clerk who sets the docket. I think Judge Weboldt is on tomorrow morning. If not we postpone so we can be sure of appearing in front of him. Weboldt can be talked to."

"Fine," I said. "And what about the bottles? I sounded like an idiot in there."

Beth paced a while longer and then an idea came to me.

"Unless," I said, "they replaced the valuable ones with cheap ones so the police wouldn't know what the real object of the killing was, wouldn't start looking in the right direction."

Beth stopped pacing and looked at me before saying,

"I know a Chinese antique dealer on Rodeo Drive, very exclusive. She'd know. So would three or four of her employees. I'll get on it and try to get permission to walk through the crime scene with my 'assistant,' Angie Woo. Good thinking, Jim."

"But where does it get us?" I asked.

"An explanation of why you didn't see bottles. If you stole them, you wouldn't have pointed out that they were missing if you'd just replaced them."

In an odd way, it made sense. Someone had set me up knowing the people I was dealing with were collectors. They knew they were going to steal the bottles. So they took my gun, shot Hill, took the bottles. Maybe they were interrupted. Maybe by Barbie, who they didn't know was there. For some reason, they didn't kill her, just ran, came back later when she and I were gone and put in the fake bottles, took the money and the jewelry and went to my place to put my gun back when I wasn't home. It was thin, but it was something.

"Or they could have found her and taken her with them," said Beth. "Anything else?"

"Not at the moment," I said, standing.

"We'll get you out of this one, Jim," she said.

"I didn't do it."

She offered her hand. We shook and then she moved into my arms for a quick hug.

She opened her briefcase and came out with a paperback.

"I always carry two," she said. "Lot of times I just sit around in hallways. I just finished this one."

I took it and stepped into the hall with Beth, who gave me a smile and went on her way.

Less than fifteen minutes later I was in the lockup. They had let me keep the book Beth had given me. There were three others in the lockup. None of us felt like talking about the current situation in Eastern

Europe or who the top draft choices might be. Suited me fine. My biggest problems, when I had been in prison, had been noise and lights at night. I could take the daily routine. I would be up running scams behind the walls. Every prison has one or two scavengers who can get you what you need. I was one of them. Angel was my assistant. I'd learned my trade and earned my nickname in the army. Fifth Regimental Combat Team. I was known as "Hound Dog" Rockford. I was young, but I'd learned fast.

But prison at night. There's a lights-out, but there's always enough light coming from the block that you have to cover your head or learn to live with it. That wasn't as bad as the noise. Cons were supposed to be quiet after lights-out, but they played radios, talked, sang, laughed, cried. It took me a long time to tolerate that. I never learned to live with it and I wound up bribing two day guards to let me sleep for four hours a day when everyone was at work. Angel logged me in at the library where we worked and no one ever noticed. I was always at my desk, making deals right after lunch.

I tried not to think about taking another fall for something I didn't do. I tried not to think about the noises and light of the prison nights. I propped up a pillow and began the book Beth had given me. Fortunately they had let me keep my glasses. The book was a biography of Boris Yeltsin. I was sure there were hundreds of subjects I was less interested in, but at the moment I couldn't think of one. The light was dim. I took off my glasses, closed the book and put it on my chest when a voice said,

"You ain't gonna read that?"

I opened my eyes. In the next lockup was a young black man, couldn't have been more than nineteen. He was thin, dirty jeans. He was wearing a white shirt with a picture of a black man with his mouth open. Under the picture was the name "Dry Now Now." It made no sense.

With some difficulty we figured out a way to get the book to him. I tore it into two parts so each one could feed through the wide mesh between us.

The young man smiled.

"Yeltsin," he said. "Man's a lucky jerk-off. You know what I mean? Case history here of how to turn your country over to the gangs. Thanks, man."

"You're welcome," I said.

"My public defender's picking up a suit from my mother," he said. "I'll wear it for the judge tomorrow."

I nodded.

"I think I'm gonna need me a real lawyer, though. You got a good one? I can come up with the bread."

I lay there, shrugged, and covered my eyes with my arm.

"You don't feel much like talkin'?"

"Not much," I said.

"What you up for?" he asked, ignoring the answer I had given him.

"Murder," I said.

"Heavyweight crime," he said with genuine awe. "I'm up for armed robbery. I didn't do it. I mean, I can't say I haven't done a thing here, a thing there. You know what I'm talking about? But I been set up on this one."

"Interesting," I said, my eyes still covered. "Let me know in the morning how you like the book."

I slept almost till dinner. The guard who served it was deadpan, near retirement, didn't even bother to look at our faces. The food wasn't bad. Spaghetti and meat sauce. After dinner I looked over at the kid with the Yeltsin book. He was almost finished with the first half.

There was a toilet in the corner of the small cell in addition to the cot.

I lay there thinking after the trays were collected. When the bored guard called lights-out, the lights did go out. The kid in the next cell with the Yeltsin book muttered, "Sheet."

And then all was silence except for an occasional unknown rattle from a pipe or someone restlessly tossing and snoring. I slept.

In the morning, they came for all four of us. There would be others from other lock-ups. They led us to an empty room with sinks on one side and a wall-length bench on the other. On the far wall were hooks. On two of the hangers were suits. The other two hangers held clean if not stylish clothes.

"What'd I tell you about my suit?" said the kid happily. He was facing up to twenty years, but his mom had come through with a suit and that was enough to make him happy, at least for the moment.

The other suit was mine. The guard gave each of us a bar of soap and a Bic safety razor. The kid who had the Yeltsin book finished first. He had almost nothing to shave. On the other side of me was an older guy whose hands shook as he shaved. He managed, but he was the last to finish. I put on my suit, checked my hair and waited on the bench.

My buddy who was either set up or had

probably come close to murdering someone during a robbery sat next to me and said,

"How I look?"

"Perfect," I said.

"Damn straight," he said.

He looked even younger with the suit on, like a kid at his high school graduation. I retied his tie for him.

"Mind if I keep that Yeltsin book?" he asked.

"Consider it a gift," I said.

"He was one real Russian cowboy," the kid said.

It was almost eight when we were ushered into the courtroom and told where to sit. We all had lawyers; even the guy with the shakes had a public defender young enough to be his granddaughter. She didn't look any too happy to be sitting next to him.

Beth had on a blue suit this morning with a tasteful string of pearls.

"Weboldt," she whispered.

"Great," I said.

"State versus Rockford," came a voice and I went through the routine I knew well.

We stood in front of the judge, who sat behind the bench. He was probably in his seventies, certainly black, and showed no sign that he felt this might be a good morning.

Flaherty stood a few feet from Beth. In the front row, Diehl and Dennis sat together.

"I've read the charges and reports," said the judge, rubbing the bridge of his nose. I had obviously had a better night's sleep than he had. "I have listened to the tape of Mr. Rockford's interview. What do you have to say?"

"Mr. Rockford is a legitimately employed private investigator," Beth said. "Circumstances stemming from his position have from time to time unfortunately placed him before the bench before. As you know from his record, he has lived his entire adult life in the Los Angeles area, has never skipped bail and has been found to be completely innocent of any and all crimes of which he has been accused, as he is innocent of this one. A reasonable bond would allow Mr. Rockford to help me in the gathering of evidence to prove him innocent. I'm sure the police will concur with my statement that Mr. Rockford has indeed been instrumental in clearing a number of crimes from the record."

Beth turned to Diehl and Dennis. Dennis nodded that he agreed. Diehl leaned back and crossed his arms.

"Mr. Flaherty?" asked Judge Weboldt.

"What say you and the jurisdiction?"

"No bail. This is a capital offense with sufficient evidence that Mr. Rockford has committed a murder, as we are confident a grand jury will agree. Mr. Rockford will then go on trial for murder. Murder in the first degree, as he and his attorney well know. The likelihood of someone with Mr. Rockford's background running from the law is great."

Weboldt nodded his head in understanding.

"If I were to set bail, Miss Davenport," Judge Weboldt said, blinking his eyes and trying to fully wake up, "would you be willing to sign for it and guarantee Mr. Rockford's appearance at any and all interviews and legal appearances until such time as a grand jury decides if he is to be continued on bail or confined?"

"Definitely, Your Honor," she said.

"Your Honor," Flaherty said, shaking his head and adjusting his granny glasses. He didn't look quite so full of energy as he had the afternoon before. Maybe I was right: At night he let his long hair down, put on washable tattoos, and jumped into pits and waiting hands and bashed into other people in a quite legal set-to-music manner. Jesus, I was definitely on my way to getting old.

"Yes, Mr. Flatery," said Weboldt.

"Flaherty," the young lawyer corrected.

"Accept my apology," said the judge.

"Your Honor," Flaherty went on, "in this case, the state must insist that —"

"Insist, Mr. Flaherty?" asked the judge, coming awake and looking not at all happy with the young man. "How long have I known you, sir?"

"About two minutes," said Flaherty, looking back at Diehl and Dennis with some confusion.

"Miss Davenport, how long have I known you as an attorney before my bench?"

"Since you were first appointed," she said.

"Twenty years, Mr. Flaherty," Judge Weboldt said. "And in that time not one of the clients she has personally guaranteed has ever jumped bail or failed to appear at a legal interview or court engagement. Mr. Rockford, how many times have you appeared before me in the past two decades?"

I shrugged.

"Would you say at least eight?"

"Something like that, Your Honor," I agreed.

"In each of the cases in which Mr. Rockford has appeared before me, I have granted bail. This includes one case of double homicide with Mr. Rockford's gun in

Mr. Rockford's trailer. Is that correct, Miss Davenport?"

"Absolutely, Your Honor," said Beth.

"In each of these cases, Mr. Rockford has managed to extricate himself with the cooperation of the Los Angeles police from all charges. I find Mr. Rockford to be of little risk, but since this is a murder charge with the defendant's weapon, though without fingerprints or other physical evidence presented by the state, the court sets bond at $100,000," he said.

Flaherty opened his mouth to protest.

"Ten percent, ten thousand dollars, will be put up immediately. You and Mr. Rockford will be informed when and where the grand jury will meet and who will comprise that jury."

"But Your Honor," Flaherty said. "This is ridiculous."

"Young man," said the judge. "I have a long day before me and a headache that I would not wish upon the most heinous criminal I have encountered in my career as a prosecutor and a judge. I do not want to cite you for contempt of court. So I suggest you say no more and accept the judgment of this court."

Weboldt's gavel came down hard. Flaherty and I jumped. Beth didn't move. She didn't smile. She simply said,

"Thank you, Your Honor."

Beth had already called Solly the Bondsman in anticipation of the judge's decision. As usual, Solly appeared and took my PI license for security. My lockup partner with the two-part Yeltsin book now stood before the judge with a public defender and another young assistant prosecutor. His bail was refused. Two felony priors and possession on this one of a semiautomatic weapon.

My lockup partner waved at me. I pointed to myself. He shook his head "no" and I pointed to Beth. This time he nodded his head "yes."

"I think you have a potential client," I said, pointing at the young man. "He already has both halves of your Yeltsin book."

While Beth looked over at the kid, I looked at Diehl and Flaherty, who were talking and looking at us. Though they did their best to hide their feelings, I had the sense that Diehl was informing the young lawyer that he was an incompetent jerk. Dennis stood back, glanced at me once and didn't allow himself a smile. He certainly would feel like one. Diehl was sure to take out his rage on Dennis, but that would be later, in Diehl's office.

There was a line Diehl couldn't cross in dealing with Dennis. There was a limit to the polluted words Dennis would take. Worst-case scenario Dennis would appear before a review board. He had done it before. There was hardly a cop in the city who didn't know and respect Dennis. On the other hand, Diehl had the political connections but no friends. It would be a stand-off. Dennis would take a little abuse — maybe quite a little with the thought of his pension and family and the possibility of being busted down. Then, in all likelihood, Diehl would simply dismiss him from his office with a wave of disgust. It wouldn't be fun for Dennis, but he had been through it before. Both Diehl and I knew that Dennis would not hold back on any investigation, though it wasn't likely he would be assigned to Hill's murder.

Beth and I had coffee at a coffee shop across the street from the courthouse where she could be seen by judges and fellow attorneys.

"Thanks," I said.

"You're welcome," she said and drank some coffee. "You want some maybe good news?"

"No," I said. "I want you to tell me that there's irrefutable evidence that I once gave Jerry Garcia an overdose. I'm sorry, Beth. I've had a bad night."

"You weren't supposed to have a good one. You want my news or not?"

"Yes," I said, putting cream cheese on a barely acceptable toasted onion bagel.

"Angela Woo and I went to Hill's house yesterday afternoon," she said. "Angela thought it was fun. I had a specific court order issued by another judge stating that my assistant and I could do a walk-through of the murder site with a police officer present and that we were not allowed to touch anything. I told the judge I doubted if we would be inside for more than ten minutes."

She reached for the second half of my bagel. I had the feeling she was on a diet and was reaching without letting herself think about it. I certainly had no objection.

"I pretended to look at the tossed furniture downstairs," she went on, slurring words as she chewed. "Then I looked at the chalked body outline with Angela beside me. Went into the room the policeman said was Hill's. No box. The police had taken it. I got on the floor and looked under Hill's bed. I didn't expect to find anything and didn't, not even a dust ball. I repeated in the guest rooms, including looking under the beds. The beds had all been overturned. There was no sign of a pill bottle or panties."

"That's what he came back for, wipe away

evidence of the witness and put back the bottles," I said. "But I still can't figure why someone would kill Hill for the bottles and then put them back."

"Wait, there's more," she said, devouring the bagel and dabbing my cream cheese on it as she went. "Angela looked at the bottle collection for about two minutes, every bottle but not long. And then we were out of there. Jim, the bottles are all recent mainland cheapies. Nothing in the collection worth more than fifty dollars tops, according to Angela."

"So," I said. "We were right. Whoever took the bottles decided to or was told to replace them with the cheapies to keep the police from considering the bottles as a motive. He came back when I left, tossed the place, and decided to take the jewelry and cash and pick up Barbie's pills and panties."

"Now all we have to do is prove it," she said.

I handed her what was left of my half of the bagel. She took it and smiled. There was a touch of cream cheese on her upper lip. I reached over and removed it. I had a lot of work to do and not much time.

CHAPTER EIGHT

It was still early in the day. I felt like getting undressed, pulling the covers over my head and going to sleep, but Beth had bought me time and I had to spend it carefully. If I didn't catch a break, I'd be putting in some long days and might find myself back behind bars slipping paperbacks I didn't want to read to armed robbers.

I went into my trailer. For a change, no one was there waiting for me, but there were messages on my machine. One was from Angel with a fake French accent telling me that he had an excellent lead on the item I was seeking. Moira called, said she wanted to talk to me live. She had a deep, sexy voice. I couldn't stop to think about Moira. Then there was Olivia Carstairs with a simple message: Deliver Douglas in three days or I was fired and she would forward a termination check of $125 and would not, if the occasion ever arose, recommend me to her friends. She added that she had heard of a real cat expert, Angelo Martini, whom she was going to consult if I did not deliver her cat. Two messages from bill collectors, and finally, a frightened young female voice saying, "Please, please stop looking for me."

Since the only one I was looking for was Barbie Lewiston, I assumed that's who it was. I took the tape out of the machine and put a fresh one in. Then I forced myself up, took off my good suit and hung it up.

I hung up the slacks, shirt and jacket I'd left at the lockup. I had also gotten back my wallet, pain pills, notebook, the list I had taken from Hill's boat and some change.

I shaved, showered, shampooed, let hot water hit my knees in a supposedly massaging setting on my shower head and came up with a kind of plan for finding who had killed Hill. If I was reading the situation right — and I probably wasn't — if I found Barbie, I'd find Hill's murderer. If I found the murderer, I'd find Barbie. And Barbie, if that had been her on the tape on my desk, was frightened and in deep trouble.

I put on a pair of blue dress jeans and a denim shirt. On my feet were white socks and my black walking shoes. I checked the cookie jar but I knew what I'd find. Nothing. Not even a stale cookie. The police had my gun.

I walked around the cars parked in the lot and knocked at the door of Fred and Connie Travis. Fred answered. He was wearing his

Hoot Gibson hat indoors. It was no longer just a face-off between him and the sun; It was a matter of image.

"Mr. Travis," I said with a grin. "I've been thinking over what you said and I've come to the conclusion that a homeowners association is still a viable concept."

Travis looked at me under the shade of his sombrero. It's possible he would have carried the dignity of a wise old sheriff if it weren't for the fact that he was wearing a very faded purple and green robe too large for him and tied at the waist with an unmatched sash of orange.

"And?" he asked.

"I'm seriously considering a payment, at least a partial payment of my dues."

"What brought about this change of heart besides my convincing argument of the other day?"

"You've mentioned that you and your wife need the dues to establish a twenty-four-hour patrol of the Cove, especially of your place, my place and the Websters'."

"And others who will soon be moving in," he said quickly.

"Yes," I said. "But meanwhile you and Mrs. Travis keep an eye on things."

"Twenty-four hours," he said. "Work in shifts. Keep a log. Connie took the night shift. She's sleeping now. I've got the day shift."

I looked around the lot and saw what I knew I could see — the front door of my trailer.

"Anybody go in my trailer the night before last when I was out?"

"Rockford," he said with exasperation. "People go in and out of your trailer all day long when you're not there. You get more visitors than McDonald's."

"And you log every visit?" I asked.

"Every one, with a description of each entrant along with the time they arrive and leave and, when possible given the light and my telephoto lens, a photograph of each. If I already have their photograph, like that lunatic friend of yours who keeps taking your father's truck, I don't take their picture. I liked your father."

"And he liked you, Fred," I said. "The day before yesterday?"

"Two men — the ones you drove off with — and another man went into your trailer, stayed about half an hour and left. I took their pictures. I had the impression that they were policemen. Then, the night before that when you were out, there had been the man who had walked in, no car. I figured he parked off the road and walked in, though why he would do that I have no idea. All our lights were out. So were the Websters' and yours. You were out somewhere. He went right for your trailer, looked suspicious. Tried your door and seemed to open it with a key or something."

"You get a picture?" I asked.

"Too dark," Fred said. "If you'd leave some porch lights on, I could get shots at night. Grainy, but shots."

"How long did he stay in my trailer?"

"I can check the log, but I'd say fifteen minutes. I figured him for a friend or bill collector. He didn't come out with anything so I didn't figure him for burglar."

I figured him for the guy who took my gun and shot Hill.

"Can you describe him?" I asked.

"Can you pay your dues?"

I fished out fifty dollars and handed it to him.

"You want a receipt?" he asked.

"At your convenience," I said. "I'll pay the rest as soon as I can. Can you describe the man?"

"Black watch cap, like in the O. J. Simpson case," he said. "About six feet tall. Walked like a young man or one in good shape. Dark sweater and dark pants. Let's see. Sweater was one of those zipper jobbies you can pull right up into a turtleneck. Had some style to it. Wife wanted me to get one like it through Home Shopping on television. I said no. I see what I'm buying and touch it before I give my credit card number or cash."

"Good policy, Fred," I said. "The man with the black watch cap . . ."

"Not much more to tell," Fred said, tipping his sombrero back and glancing at his enemy, the sun. "I think he had a sports car parked by the highway. I didn't see it, but it made that *vrooom-vrooom* sound. You know what I mean?"

"I know," I said. "Anything else you noticed about him? Did he walk funny, have a beard? Could you recognize him if you saw him again?"

"No funny walk, no beard, couldn't recognize him again. What I can do is tell you when he went in and when he went out and give you some advice: porch lights."

"Porch lights," I agreed.

Fred left the door open and disappeared into his trailer against the rocky cliff. He came back less than a minute later with a book in his hand. "Thirty-seven minutes after he left, your friend Mr. Martin arrived and went in. He didn't come out till the following morning. You arrived at —"

"I know," I said, wondering what, if anything, Beth could make of Fred's log. When I had been waiting in the rain on the deck of the *Gordo*, someone had taken my gun already planning to kill Hill. It made no sense, or none I could come up with.

"Handwrite it in the log," Fred said, pointing to the book. "Then put it on the computer, with a backup disk. Here it is. Man came night before last at around nine. You were out, sun was down, surfers were gone. Had a clear view but not enough light for a photograph."

"Thanks, Fred," I said.

"More advice," he said.

I turned and gave him my attention. The sombrero was back down.

"Wear a hat and sunscreen yourself at least twice a day, minimum of 45-power stuff."

"I'll do that," I said.

"Your father wore one of those baseball caps most of the time," he reminded me.

I smiled, waved adios and walked into the afternoon sun to my car.

When my notebook and wallet had been returned, Doc Lewiston's list of people in show business who Barbie might have seen and Hill's list of collectors of Chinese bottles were still there, but they had been gone over and certainly copied. Given the workload and inclination, the police would be checking both lists, probably by phone. There was nothing on the lists to indicate the connection of the people named. But Hill's name was on the list of collectors and so were Lewiston's, Cameron's and others. It would only take a call or two to figure out the bottle collection connection even though I had handed it to them when I was interrogated. If the cop in charge were smart — if it were Dennis — he would have had someone immediately appraise Hill's bottle collection and find it phony. But Dennis wasn't on the case, and it might take whoever it was a long time if ever to come up with the angle Beth had thought of.

I went to my trailer considering a sombrero or a Raiders cap. I rejected both and ate a cheese sandwich with light salad dressing and a plastic carton of Jell-O pudding plus a Diet Coke. I felt a little better. I glanced at Fred in the window of his trailer. He was, I knew, about to log me out.

Reaching Lewiston proved to be a problem. I put in a call. He was making rounds, would get back to me as soon as he could. It was all right. I had another source. I called my former and generous client Dwight Cameron. He was home, answered the phone himself. When I said I'd like to talk to him, he invited me right over. In less than fifteen minutes, I was parked on the driveway in front of his house, being careful not to block any of the doors on his six-car garage.

I rang the bell and Cameron met me at the door in a University of Idaho sweatsuit, an orange towel around his neck. We shook hands and I stepped in. He was sweating.

"Middle of a workout," he explained, shaking some sweat out of his hair. "You mind?"

I didn't. He led me through the house past his office-study and into a room I hadn't seen before, a workout room. The treadmill had an operating board that looked like it required a United Airlines pilot. There were two snow-white mats on the floor, a rack of free weights going up to seventy-five pounds, a stationary bike and a wall-covering mirror. The room, however, was dominated by a black metal Universal machine with six workout stations. I could see from the weight settings that Dwight Cameron was in shape. He saw me looking at the machine and said,

"Machines aren't enough. Swimming. Sit-ups for the abdomen. Lots of them, hundreds a day."

He didn't bother to look at me but sat at

one of the stations and began to pull a pair of handles connected to weights on the Universal machine toward him. He turned red after five pulls, blowing out air, and kept going for five more. He let the weight back gently, took a deep breath and blew out one last time before looking over at me. I was leaning against a stationary bike.

"Wanted to finish the set," he said. "You understand?"

"Perfectly," I answered. "I'd like to show you a couple of lists and have you tell me what you know about anyone on either list."

Cameron mopped his face with the orange towel and dried his hands before taking the two sheets of paper.

He looked.

"Andy Lewiston, of course," he said.

I nodded, and he went on,

"And every other name. All collectors."

"What can you tell me about John Stuart Hill?" I asked.

Cameron shook his head.

"Collects as an investment," he said with a touch of disdain. "Waits for the price to go up. Tries to get to auctions, dealers, before the rest of us and then offers us the pieces at ridiculous rates. I know a few on the list who've paid what Hill asked for some of the better pieces."

"Then John Stuart Hill was not liked?" I asked. Andy Lewiston had already indicated his lack of affection for the dead producer, but now I was finding that there were probably half a dozen others who felt just as strongly as he did.

"Was?" asked Cameron. "Past tense. Do you think we suddenly found the goodness deep in his heart and forgave him everything?"

"He's dead," I said. "Murdered."

"That was my conclusion," Cameron said, moving to a station that required standing straight up and lifting a bar by bending his leg. I didn't count. He blew out and toward the end grunted.

"He was the one who had your bottle stolen."

Cameron looked at me and switched legs for the same exercise.

I watched him. No music. No television. Just Dwight Cameron in his workout room. When he was finished with the second leg, he mopped sweat from his face and looked at me.

"The police know any of this?"

"I don't think so," I said.

Cameron nodded and tossed the towel into a hamper about ten feet away, a three-pointer.

"I'd rather not deal with the police," he said. "I'd rather not have my name in the papers or on television suggesting any . . ."

"Possibility of your having a motive to murder Hill?"

Cameron cocked his head to one side and said,

"I wouldn't kill anyone over a painted bottle no matter how beautiful it might be. Not that I wouldn't be willing to beat the crap out of someone who took one of my bottles, but murder . . . pointless. Besides, I got my bottle back. You got it back. What's the scenario here? I got so angry thinking about it that I went to Hill's and shot him?"

"Shot?"

"Or strangled," Cameron went on, walking around the machine. "Or beat to death with a rock, anvil, log or . . . What difference does it make? You want to take a swim with me? I'm sure I've got a pair of trunks that'll fit you. A little exercise wouldn't hurt you."

"Another time," I said, following him. "The problem is the police think I murdered Hill. He was shot with my gun. Someone stole the gun. Take a look at this list."

I handed him the list of former patients Lewiston had given me as references.

"I know some of these people," he said. "And of course there's my name. Let's see.

I've met Corbin at a party or two. Recognize Crystal Fontaine's name, but I've never met her. The rest . . ."

He shrugged and started out the door. I followed Cameron out of the room and down the stairs. We walked out on the pool deck behind the house. The pool was big and very blue. Seated in a deck chair wearing a straw hat as big as Fred Travis's sombrero and a pink two-piece bathing suit was a blonde in sunglasses reading a book. I could see one reason he stayed in shape. Mrs. Cameron looked up at us as Cameron took off his sweat suit, revealing a white bathing suit beneath.

He dropped the sweat suit in a chair. There was no sign of any surgical scar on either leg. Lewiston had done one hell of a job.

"Tip, Rockford: Don't swim before you work out. Makes your arms feel heavy. Hard for your legs to run."

I nodded and got back to the subject.

"I may have to tell the police my connection to Hill through you," I said.

"I really would prefer that you not do that," he said. "I'll give you an added substantial fee for continuing to represent me and maintain my privacy."

"I don't plan to roll over on a murder

charge," I said. "I'm out on bail. And I'm running out of time."

"Then," he said, "you'd best find whoever killed Hill as soon as you can. I'll pay for your services in investigating the death."

"I've already got a client for this one," I said. "But I appreciate the offer. Do you know if anyone else on that list of collectors is in show business?"

Cameron moved to the edge of the pool.

"Jerry Richter," he said. "Claims to be a screenwriter. Mentioned something once about some television shows he had done. Dabbles in the bottles. Relatively small collection. More of a broker than a collector, really; a third-rate John Stuart Hill. I've done some business with Richter. Any other questions?"

I couldn't think of any.

"Can you find your way out?" he asked.

"Yes."

Cameron got in position to dive in the pool and then stopped and turned to me.

"Rockford, what happened to Hill's collection? Who gets his estate? If you can find out before it becomes public, I'd be willing to pay you a finder's fee of two thousand dollars. As you can guess, I'd like to make an offer to his heir before the rest of the collectors hear about it."

"Strange thing about those bottles. Whoever killed Hill took the bottles and ran. Later, after I found Hill's body and went to the police, the killer or someone else filled Hill's display cases with cheap bottles and imitations."

"How do you know they were imitations?"

"My lawyer had an expert look at them."

"An expert?"

"Angela Woo," I said.

"Nobody better, at least in this state, with the exception possibly of one or two people on your list," he said. "Do the police know the bottles are fakes?"

"Not yet," I said. "But I'd say they'll figure it out eventually. Maybe not."

Something was on his mind that he wasn't sharing. He bit his lower lip in thought, glanced at his wife and then back at me.

"I think you should know this, get it from me rather than Richter or someone else if you haven't already. I was tried for murder back in Vermont almost twenty years ago. I was tried, acquitted. The victim was my wife. Her real killer has never been apprehended. My business success has been decidedly well within the law and I've never even received a ticket for a moving violation."

"And I should know this because . . . ?"
I asked.

"You have discovered, Mr. Rockford, that
people with a passion for these bottles can
be manic. I imagine it is no different for
those who collect precious gems, antiques,
rare first editions and possibly even barbed
wire and cigar wrappers. But a man has been
murdered. You worked for me. If my name
comes out in all of this, that twenty-year-old
tragedy may be dug up by some zealous
reporter with a knowledge of computers and
how to retrieve information from them."

"I understand," I said, trying not to glance
at the blonde who had now stood up, taken
off her hat, shaken out her long golden hair
and taken off her sunglasses.

I said I tried, but I didn't fully succeed.

"Carol is beautiful, isn't she?" Cameron
said. "Loyal and beautiful. She knows all
about Vermont. I tell her everything. She
handles most of my business dealings, an
MBA from the University of Chicago."

"How long have you been married?" I
asked softly.

"For the past four years," he said. "And
I hope for the rest of my life. Any other
questions?"

"Not now," I said.

He dived in the pool. Carol the beautiful

MBA dived in from the side. They met about in the middle of the pool, hugged, kissed and began what I assumed was the first of who knows how many laps. I let myself out.

Back in my trailer, behind my desk, ignoring my messages, I looked up Jerry Richter in the phone book. Next to every name on the list of collectors I had taken from Hill's boat was a phone number, with the exception of Jerry Richter. That could mean a lot of things. One of those things might be that Hill knew the number so well he hadn't bothered to write it on his list. I found a couple of Jerome Richters and a few Jerry Richters in the fat LA phone book. I started calling. One Jerome was a house painter on disability. Another was a teacher at Loyola Marymount in the philosophy department who clearly knew nothing about Chinese bottles. Besides, he was emeritus, seventy-one, and busy working on a book designed to renew interest in the work of Bertrand Russell. I also found a J. Richter whose answering machine voice was male, but the use of an initial suggested this J. Richter was a woman. The next call seemed promising, a Jerry Richter in Encino. He answered the phone, young voice, a little wary. I said I was aware of his work and wanted to know if I could meet him to discuss the purchase of a particular Chinese bottle.

"Sure," he said, "I don't know what the hell you're talking about, but you must have got my name on the Internet. Are we talking about the bottle on level six of Ninja Masters in San Francisco?"

"Ninja . . . no," I said. "Real bottles. Collectors bottles."

"Look," he said, "I've got to get back in bed. My mom's due home to check on me. I'm supposed to be asleep in bed with a late case of chicken pox."

"How old are you, Jerry?" I asked.

"Almost fourteen," he said.

"Forget the bottle," I said. "And get back in bed. One more piece of advice. Don't agree to meet men you don't know who call you on the phone or write to you on the Internet."

"You mean sex scum," he said.

"Exactly," I said.

"I would have checked you out," he said. "Set up a meet, spied on you. Set up a second meet if you looked okay and checked you out on the computer Net. Second meet would have been right across from the Encino police station."

"Good-bye, Jerry," I said. "Get in bed."

I hung up. It didn't look as if my Jerry

Richter was listed. I checked the phone books for Richters with the middle initial "J." There were a few. I tried them. Not even the hint of a possibility. Desperate, I called the Writers Guild of America. Richter was supposedly a television writer. The guild had a listing for two Richters, neither Jerry or Jerome, both well established. Then I got an idea I probably should have had in the first place.

I called the office of Dr. Andrew Lewiston and made my way through to his bodyguard Janet Caples.

"This is Jim Rockford," I said. "I'd like to know if Dr. Lewiston has a phone number or address or both for a Jerry Richter. Not a patient. A collector."

"One minute," she said.

I timed her. She was back on in one minute and two seconds. Miss Caples was to be taken literally.

She read slowly, enunciating carefully, as if I were a brain damage victim. I wrote on the back of an envelope that I hadn't opened. I knew it was a bill from the exterminator.

"Doesn't the doctor want to know why I want Jerry Richter's address and number?"

"I don't know. He was busy with a patient. Told me to get the information from a book he keeps on his desk. He did ask that you call him this evening."

"Have a good day, Miss Caples," I said.

"And you too, Mr. Rockford," she returned, hanging up the phone.

I looked at the address and phone number of Jerry Richter. It was on Melrose, though I couldn't quite place the block. I listened to my calls. Bill collectors, a promise from Angel that he was in leaping distance of Mrs. Carstairs's cat, a call from Mrs. Carstairs reminding me of both her grief and my deadline, a call from Beth Davenport.

I called Beth. She came out of a meeting with a client.

"Jim," she said. "You tore my Yeltsin book in half."

"What?"

"The Yeltsin paperback I gave you when you went into the lockup," she said.

"I gave it to a kid in the next cell," I explained. "It wouldn't fit in one piece. How do you know?"

"I took his case pro bono," she said. "He's smart and I think there's a distant chance he can be saved or partially salvaged."

"I like him too," I said. "But he goes around with an automatic weapon shooting places up and threatening innocent people."

234

"I didn't say it would be easy. You're not easy."

"You called?"

"Angela Woo suggested a number of collectors and dealers who might go in for robbery, but not murder. She did mention one whom she didn't know personally, but he supposedly has a questionable background. She was vague on the background, but she thought he had gotten into trouble with the police."

"Jerry Richter," I said.

Beth laughed.

"Jerry Richter," she confirmed.

"I'm on it — dinner? Talk about the case?"

"I'll get back to you on that," she said and hung up.

I looked in the refrigerator freezer, found the remains of a half-pint of Ben & Jerry's Cherry Garcia, finished it and went off in search of Jerry Richter, who might have nothing to do with the case. I called first and got no answer, just an answering machine that said "Jerry Richter. At the tone, leave your message." I didn't leave a message. I headed for Melrose, not bothering to see which of the Travises logged my departure.

I found a spot half a block away from the

Richter address, put a couple of quarters in the meter and walked past a pastry shop that smelled great to a We-Mail-Anywhere-Fast shop, which was the address of Jerry Richter. My leg was definitely informing me that it would not tolerate not getting the attention it needed for much longer. The signs on the window indicated that the shop not only did mailings but also printed copies, faxed and received messages, gift-wrapped boxes and had a variety of other services including mailboxes.

I went inside. In front of me was a counter behind which stood an erect woman in her late sixties gift-wrapping a box. She smiled up at me. I smiled back. On my right was a counter with pens chained to it so the customers could fill out the necessary envelopes and forms but couldn't walk off with the fifty-cent pens. On my left was a wall-size bank of metal mail cubicles with locked doors.

"Good afternoon," I said, handing her one of the cards I dug up out of my wallet. This one read: "J. W. Farnsworth, Arizona Crude Oil, Phoenix, Arizona." They were left over from a scam Rocky, Angel and I did on some people who had bilked Dennis Becker out of most of his life savings. We got it back for him. It had been a fun scam with a few unexpected sidebars when some syndicate types got involved. It was a favor I could always play if worse came to worse with Dennis. But then again, Dennis had some cards he could call in on me.

"Yes, Mr. Farnsworth," she said, pushing the gift package to the side, giving me her full hands-folded attention. She reminded me of a teacher I had in grade school in Oklahoma. Her name was Miss Bright and she did her best to live up to the name, though occasionally a class of eight-year-old enemies got the best of her and she hurled the first thing she could reach on her desk at the blackboard behind her. Once the object was an ink bottle. She cracked the blackboard. The crack remained unrepaired. It might still be there.

"I was wondering," I said, showing all the teeth I could, "if I were to rent a mailbox here, a sort of branch office for the coast, if there would be anything on it to indicate that it was a box and not an office or home."

"Normally we ask our clients to include the box number on any return address or mailing address they might give, but for a small extra fee for the additional work required, we can accept mailings without box numbers."

"I see," I said. "Do many people take

advantage of this service?"

"You mean not listing their box number? Quite a few," she said.

"I came to you because I have a friend who uses your service, Jerry Richter," I said.

A look of disapproval crossed her face.

"Actually, I'd have to admit that Mr. Richter and I are not friends at all," I said sadly. "We met at a dinner and had a bit of a skirmish. This was after he told me about your excellent service."

"Did you punch him out?" the little old lady asked with one fist clenched, definitely a sign of impending blackboard damage had she been Miss Bright.

"I regret to say that in spite of my Christian upbringing," I said, "my temper got the best of me and I got him square in the nose. Think I broke it. Fight was over with one punch."

The old lady behind the counter looked definitely pleased.

"Can I tell you something?" she said, leaning over and whispering, though no one was in the store.

"Whatever you like," I said sympathetically.

"Mr. Richter is a demanding, overbearing, foulmouthed, impolite bastard," she said.

"That's the way I'd describe him," I said.

"But I'd like to be sure we're talking about the same Richter. I'd hate to slander an innocent man."

"About thirty," she said. "Shorter than you. On the wiry side. Dark hair a little on the long side for me. Not neat and straight across the back like yours. Though a few times he came in for his mail with his hair slicked down."

"He ever come in with anyone?" I asked.

"Blond man, about his height, better built. I'll give Richter that: He has good teeth. You should have knocked one of those out."

"Maybe next time," I said.

The blond man sounded suspiciously like Hanson, who very recently had to be talked out of killing me.

"Information on mailbox renters is strictly confidential?" I asked, also whispering.

"Couldn't give you more no matter how much I wanted to. Probably gave you too much already," she said. "You open a box with us, it'll take a federal court order to get into it."

"Good," I said. "Richter was right about one thing. I'll get back to you the minute we decide on establishing a branch mailing address. Thank you, Miss . . ."

"Mrs. Pettyfony," she said. "Mr. Pettyfony and I are the sole owners."

"One last question," I said as I moved to the door. "Curiosity, mostly. Does Richter come regularly for his mail?"

She smiled.

"So you could come back and maybe take out a few of his precious teeth?"

"It's a possibility," I said.

"Sorry," Mrs. Pettyfony answered. "He comes at odd times. Odd days. Usually once a week. Sometimes every other week or so. Gets a good amount of mail."

"Thank you," I said, opening the door.

A man with his arms full of packages was on the way in. I held the door open for him and left, heading into the pastry shop. I ordered a coffee and a big thing with chocolate and whipped cream and asked if I could use their phone, local call.

The man behind the counter, dressed in a white apron, pointed to the wall behind the counter against a rear wall. I walked to the end of the counter, reached over and made an illegal call.

"I'd like the address of the following phone number," I said. "This is Lieutenant Dennis Becker."

I gave her Dennis's badge number, precinct and phone number.

The woman looked it up and gave me an address. It wasn't on Melrose. I thanked her, wrote down the address and hung up.

The coffee and the chocolate thing were fine if a little pricey for the neighborhood, but there was a chance I might soon be eating prison food again and I wouldn't be getting good coffee and things with real whipped cream.

Richter's address was definitely not that of a successful writer and collector of rare Chinese bottles.

CHAPTER NINE

It was a neighborhood — if the word *neighborhood* could apply to this crumbling collection of three-floor apartment buildings almost touching each other — like hundreds of others in and around Los Angeles. Their small studio and one-bedroom apartments held determined or discouraged young people looking for their break in movies and television, peddling their scripts, videos and flesh to agents, or if they were lucky enough to get an appointment, to fringe producers, writers and flesh sellers who strung them along until the eager youth got the point. Some of the people in these apartments had lost their eagerness and their youth and hung on and in, with a determination that was admirable but that didn't match their meager talents and bad luck.

Barbie Lewiston had more going for her at first sight. Good connections, real youth and beauty, and something to fall back on when things went inevitably bad: Dad the urologist or Uncle Andy the bone doctor.

There were others in the apartments: the occasional drug dealer, the freelance prostitute, the aged living on a pension. No one lived in this grafitti-covered neighborhood unless they had to. And that would surely include Jerry Richter, whose front door I was now knocking on.

I knocked hard. I knocked long. Eventually the door across the hall opened a crack. I could see the trio of chains still attached and a bespectacled eye.

"He's not home," came a young man's voice. "Just leave him a message or something. You're making so much noise I can't work."

"Sorry," I said. "Someone recommended Mr. Richter to me."

I went into my wallet and found my R&R Industries card and shoved it through the crack of the heavily chained door. He took it with two fingers.

"I'm going to start production of some interactive CD-ROMs and I'm looking for writers, actors," I said with my Texas accent coming to life. "I met with Carl Corbin and Dick Lamotta for lunch a few days ago and —"

"You lunched with Corbin and Lamotta?" the young voice said behind the door.

"I did," I said. "And I found them very cooperative and receptive. We've got a lot of oil and cattle money to invest in this and

I'd like to keep the budget down somewhat initially. You know, talent unknowns, actors, directors . . .."

"Writers?" he asked. "Maybe writer-directors?"

"Absolutely," I said.

"And someone recommended Richter?" he asked with more than just a touch of incredulity in his voice.

"Let's say his name was given to me by a wealthy client of mine," I said.

The door closed and chains opened. Then the door opened.

The man standing there was probably in about his mid-twenties. He looked twelve. He wore torn-off jean shorts and a gray sweatshirt whose sleeves were cut short and a little raggedy. The front of his shirt read UNIVERSITY OF TEXAS LONGHORNS.

He was thin. He was barefoot, but his hair was combed, and assuming he shaved, he was clean-shaven. He adjusted his glasses and invited me in. In I went. The place was clean, neat and the furniture was old but in good shape. It all went more to 1960s Swedish modern than I liked but I was impressed. There was a desk at the window looking out on the street. On the desk were a small computer and a printer with a telephone between them. In a bookcase along one wall were dozens of scripts with different colored covers.

I can't say he was a good-looking kid — too many freckles, too big an Adam's apple, large bewildered eyes — but I can say there was an honest hope in his eyes.

"Louis Feinberg," he said, holding out his hand.

"James Rockford," I said, taking it.

"Get you some orange juice, water?" he asked.

"No, but I'd just like to ask you a question or two."

"You noticed my scripts. I've got one-page synopses and six-page treatments on all of them. Work is in every genre. Name it, I've written it: comedy, horror, science fiction."

"Interesting," I said, looking at the rows of scripts. "Like to talk about some of your work?"

"Sure," he said with a sincere grin. "You want to sit?"

"Won't be here that long," I said. "You know when Richter gets home?"

"Different times, hours. Usually I hear him, but sometimes I don't. Sometimes he's gone for days."

"Proposition," I said. "You call me when Richter gets home and I'll get you an appointment and an honest reading from an agent I know. I've got one who owes me a favor or two."

"Sounds great," he said. "You want to take some of my treatments or scripts with you? I can make copies after you've gone."

"Let's leave that up to the agent," I said, taking out my notebook and writing my home number on it. I handed it to him. "Local number. You call me the second Richter gets in. I won't tell him where I got the information."

"Okay," said Feinberg.

I gave him the name of the agent. He was impressed. I said to be sure to use my name.

"Two last things," I said. "Ever see Richter with a big blond guy with —"

". . . A loud voice," said Feinberg with a frown, taking off his glasses. "Name's Hanson. At least that's what I've heard Richter call him."

"Last question," I said. "Ever see Richter with this girl?"

I showed him Barbie's photograph, for which his glasses were required. He looked at her and then up at me.

"You're not a CD-ROM producer," he said.

"I'm not," I said. "But that agent will see you if you use my name."

"Are you a hit man?"

"No," I said. "A private investigator looking for the girl. Trail brought me to Richter's door."

"I've seen her," he said, handing the photograph to me. "Last night. They almost caught me looking. She looked scared. Then Hanson showed up. This morning Richter and Hanson left. I think the girl is still in there."

I thanked him and went back to Richter's apartment as Feinberg closed the door, now eager to get back to Virtual Reality in Outer Space or Looking for Lost Love.

I knocked louder this time, looking down the hall in both directions to see if anyone was going to come out and tell me to shut up. Nobody appeared. I put my ear to the door and thought I heard some familiar music and the voice of a man saying something about Infinity. I knocked again, very loudly, and said,

"Miss Lewiston, this is Sergeant Hill of the Los Angeles Police Department. I have a warrant which I can exercise to enter these premises. You have been reported as a missing person. Please open the door."

"No," a girl's voice said so softly I could barely hear it.

I couldn't carry on more of the conversation in the hall for neighbors, certainly my pal Feinberg, to hear. I considered telling her I would huff and puff till I blew the door down, but I was fairly confident it wouldn't amuse her.

I took out my pocketknife — simple, three blades, one of which had been modified by a friend of Angel's as a lock pick, providing the lock wasn't too tough. I checked the hallway again, including Feinberg's definitely closed door, and went to work on the lock. The doors to these apartments were thick. They were probably chained. Some of them, but not this one, were dead-bolted. It took me about twenty seconds to open the door.

When I stepped in, I found myself in a living room with one good-sized window and a lot of light since the drapes were open. The room was clean, the furniture showing age but a stylish dark couch with matching chairs and a table that didn't destroy the image. There were paintings on two walls, none familiar to me, all bright with flowers. The wall behind me held a large mirror with an ornate frame painted gold. A small-screen television on rollers was a few feet from the couch where Barbie Lewiston curled in a near-fetal position. She was wearing a yellow dress and very little makeup. Her hair was down. Her feet were bare and she looked a lot closer to fifteen than eighteen.

"Barbie," I said. "There are people worried about you. I'm one of them."

"I don't know you," she said in a very high voice that would need a lot of work if she could act, which, according to all reports, she couldn't.

"I've been looking for you, trying to make sure you're all right."

"I'm all right," she said. "Jerry's taking care of my career. He's out right now talking to a producer and setting up an audition for a movie-of-the-week."

I doubted it but wasn't about to say so. Instead, I said,

"Good. I hope you get the part. You stayed with John Stuart Hill for a few days."

She looked at me with fear in her wide brown eyes.

"You were there the other night when he was killed," I said.

"No," she answered. She really was one hell of a terrible actress.

"You were," I said with a show of reluctance.

"I heard them talking," she said. "Arguing. Mr. Hill was laughing. Then they were arguing. Then there was shooting. I think three shots."

"And what did you do?"

"Hid in the closet for more than an hour. Then I went out and found Mr. Hill's body. I packed my things fast and left."

"Not all of them," I said. "You left a prescription and a pair of panties behind. I saw them. Later they were gone. Why didn't you go back to your uncle's house?"

No answer.

"Did Jerry go back and get them for you?"

She didn't answer.

"Hanson?"

Still no answer.

"Did Jerry promise you a career if you moved in with him?" I asked.

"Yes," she said. "That's why I called him, came here."

"And Hill had done the same thing?"

"Yes. But I didn't go to bed with him. He left me alone the first night. Started to get fresh the second night and backed away when I showed I didn't think I knew him well enough yet. He said something about my career. I said something about my being careful, that it was my period. He said he didn't care. I said I was having pain. He backed away, said he hoped I'd be all right in the morning. He kissed me and left. I'm naive, Mr. . . ."

"Rockford," I said.

"Rockford," she repeated. "But I'm not

stupid. I knew I had to get out before the next night. I planned to tell Mr. Hill that I had called my favorite cousin and found she was sick. I had to leave for a few days. I had decided that I was going someplace else and Mr. Hill was just using me. He might get me work, but I'd have to pay for it. I had met Jerry a few days before. He had come to see Mr. Hill on business, something to do with Mr. Hill's bottle collection. Can you imagine collecting little bottles?"

I shook my head to show I agreed with her.

A talk show came on softly on the television. She glanced at it and then back at me.

"Jerry had given me his number and said if I ever needed a hand up, he was probably a better choice than Mr. Hill," she said. "Jerry has a wonderful, kind personality and he knows a lot of people in the business. He knows Kevin Costner personally. They went to school together, roomed together when Kevin was just starting."

"Why didn't you go back to Gail Chernowitz's apartment?"

"She had enough problems," Barbie said. "I didn't want to bring her more."

"So," I said. "You called Jerry, told him what had happened and he picked you up."

"Sort of," she said, retreating. "He wasn't

home when I called from the restaurant on that big street near Mr. Hill's house. I had my two suitcases. I couldn't eat. I kept drinking tea and ordered a grilled cheese, but I couldn't eat it all. I kept thinking about Mr. Hill lying dead and wondered if I should call the police or something. I kept calling Jerry and finally reached him. That's all there is."

"Did you recognize the voice of the man who was arguing with Hill?" I asked.

"My door was closed," she said very softly.

"But you think you may have recognized the voice?" I persisted.

"I thought I did," she said. "Then I realized I must be wrong. Then I heard the shots."

"Who did you think the voice was?"

She shrugged, turning her eyes back to the television screen.

"Did the person sound like me?" I asked.

"No," she said.

"You're sure?"

"I'm sure the person who killed Mr. Hill wasn't you," she said. "At least the voice wasn't yours."

"You might have to tell the police all this," I said.

"You're the police," she said.

"I'm a private detective hired by your uncle to find you," I admitted. "Not to take you anywhere, just find you and report to your family that you're all right."

"You lied," she said.

"People around this town do it all the time," I said. "Most of us do it for a living. I'm sorry, Barbie. The police think I killed Hill. I found the body when I went there to look for you."

"It wasn't you," she whispered. "You don't have a warrant. Jerry's not going to like this."

"One more question," I said. "Whose voice did you hear arguing with Hill? The person whose voice you heard killed him."

She closed her eyes, shivered once and looked as if she were about to answer the question, but she never got it out.

They must have come in very quietly. I had a sense someone was behind me but before I could turn, something hit me in the head. Barbie looked up from the television set with fear. I almost went down. Arms grabbed me and I stumbled forward.

I woke up two hours later in a hospital bed.

Dennis stood next to my bed next to Beth. Angel was there, too, along with Lionel, one of my father's friends who had helped him with his trucking from time to time. Lionel was a black man even older than Rocky had been, but he looked fit and was dressed up complete with suit and tie for the visit.

When I opened my eyes, Beth smiled.

"Jimmy," Angel said. "You almost bought it."

Angel was in a dark jacket, even darker slacks, and a blue shirt open at the neck.

I didn't answer. I turned my eyes to Dennis, who looked worried, and Lionel, who looked relieved that I was alive.

"You went through a second-story window," said Dennis. "Landed in a bush and rolled onto a patch of lawn."

"Water," I said.

Beth handed me a plastic cup with a plastic lid and a plastic straw. My throat was sore.

"You were lucky, Jim," she said. "Doctor says you have a concussion. Not a bad one. You've got a few cuts on your arm from the window that took some stitches to close and some scratches from the bush you fell in, but you're going to be fine."

"Dennis," I said in a croak. "There was a witness to Hill's murder. Person was in the house, heard the voice, can swear it wasn't me."

"So he threw you out the window?" Dennis said.

"No," I said. "Someone, probably Richter, snuck up behind me and pushed me through the window. I had the feeling he had help but I'm not sure."

"Mr. Richter is a month behind in his rent," said Dennis. "Now he's gone — must have thrown some things together and ran after he sailed you through the window."

"Sounds reasonable," I said.

"Who was the woman?" asked Dennis.

"I'm getting tired," I said, closing my eyes.

"Doctor says you can get out of here tonight," Dennis said. "There were signs of a woman. Is she the one who was at Hill's, the one who can swear it wasn't you who killed Hill?"

I looked at Angel and closed my eyes. He nodded. We'd known each other so long we didn't need much of a visual code.

"I'll be back, Jim. We're going over Hill's friends, enemies and anyone he knew," said Dennis. "If we come up with anything, I'll let Beth know. When you decide to stop faking it and give me the woman's name, call me. I want to know what you were doing at Richter's apartment."

Beth kissed my cheek. Dennis touched my arm. Angel whispered, "Jerry Richter, right?"

I blinked my eyes without opening them.

When I thought they were gone and the door was closed, I opened my eyes. Lionel stood there, hands folded.

"Thanks for coming, Lionel," I said.

"Rocky asked me to check in on you from time to time," he said. "Said that in case he died first. Checking in on you is going to be a bigger job than I thought. Anything I can do for you?"

"Look in that locker in the corner and see if my clothes are in it."

He walked across the room, opened the locker and came out with my clothes.

"Pockets," I said. "See if they left anything."

He checked.

"Empty," he said.

I threw the cover back and started to sit up. I was dizzy. My head didn't hurt as much as I expected but I had a bandaged and stitched cut on my left arm. The cut hurt. I couldn't tell how many stitches were in it. I didn't dwell on it. Lionel put my clothes on the bed and helped me up. I went into the bathroom and looked at myself in the mirror. A small scratch over my left eye and a good-sized one on the outside of my right ear. I examined the rest of my body. Nothing looked too bad. I ran the water till it was cold, filled the bowl and stuck my face in it for about thirty seconds. My face was wet but I looked better. I toweled off and walked out of the bathroom on my own weak legs.

"You're angry," Lionel said, helping me dress.

"Angry as hell, Lionel," I said. "Someone sets me up for murder and then tries to kill me by throwing me out a window. I've got every reason in the world to be mad."

" 'Cause you just lost the only gal you had?" He came back with the Beatles line.

"The only gal I had who could take away my murder charge," I said. "I'm going to find her before she gets thrown out of a window or worse. Then I'm going to get my knees fixed and then I'm going up north to a stream Rocky liked to fish. Feel like joining me?"

"When the time comes," he said, "give me a call. I know the stream. Meanwhile, Jimmy, I'm talking to you the way Rocky would. Don't do anything stupid 'cause you're mad. You're lucky to be alive."

"I know, Lionel," I said. "But there are times when a Rockford has to do what a Rockford has to do."

"Sound like your father," Lionel said with a grin. "You know where to find me."

"How did you know I was in the hospital?"

I asked, touching the back of my head carefully. There was a small lump, but it only hurt when I touched it.

"Hospital called the police," he said. "News made its way to Dennis because you're out on bail and he's the arresting officer. Dennis called Miss Davenport, who called me and Angel."

I stood up straight, my pants and jacket punctured with holes from the fall into the bushes.

"Let's go," I said.

I opened the door myself and Lionel walked next to me down the hall to the nurse's station. A heavyset woman in a white uniform and a bun of gray-black hair was reading a chart.

"I'd like to check myself out and get my things," I said.

She looked up from the chart. Her eyes were so blue they were almost white.

"Rockford," I said.

"Six-two-zero," she said. "Dr. Abduraman said he wanted you to stay till you could be examined later tonight."

"Dr. Abduraman will have to live with the disappointment," I said. "Just give me the form and my personal effects."

She handed me two forms. One was nice and simple. Just a statement that said the hospital was not responsible for anything that happened to me as a result of my checking out without a doctor's permission. The other form asked for a list of my personal goods with a space at the bottom that I had received them all. She handed me a plastic bag with what had been in my pockets. I checked my cards — credit and identification — and my money; all there. So were my notebook and my car keys. I signed that form.

"Rockford," the nurse said, turning her attention back to the chart in her hand, "you are one lucky son of a bitch."

"Time will tell," I said brilliantly.

Lionel drove me back to where I had parked my car in front of Richter's apartment building. It wasn't far.

"Lionel," I said, shaking his hand, "you know anytime you want to use Rocky's truck, you're welcome to it."

"You're not selling it?"

"Never," I said.

"Might take you up on that offer," he said as I got out of the car.

"And don't forget that fishing trip," I said.

I closed the car door and looked up at the windows. The hole in one of them on the second floor was big. Fortunately the ceilings were low and the fall not as far as I thought. Instead of getting in my car, going home and getting some rest, I made my way up to Louis Feinberg's apartment and knocked at the door.

"Rockford," I said.

The door opened slowly and Feinberg's mouth opened.

"I thought you were dead," he said.

"Not hardly," I answered. "The police come to talk to you?"

"Nope," he said, letting me in and closing the door. "You don't look great, but you're alive." He shook his head. "I went downstairs and saw you lying there," he went on. "So did a lot of others. We heard the window break. I thought you were dead."

"You said that, Louis," I said. "Mind if I sit down?"

"Wherever," said the thin young man with ideas for hundreds of movies. Maybe a guy's being thrown out of a window and surviving would appear in one of them.

I sat in the nearest chair. Feinberg didn't ask. He just got me a cup of water from a dispenser in the kitchenette.

"Thanks," I said.

"I called your friend, the agent," he said as I drank. "Used your name. Said I should bring him samples with treatments, particularly low-budget action or comedies with dirty words from teenagers."

"I'm happy for you, Louis," I said. "Who threw me out the window?"

Feinberg took my now-empty cup.

"More water?" he said.

"Information," I said, feeling decidedly queasy. "You heard the window break, opened your door a crack, saw Richter's door open, maybe even saw the broken window. What else did you see?"

"I owe you," he said. "I saw Richter and his blond friend Hanson, and the girl. She was on the couch with her eyes closed. The blond guy was at the window looking down at you. Richter said, 'We gotta get out of here fast.' That's when I closed my door. I heard his close. Then about two minutes later I heard his door open. I looked. Richter had a big suitcase and was holding the girl's hand real tight. She looked confused. The blond guy came out last carrying another suitcase and a little television set."

"Probably the girl's suitcase," I said.

Feinberg shrugged.

"Then I went downstairs with everyone else and you were lying there with some guy on his knees trying to help you. Medics came fast and took you away. End of sequence."

"Thanks, Louis," I said, forcing myself out of the chair.

"No, thank you," he said. "I'm going to be considered by one of the best agents in town because of you."

"Louis," I said, moving to the door. "I'm going into Richter's apartment. You are going back to your computer. You will neither see me enter nor leave, nor will you hear me. Understand?"

"Fully," he said seriously. "I'm glad you're all right."

I was sure he meant it. I went into the hall, opened Richter's door as easily and in the same way as I had earlier. I closed his door behind me when I got inside. I looked at the shattered window. I was suddenly filled with panic and felt as if I were going to pass out. It wasn't my wounds. It was the visual reminder that I could have been killed, that someone had tried to kill me. It hadn't been the first time someone had tried to kill me, but it had come the closest to succeeding. Another foot either way and I would have missed the bush that saved my life.

I searched the place. My guess was that the cops had done a halfhearted job. After all, I was alive. They probably had it listed as a routine neighborhood fight; plenty around here. Still, someone would eventually come from building management to clean up broken glass and board up the windows. They'd get the picture soon enough that Jerry Richter was no longer a resident. Whatever remained would be sold and used to cover his back rent. So, maybe I had some time. I pulled myself together and started a quick search, as quick a search as I could. There were a few women's items — a pair of stockings, a right shoe — nothing I could find with Barbie's name on it. The case wasn't big enough for the police to dust for prints.

There were plenty of signs of Richter. Clothes in the closet and on the floor, a medicine cabinet in the bathroom with the door open and a bottle of Pepto-Bismol cracked and on its side in the sink, with disposable razors on the floor and a few ancient prescription drugs. Richter had cleaned out whatever he needed from the cabinet.

Back in the bedroom I checked the dresser drawers. They were open, plenty of clothes still in them, nothing that would give me a lead or an idea. There was a small desk near the wall. Its drawers were empty, dumped on the floor, gone through hastily. In the closet, however, was where I found the big it, a box on the shelf, a big box. I took it down. It had a handle on top and a row of eight shallow drawers. I opened it. There were empty cubicles in each drawer. The cubicles were couched in felt. Some of the drawers had larger cubicles. This was a box made for Chinese bottles just like the ones that were stolen from the home of John Stuart Hill. I placed the box on the bed and looked at the empty drawers. Richter and Hanson had left with two hastily packed suitcases, maybe with a bottle or even a dozen, but nothing like the collection he told people he had.

And this box on the bed was empty.

The phone rang. I ignored it, closed the drawers and picked up the box. It was about the weight of a small, almost-empty briefcase. The phone was still ringing as I walked back into the living room with the box.

I put down the box and picked up the phone. I didn't know what Richter's voice sounded like, but I knew Hanson's. I did my best to come close to it and said only, "Hello."

"Rockford," came a voice I didn't recognize. "You're lucky you're alive. My mistake. I want you to walk out of that apartment. I want you to get in your car and go home and stop trying to find Barbie or who killed Hill. Am I clear?"

"Clear," I said.

"You understand the consequences I'm

suggesting?" he asked, making me wonder why he was not just coming out and saying he'd kill me if I didn't do what he said.

"Good," he said. "Be smart. Your lawyer's smart. She'll find a way for you to beat the rap."

"One problem," I said, figuring out why Richter was being careful about what he said.

"What?"

"I want to hear Barbie's voice, now."

There was a pause and then . . .

"Mr. Rockford?" she said. "I'm fine. And I'm glad you're all right. Jerry didn't try to kill you. He thought you were there to hurt me. I'm sorry I can't help you. You've got to understand that Jerry is in a difficult situation, but we're on our way to —"

Richter had taken back the phone.

"Satisfied?" he asked.

"You coached her well," I said, "but she's not much of an actress."

"Walk away, Rockford," he said and the line went dead.

I hurried to the broken window and looked out. It wasn't high but it was a case of instant vertigo. I looked up and down the street for a car. Richter had to be calling from a car phone. He knew I was in his apartment. He had to be watching.

I spotted the car half a block down parked next to a fireplug, its engine running. It was a late-model Nissan, red, clean as far as I could tell, the kind of car for the business Richter seemed to be in. I couldn't make out who was in the car but there were definitely two people in the front seat and one in the back.

I left the apartment carrying the box, went downstairs, my vertigo gone, my arm not throbbing, my head not aching. My knee wasn't great, but it wasn't as bad as it had been before I had gone through the window. I must have been given painkillers in the hospital. They had dulled the pain in my knee, but I knew it would soon be back bigger than ever. I was well beyond angry. I was well into out of control.

I went through the front door and out on the sidewalk, where I looked directly down the street at the Nissan. I held up the box so Richter and anyone else in the car could see it. Instead of heading to my car, I went toward the parked Nissan. I did my best not to limp, to stand straight and to look like a man bent on mayhem.

It was stupid. There were two of them, probably armed. I was attacking with an empty box.

I was about forty feet away when the Nissan screeched from the curb and broke the speed limit going down the street.

When I got home, I was exhausted and wondering if I should have stayed in the hospital. Fred Travis was logging me in. Angel's Feline Finesse van was parked in front of my door. I made my way into my trailer. Angel was seated at my desk in the middle of a phone call. I put down the box I had taken from Richter's closet and closed my door.

Angel looked up, smiled and indicated with his free hand that I have a seat on my couch. I did as Dr. Martin suggested.

"We specialize in long hairs," he said with that hint of an accent and a tone of reassurance. "A Manx? Wonderful. I can pick up Prince William within the next few hours . . . Not at all . . . I'm so glad that the Stones recommended me. You know, of course, that since you want this grooming done overnight, I shall have to charge — Of course. I'm glad you understand. To do a Manx properly is not just grooming. It is art."

He hung up the phone and in his normal voice said,

"Jimmy, you look terrible. You know what a goddamn Manx cat is?"

"All I know is they have no tails and come from the Isle of Man off the Irish coast."

"Thanks, Jimmy," he said. "Now I've got one for you."

He took out a revolver that looked as if it had belonged to Bat Masterson as a backup.

"This is what you want, right?" asked Angel, getting up. "I got the right signal in the hospital?"

"You got the right signal," I said, taking the weapon.

"Best I could do on short notice," he said. "It's legal. Belongs to a friend named Phil Nelson. You get picked up with it or use it, say Phil let you look at it overnight. It's officially registered as an antique. Box of cartridges in your desk drawer. It's loaded now. Six-shooter just like on the television."

"Thanks, Angel," I said.

"Hell, Jimmy, you got me into this great cat business. Least I can do. But, like they say on one of those TV game shows, Wait, there's more. Put the gun in your pocket and come with me."

"I'm tired, Angel," I said. "Someone tried to murder me, remember?"

"Come on. Come on," Angel said, taking my arm and helping me up.

We went outside. The sun was going down fast. I followed Angel down the stairs and to the back of his van. He opened it and said, "Douglas."

There were four cages. In the one right in front of me was a Self. The markings looked right. The cat looked bored.

"Heard through Raul, one of my groomers, about a guy trying to sell a Self," said Angel. "Followed up. Guy can't speak English. His girlfriend works for Mrs. Carstairs. Housecleaner. Easy snatch. I cleaned him up. Old Doug is sitting quiet now, but he's got a temper, Jimmy."

"Angel," I said. "Sometimes you amaze me."

"I often amaze myself," he said. "Who would have thought a week ago I'd be making big quick bucks and shaking the hands of the rich and famous just by driving around a bunch of funny-looking cats, handing out cards and talking in an Italian accent. I tell you, Jimmy, America's a great country."

He reached in and took out the box with the cat in it.

"It'll fit in your trunk," he said. "You might have to tie it down with a bungee cord or something. But I warn you, Jimmy, don't take that little son of a bitch out of that cage or he'll rip your arm off."

I took the cage. Douglas shifted. It was about as heavy as the box I had taken from Richter's apartment.

"What did you have to pay the thief?" I asked.

"That's the beauty part of the whole thing, Jimmy," Angel said, grinning. "I hired him. He's an illegal. I'll pay him cash. He was ready to kiss my new Florsheims."

"What did you hire him to do, Angel?" I asked.

"You don't want to know, Jimmy," he said, putting a hand on my shoulder. "You really don't want to know."

I knew. Angel's new employee was going to steal cats from the rich and Angel was going to return them for a suitable reward. I had a feeling that the fact that I was a private investigator who had recovered the rare Self of Mrs. Olivia Carstairs might occasionally creep into his conversation and that he would be telling people whose cats he was stealing that private investigator James Rockford who specialized in such cases would be on the job.

"When are you branching out into dogs?" I asked.

Angel shook his head.

"Think I'll stick with cats," he said. "I hate dogs, but if one or two come my way for the right price . . . Take care of yourself."

Angel moved around to get into the van.

"Thanks, Angel," I said.

270

"What are friends for, Jimmy?" he shouted cheerfully, closing his door.

I was afraid I was going to find out the answer to that question in the not-distant future.

I took the currently benign Douglas in the trailer, took off my clothes, showered, being careful not to get my bandaged arm wet, and managed to shave. I felt a few stings from the scratches, but I got through the cleansing and even shaved without cutting myself. I put on a pair of shorts, an extra-large Rams T-shirt, and a green baseball cap and took Douglas out in his box to watch the sun set with me. It felt good to watch the sun, sand and surf. It felt good to be alive.

I cradled the pistol in my lap and sat there for at least an hour. I'd return Douglas to Mrs. Carstairs in the morning. I wasn't up to it now.

CHAPTER TEN

It wasn't easy getting out of bed the next morning, and it wasn't early either. I got up aching, my bandaged arm reluctant to bend, and with a headache. But I was alive. Dressing took a little longer than usual, but I managed and checked my face in the mirror. It was passable.

I had no intention of feeding Douglas. Anything I had might kill him. Even the tap water wasn't safe for nonhuman consumption. I checked the cage. Douglas was standing but looking at me lethargically.

I microwaved a cup of day-old coffee and drank while I checked my message machine. One call from Dr. Andrew Lewiston asking if I had any news about Barbie. That call came after I'd gone to bed the night before. There was another call from a woman who garbled her name. I think it was Ann Skpernk. She left a number. She was full of no-nonsense enthusiasm. She was writing a book about real private detectives and she wanted to interview me. I didn't feel a whole lot like being interviewed. There were plenty around who did. On the other hand, if she used my name and didn't make me look bad, the book might bring a few customers. If she wasn't an amateur. If the book ever got published.

I wrote her name and number on my pad with the notation: PI Book.

Then it was time to get going. Actually, it was close to ten. I called Mrs. Carstairs. Her maid answered with a slight Spanish accent. I told her I had some very good news for Mrs. Carstairs. Seconds later Olivia Carstairs was on the phone and I told her I was bringing Douglas right over.

I also called Andy Lewiston's office and told his receptionist that I'd be there just before noon. I hung up while she tried to tell me that the doctor had patients at eleven-thirty and noon. I told her he'd want to see me and I hung up.

With my slightly disabled arm, headache and bad knee, I managed to get Douglas's cage into the trunk of my Firebird. Angel was right: It took a bungee cord to hold the trunk door down, but when I ached my way into the driver's seat, I could still see through the rear window.

Mrs. Carstairs was waiting at her door when I arrived at her house. She stood in the doorway, erect, trying to show no emotion. Mrs. Miniver. I got out, opened the trunk and shlepped the cage to her doorway. Mrs. Carstairs knelt and gave a small smile and then looked worried as she stood up.

"He doesn't seem to recognize me. He should be full of energy, pawing to get out."

"You see these scratches on my face?" I rolled up my sleeve. "See this arm? Douglas is sedated."

"He did that to you?" she said, rising and looking at my face.

"Let's just say I had a bad day yesterday and I'm hoping for a better today."

"I'll bring him in," she said. "I'll let him out and return your cage. If he doesn't like you, it might be better if you waited here."

I waited there while Olivia Carstairs, with surprisingly little effort for her age, carried in the cage and turned to close her door. I stood looking at the stone path, the green grass, the fence and bushes to keep wanderers and idlers out. She was back in about five minutes.

"Douglas is hiding behind the refrigerator," she said with concern. "What happened to him?

"He was kidnapped," I said. "One of my sources helped me find him before the kidnapper could sell him out of state."

"Did you turn the thief in to the police?" she asked.

"He got away," I said. "Without the cat-napper in hand, the police aren't likely to make this a high-priority case."

"Did you at least punch him?" she asked.

"Twice," I lied. "Once in the nose. Once in the stomach. I told him there'd be more if Douglas was ever missing again."

She nodded her head yes and handed me a check.

Her hand was thin but remarkably free of liver spots and loose skin. The check was for more than she owed me.

"Consider the extra few dollars a bonus," she said.

She closed the door to resume her attempts to get Douglas out from behind the refrigerator.

I went to my nearest branch bank and deposited the Carstairs check along with some of the cash I was carrying. I'd been lucky that no one had taken my money when I was unconscious in front of Richter's building or in the hospital.

I had two stops on my schedule. I hoped they would lead to more before another day closer to my trial date came off my Williamson's Fine-Tuning calendar.

I was a little early when I hit Doc Lewiston's neighborhood. I stopped for something to eat at a diner where I could find a parking space. It wasn't the kind of place I'd normally eat, but it was only a block from Lewiston's and I was hungry. My morning coffee didn't quite agree with me.

There weren't many customers at this hour. My guess was the place was jammed in the early morning and the lunch hour.

I had my choice of the breakfast or lunch menu, according to my slightly overweight waitress with dark hair in a kind of long bob. I took the breakfast menu and wound up with a large, round, brown wheat pancake with sunflower seeds. I had tea instead of coffee and asked for syrup.

The syrup wasn't almost transparent. I smelled it. It didn't smell bad. I poured it on my pancake and took a bite. Then I motioned for the waitress.

"What is this pancake made of?" I asked.

"Wheat germ, sunflower seeds and soy meal," she said.

"Soy meal? Have you ever eaten one of these?" I asked.

"Yes," she said with a smile.

"You like it?"

"Hell, no," she said in a whisper, looking around to see if anyone heard her. "I could lose my job over this, but I can't stand anything we serve here except the carob shakes, and they're not all that good."

"Why do you stay?" I asked.

"Meals are free. Job is taking a pound a week from me. Tips are good. I get to meet healthy guys. Enough?"

"Enough," I said and off she went.

I ate the pancake and decided that it was tolerable. I wasn't hungry when I left, but I knew the place had seen the last of me.

I carried the illusion that I felt better as I walked down the street. I had consumed a healthy meal. I was wide awake. My pain was . . . well, painful.

There were three patients in Dr. Lewiston's waiting room. They were looking at *People* magazines, *Vanity Fair* and *U.S. News & World Report*. The *Sports Illustrated* receptionist looked up at me with a smile.

"Fingernails are just a tad too bright," I whispered to her, leaning over her desk.

"You really think so?" she asked with some concern, looking at her hands.

"Trust me," I said with confidence. "You've got natural beauty. You don't want to distract from it. You want to enhance it."

"You're Mr. Rockford from the other day?" she said. "You called this morning and I told you Dr. Lewiston couldn't see you."

"Nails are still too bright," I said.

"I'll consider it," she said seriously and

277

picked up the phone to say, "Mr. Rockford is here."

She put down the phone and looked at me.

"You think I should find ways to enhance . . . ?"

"Your natural beauty," I said.

I went no further. I was trying to flatter her, not date her. I was not only old enough to be her father, but if I had started early enough I could have been her grandfather. Age differences didn't bother people much in this town, but I had my own rules and I tried to stick with them.

Nurse Janet Caples appeared in white still looking like a society matron slumming as a nurse. She did not smile. She said,

"Mr. Rockford."

"Miss Caples," I responded.

"You look as if you've had an accident," she said.

"No," I said. "There was nothing accidental about it."

Since it was clear I wasn't planning to say more, she turned and walked through the door behind the reception desk. I followed her. She led me to Lewiston's office and wanted to know if I wished some lemonade or ice water. I declined both and she left me sitting in a chair next to Lewiston's small antique table. Lewiston's desk was on the other side of the room near the window. I'd say he appeared in less than three minutes.

He shook my hand, looking at me over his half-glasses. He was wearing a white lab coat and it seemed to me that his brushed-back graying hair had been cut since our last meeting. He sat across from me, the table between us.

"Did you find Barbie?"

"Found her. Lost her," I said. "She's with a man named Jerry Richter."

"Richter," he said through an almost closed mouth.

"Ever do business with Richter?"

"No," he said. "He's a fraud. Barbie's with him?"

"I'm afraid so and I don't know where they are, but I'm working on it. John Stuart Hill?" I tried.

"I think I told you on the phone that I had little to do with Hill," he said.

"Ever been in his house, seen his bottle collection?"

"Yes," Lewiston said. "Twice."

"What would you say it was worth?"

"Worth? I don't know. I really don't think that way, but Hill claimed it was worth more than a half million dollars. I think he was right. What has this got to do with Barbie?"

"She stayed at his place two nights," I said, moving uncomfortably. "I don't think anything went on between them. Hill, as you know, is dead. Barbie knows who did it."

"Barbie knows? Who was it?"

"She wouldn't say, only heard the voice. I'd put my money on Richter or his buddy Hanson, the one who stole the green bottle from Dwight Cameron to sell to Hill."

Lewiston stood up and moved to the window. He played with the stethoscope around his neck.

"Police think I killed Hill," I said. "My gun was used. Someone set me up, but Barbie can say it wasn't me. So I've got lots of reasons for wanting to find your niece — her testimony, my knees and the fact that I think she might be in danger from Richter."

He turned from the window and faced me, his hands now in his white pockets.

"Find her," he said. "Not only will I do your knees, but I will pay your normal fee."

"I'd look for her anyway," I said, getting up. "And your money won't give me any more incentive than I've already got."

"Nonetheless," he said. "I wish to be billed at your normal rates when you find Barbie and she is safe."

He took his right hand out of his pocket and we shook again. This time it was a harder, seal-the-deal shake. Dwight Cameron could swim a thousand laps and lift K2; he still wouldn't be as strong as Doc Lewiston.

"I might have to tell the police who I'm working for and what this case is all about," I said.

"I understand," said Lewiston. "But if you can possibly keep this private . . ."

"If I can, I will," I said. "One more thing. I wonder if you could prescribe me a stronger painkiller."

"Your knees are that bad?" he said with medical interest.

"A little of everything, Doc," I said. "Richter and his friend Hanson hit me on the head and threw me out a window yesterday."

"Threw you out . . . ? Was Barbie there?"

"Yup," I said.

"You're a remarkable man, Mr. Rockford," he said sincerely.

"I'll accept the compliment and show you my wounds."

I showed him my bandaged arm and the scratches and punctures. He felt the back of my head and gently touched my bandaged arm.

"You've been hit in the head before?"

"I have," I said.

"I suggest that when you find Barbie you

consider another line of work," he said. "Enough concussions and you can develop clots, possibly even experience seizures."

"I'll consider becoming a surgeon when this is over," I said. "I'll call you when I have something."

"What are you going to do now?" he asked, escorting me to the door.

"I just thought of one more question," I said. "Anyone on your list of bottle collectors who might be willing to buy Hill's collection from Richter if he put it in front of them in a neat felt box?"

Lewiston stood for a few seconds thinking and then said,

"I don't know. I suppose Daniel Cohen or Sally Brightman might . . . But no, I can't really think they'd —"

He stopped in the middle of his sentence and shrugged.

"One moment," he said, walking to his desk and coming back with a pill bottle. "Take one of these as needed for the pain. No more than four a day. They should work, but you might need some coffee and determination to stay alert."

I opened the bottle full of large white pills, gulped down a bitter pill dry and went out in search of Barbie Lewiston.

By the time I got to my car, I was feeling

better already. Not a hundred percent, but decidedly better. I had two choices: I could check out the last two collectors on Lewiston's list, the ones he had hesitated to name as possible purchasers of the stolen bottles; or I could go in search of Hanson and Richter. Hanson and Richter had Barbie. There wasn't much choice. I headed for Hanson's house on Camino de Fernandez.

There wasn't much of Old Mexico about the street. Small one-bedrooms with small lawns. Hanson's wasn't much of a house: fake adobe with wood and bricks showing through above a window next to the back door. There was a house just like it next door, but that one was in good shape. I had my miniature peacemaker in my pocket, and after I'd opened Hanson's back door I took it out.

I imagined Hanson or Richter, who I still hadn't seen, stepping into a doorway, automatic weapon blazing away while I got off a shot or two with my Bat Masterson backup six-shooter.

I had been here once before, but I wasn't ready for the stench of dirty dishes in the sink and overflowing garbage. The counters were filthy with something that came in a rainbow of putrid colors and might once have been edible. A dirty yellowish linoleum with patches that showed through to the wood below covered the floor. My footsteps squeaked as I went toward the open door to the living room, passing the bathroom on my way. I hoped I wouldn't have to search the bathroom.

The living room was as bad as the kitchen: pillows strewn around, unboxed videotapes thrown across the floor, full and foul-smelling ashtrays. The sofa and two chairs wouldn't have been accepted as donations to the Salvation Army or Goodwill.

There was only one other room in the house, Hanson's bedroom. The sound that came from it was distinct and familiar, someone sitting on a bed with rusty springs. The bedroom door was open. I moved carefully, gun ready to the left wall so I could keep my six-shooter ahead of me when I went into the bedroom where I hoped to find Hanson on his back in bed and completely surprised.

I took a deep breath and stepped quickly into the doorway, leveling my peacemaker where I remembered the bed had been. It was still there. The room was dark, but enough light came through the torn Venetian blinds to reveal as much of a mess as the rest of the house in addition to a woman with long, dark hair sitting on the bed. She didn't look up at me, simply sat there hands in her lap, staring at a blank and dirty wall. She was thin, probably around fifty, on the pale side but definitely a former beauty.

"You're one of Jamie's friends?" she asked, still looking at the blank wall.

"Not exactly," I said, checking both sides of the room and making my way carefully to check out the closet.

"What's he done now?" she said with a very small sigh.

"My name's Rockford," I said. "Jim Rockford. I'm a private investigator. I think Hanson's involved in a possible kidnapping, a certain theft, a likely attempted murder of me, and maybe the murder of a man named Hill."

"My name is Jackie Romaine," she said. "Jamie, God help me, is my sister's son. Annabella died ten years ago and I agreed to do what I could to take care of him. I have, as you have just recounted and can see by looking around this house, failed miserably. I live next door and I've been hearing promises from Jamie for the last three years that he had or was soon getting a job and would start paying rent."

"Jackie Romaine?" I said, moving in front of her and looking down. I could see clearly now what I had already assumed. She was blind. "You were in movies with Cornel Wilde, Erroll Flynn."

"Flynn was at the end of his career and life; I was nearing the end of my eyesight," she said. "I worked as much as I could as quickly as I could, bought five of the houses on this block and made some safe investments of other real estate at Big Bear Lake. Married once when I was a kid. Divorced before I was twenty. No kids of my own. Rockford?"

"Right," I said.

"After you leave here, I will go to my house, which is right next door, call an old friend in the construction business and have him level this less than vile hovel in which we stand. I said something like that in *Satin and Swords*. I will then take an income tax loss on the property and attempt to sell it at a reasonable price. It is my hope that when Jamie returns, as he always does, he will find an empty grass-covered lot with a sign saying the property is for sale. He will then knock at my door and I will get to play Olivia DeHaviland, refusing to allow Montgomery Clift back into my life and out of the rain."

"Sounds like a good idea to me," I said.

"I talk too much," she said. "I don't know if it's true of most blind people. I know it's true of the partially deaf."

"Since we're talking," I said, putting my gun in my pocket, "you have any idea where I could find Jamie? It would save me the trouble of going through the mess in here and possibly coming up with nothing."

"If he's hiding, Jamie is probably at the cabin on Big Bear Lake," she said. "My father built that cabin before I was born. We used to vacation there. I check with Harlan Williams — he looks in on it from time to time for me. I can't bring myself to sell it, and since I lost my sight I haven't the heart for the place. Harlan offered to come and get me and drive me down. I tried it twice. I could smell the trees and hear the water and the animals, but it wasn't the same and I was too dependent. I'd guess that's where Jamie would go. He doesn't have much of an imagination."

"Harlan Williams?" I asked, taking out my notebook.

"Owns a boat dock on the lake," she said. "Rents canoes, rowboats to the people who rent or own the cottages. He's also got a hardware store in town his son runs. Should mention that Harlan's been mayor and town marshal of Big Bear Lake for over thirty years. Whatever office he doesn't hold, his son Rusty does. Most of the eligible voters who live there full time are his relatives."

"You're suggesting I check in with Harlan before I go to the cabin?" I asked.

She laughed.

"Mr. Rockford," she said. "If Harlan or one of the locals doesn't show you the cabin, you'll never find it. That's the way my father wanted it and that's the way it's stayed. Harlan tells me the population has more than tripled and cottages and cabins have been popping up here and there, which is fine with me and Harlan since we own almost all the lakeside land."

"I'm sorry about your nephew," I said.

She shook her head and stood up.

"Bad genes," she said. "And bad company. His father was worse than Jamie. I think they might be carrying that extra Y chromosome."

"Jamie's father?"

"Doing life in Illinois for murder," she said facing me, her dark eyes blank and unseeing.

"Can I see you home?" I offered.

"Not necessary," she said, picking up a white cane I hadn't noticed leaning against the bed. "I've done it thousands of times. My friend Kate is coming over this afternoon. We're going to listen to television and talk about the old days. She used to be a film and television writer."

She made her way confidently toward the doorway. My only fear was that she would trip over some of the garbage her nephew had left around, but she was moving carefully.

"Television isn't much different from radio," she said. "Especially the comedies. You can get almost every one of the jokes without seeing what the characters are doing. Remember, tell Harlan I sent you."

"I'll remember," I said. "Can I ask you a question?"

She paused in the bedroom doorway.

"Why are you helping me?"

"I think I'd rather not have to act out that scene from *The Heiress*," she said. "I think Jamie might not just walk away in the rain. The world and my nephew and I might all be better off with him behind very secure bars."

"Thanks," I said.

"One thing you can do for me," she said. "Give me a call or come by and tell me how it comes out."

"That's a deal," I said.

I walked to the bedroom doorway behind her and watched her make her way to the front door and out.

In spite of my strong desire to get out of Jamie Hanson's filth, I forced myself to search the place. I came up with nothing that could help me. Hanson's clothes were gone. He hadn't had much in the closet and drawers when I had been here last. Now there was nothing.

I got out as fast as I could, got in my car and looked up Big Bear Lake on my California map. It was about halfway to Fresno, past Bakersfield and well off of I-99 not far from Woody. Hanson might be in Mexico or someplace Richter knew about by now, but I felt like driving and thinking and arguing with Rush Limbaugh for a few hours.

I put the map on the seat at my side and headed for Big Bear Lake.

CHAPTER ELEVEN

I stopped at Gilda's diner outside Bakers-field. It was a place Rocky used to stop at back in his big-rig days. He said the food was solid, the service fast, the price right and the place clean, not to mention the owner-waitress named Gilda who was worth the price of admission.

It was late afternoon and the place wasn't crowded. Gilda's had hit hard times; I knew the diner was on the way down by the fact that there were no rigs parked nearby and no one gassing up at one of the three pumps outside. A big Mobil station and a BP a little farther down on Gilda's side of the road were doing afternoon business, as were the Waffle House, Burger King and McDonald's across the road.

I pulled up to a gas pump, and a kid in jeans and a clean blue polo shirt came out. He was wearing a Wasco Oil cap and a grin.

"Fill it up," I said, opening the gas tank and throwing him the keys. "I'm going in for something to eat."

He nodded and I went inside. There had been a car parked in front of the place and a couple at the side. A family of five sat at one table. Two kids. Two parents. One overweight apparent grandfather who looked at each of the two kids who were battling with less than total favor. I went to the counter and a woman in a waitress uniform came to take my order. She wasn't a kid, but she had outdoorsy, freckle-faced good looks and red hair. I checked the menu. Rocky had said they had a stuffed cabbage special. I didn't see it on the menu but I ordered it with a cup of coffee.

She wrote my order, ignoring the family battle behind us.

"Gilda?" I asked.

The waitress looked at me.

"Gilda's my mom," the woman said. "Left it to my brother and me and died with a trucker in a motel in Sacramento, leaving us a lot of debts."

"How long ago she die?"

The woman shrugged.

"Four, maybe five years ago, maybe longer," she said. "You didn't pull in a rig."

"My father, Joe Rockford — Rocky — was a trucker. Recommended the place."

"Name sounds vaguely . . . ," she said as the boy with the Wasco Oil cap came in and handed me the keys to my car.

"Ten even," he said. "My sister'll add it to your bill."

"Richie," the waitress said, "see if that family of hamburgers wants anything."

Richie went to check and I waited for my special, trying to decide if I was doing this the right way. Something was wrong. Something always is, but it was usually pretty straightforward: money, lust, power, even insanity once in a while. But I didn't have much experience with people who went around killing other people for cookie jars, rare books, Greek urns, paintings or little Chinese bottles painted from the inside. I knew a shrink I could ask when this was all over if I was still interested, and if she would still talk to me after our last disaster of what might be called a date.

The stuffed cabbage was good. The Simpsons had left before I was finished, and I ended my meal in peace and with an ample slice of fresh peach pie and a cup of coffee.

"Rocky?" the freckle-faced waitress said, filling my cup a second time. "Shorter than you. Smoked a pipe. Laughed a lot."

"Sounds like him," I said.

"He had a thing for Gilda," she said. "Most of the truckers did. Some of the oil rig workers did, too. Then the truckers retired with bad backs, the oil rigs went dry,

Momma died and Kentucky Fried Chicken moved in."

"Great stuffed cabbage," I said.

"Thanks," she said, cleaning up my place. Her kid brother Richie was sitting at one of the three booths in the diner. He had cleaned up after the family and kept looking up from his book to see if any customers were coming.

"You know a place called Big Bear?" I asked.

"Been there," she said. "Not my kind of action. Place is quiet, dead except for the loons at night and once in a while a fish jumping. My ex-husband, a trucker, took me there a couple of times. Rented a cabin for a week each time. Longest damn weeks of my life."

I nodded.

"Anything else I can get you?" she asked.

The way she said it indicated that she might be talking about more than another slice of peach pie.

"Maybe on the way back," I said, dropping a twenty next to the check, which covered the gas, food and a big tip.

"I'll be here," she said with a sigh.

I waved to the kid on the way out. He was wearing glasses to read. The book was *Great Expectations*.

There was a phone booth outside. I took

out my pocket telephone message retriever, punched in 213-555-9000 and listened to the messages:

— *This, on the slight chance that you do not recognize my voice by now, is Olivia Carstairs. This morning a filth-covered, underweight Self cat with a small piece of his ear missing turned up at my door. There is no doubt that the cat is my Douglas. I have taken Douglas to his veterinarian who is sure that he can restore Douglas to his former state sans the small piece of ear, which will be sufficient to keep him from competition. You have deceived me, Mr. Rockford, with an impostor cat. However, the cat you brought me, which I have named Richard, is, according to my veterinarian, a purebred more than worthy of competition. Hence, while you have sought to defraud me, I will press no charges, put no stop on the check I gave you and retain Richard. My impression is that Douglas and Richard will get along quite well. I have, meanwhile, warned and will continue to warn my friends about seeking out or using your services. Please do not contact me again.*

— *Jimmy, Jimmy, Jimmy. This is Angel. Where the hell are you? I need you. Just when the cat business money really started to roll in someone asked to see my license. You need a license to clean cats? I told him I left it home. I had Little Charlie Corascos make up a license and I brought it to the guy. He said it was a fake and he was calling the authorities. I ran like hell, packed up the cats in the truck, closed my place of business before the paint on the sign was even dry and hand-sprayed the van blue to cover the sign. Jimmy, I'm driving around town with a bunch of screaming cats. I can't just return them. Their owners may know I don't have a license. They may have called the police. There could be ambushes for me all around Bel Air and up and down Beverly Hills. I'll keep calling till I reach you. These cats are driving me nuts.*

— Jimbo, Dennis. Captain Diehl wants you to stop by in the morning. Give Beth a call and come by or give me a call so I can set up the time. Take care of yourself.

— Carl Corbin. Call me.

I called Dennis and tried to find out what Diehl wanted from me. Dennis was guarded but said the news wasn't entirely bad. I told him I couldn't make it till tomorrow afternoon, as late as possible.

"Diehl won't be happy," Dennis said.

"I'm not happy, Dennis," I said. "And I

certainly don't care if Diehl is happy. I can't make it till tomorrow afternoon. Has he got papers on me?"

"No," said Dennis.

"Then I definitely can't make it till tomorrow afternoon," I said. "Dennis, I've got a few names I'd like you to check to see if they have records for anything."

"Jim, I . . ."

"We're talking about keeping me on the streets, Dennis," I said, nodding at Richie who had come out of the diner to take care of a customer at the pump. "You know I didn't kill anybody."

"The names," Dennis said with a sigh.

"All collectors of Chinese bottles," I said. "Carl Corbin, Crystal Fontaine, Dwight Cameron, Daniel Cohen and Sally Brightman."

"Cohen, the all-pro?" asked Dennis.

"Former all-pro," I said. "Retired five years ago."

"Great middle linebacker," said Dennis. "Right up there with Butkus, Singletary and Nitschke. He's not gonna have a record."

"Humor me, Dennis."

"Tomorrow afternoon," he said. "Four o'clock."

"I'll be there early to see what you've got," I said.

"Don't," he said. "If I find anything, I'll put it on your machine."

I thanked him and hung up.

Beth was in her office. She said she'd meet me with Diehl tomorrow afternoon. She asked more questions and I told her where I was and where I was going.

"Does the place have a second-floor window Hanson can throw you out of?" she asked with more than a hint of sarcasm.

I told her I should probably have married her when I had the chance. She reminded me that I had had at least a dozen chances.

I called Corbin's office. He wasn't there. I left a message that I had called and would call him sometime the next day.

I got in my car and headed north. Rush Limbaugh was long over. I listened to a sixties pop station and took one of Dr. Andy Lewiston's magic pain pills. It went down dry. In a few minutes, my legs weren't bothering me much and the scratches from my flight through the window and into the bushes were insignificant.

I ignored the feeling of sleepiness that tried to take over. I sang along, as best I could, with the Stones, the Beatles, the Who, Frankie Avalon, and the Supremes.

An hour later, there were no signs for a turnoff to Big Bear Lake but I followed the map, turned right at what looked like the right place and stayed on a reasonably maintained two-lane for about fifteen miles. Then I saw a sign on my left. It was a bit rusty, but it did say BIG BEAR LAKE in brown letters against a cream background and it did point down the road. I made a left and found myself on a single-lane asphalt-paved road with just enough room to pull off of it if another car came at me head-to-head. There were thick woods on both sides. No houses. There were also a few snakelike curves in the road. I drove slowly for about fifteen minutes and came to an open parking lot on my right.

The lake was bigger than I had expected and I had been lucky. There were two cars in the small lot of Harlan Williams Boat Rentals and Sales, according to the sign on top of the wooden building across the lot. I pulled as close to the building as possible. A narrow gray pier fingered out into the lake. There was a boathouse alongside the pier. At the end of the pier sat a man in a yellow beach chair. He was wearing a big straw hat and fishing. The door to Harlan Williams' boat shop was open but there was no one inside, so I headed for the fisherman at the end of the pier.

I was no more than six feet behind him.

He must have heard my footsteps but he didn't turn around. Instead, he said in a gravelly voice,

"Jim Rockford."

"That's right," I said.

"Jackie called. Said you might be coming. You a fisherman?"

"Yeah, when I can. My father was the real fisherman."

Williams reluctantly propped the fishing pole in a round metal pipe cut into the pier and turned to face me. The sun was almost down. He took off his hat and held out his hand.

"Give me a hand up out of this thing," he said.

I helped him up. He was a big man and not young, but there was a look in his eyes that I knew well. I had a feeling he might play the yokel if it suited him, but he was smart, not just street smart, but educated smart.

I put him somewhere in his late sixties, but maybe the outdoor sun had turned his face a permanent light, leathery brown. His hair was white, his nose as ample as his stomach and his casual clothes — blue chinos, short-sleeved soft white shirt — were right out of L. L. Bean.

He squinted at me to get my measure and

then pointed across the lake. There were about a dozen houses visible lakeside. A few already had lights on.

"One set back," he said. "Smaller than the rest."

"With the little pier, a log cabin?"

"Real log cabin," Williams said, examining his straw hat. "Used to be the only house on the lake besides the Bedford place over on the left. Jackie tell you how much that developer offered us for our land?"

"No," I said.

"I'd say I'm more than comfortable now," he said, looking around. "Nothing much more that I want except maybe to see the Kremlin. Never did that. Jackie and I sell and we'd be millionaires. But we both agree there's not much more we want, and we like Big Bear the way it is. We did let it build up a little, but that's the end, at least till Jackie and I die. My son can do what he wants and Jackie's got a niece back in Indiana who can do what she wants. Till then . . ."

"It's beautiful," I said.

Williams smiled.

"Love the water," he said.

"Me too. I live on the beach. Malibu."

He looked at me with some suspicion.

"Trailer," I said. "Small trailer park. I

have to sink whatever I can earn into keeping it from dropping from its struts and sailing out to sea."

"But . . . ?" asked Williams.

"I like the view," I said.

"I know what you mean," he agreed, looking out across his lake. "Lake's deeper than it looks. Good fishing. Geologists think it was dropped off when a glacier retreated a few million years back. My son can take care of himself and I could leave it to the park service or something, but I don't care much for turning things over to the government unless I have to. I trust my boy first, but . . ."

He looked across the lake at the log cabin he had pointed out.

"What do you think of Jamie Hanson?" I asked.

He looked as if his stomach had gone suddenly sour.

"You don't like him," I said.

"Understatement of the week," he said. "I think he's lower than a slug. His father was worse. Hauled him in must have been six, seven times, back when I was your age. Mean man. We've got a little lockup in town. Jackie tell you I'm the town marshal?"

"And everything else," I said.

"Must have been fifteen, twenty years

back. I talked to Jackie about it and it came down to me telling Hanson, the older one, that he wasn't welcome in Big Bear Lake anymore. We had a nice talk the night before he left for good. He fell a couple of times, almost lost his left eye. Haven't heard from him since."

"Jamie?"

"I think he spent last night in the cabin," Williams said. "How bad do you want him?"

"I think he may have killed a man and helped kidnap an eighteen-year-old girl. I know he's a thief."

"So Jackie said," he answered, looking at his fishing pole. "Suggestion: We wait till morning and go over together with some shotguns and my son fully deputized. Meanwhile, I've got a bucket of fish I'm gonna have to throw back except for the one I'm going to panfry. You're welcome to join me."

"Sounds tempting," I said, "but if the girl's over there . . . ?"

He nodded in understanding, wrapped up his gear, threw most of his fish back in the lake and nodded for me to follow him back to the boathouse. I did, and he opened the door.

"I could tell you how to drive over there," he said as we stepped in. "Gets a little tricky, but I think you could make it. Problem is Jamie and whoever the hell else might be with him would hear you coming a good five minutes before you got there."

"Can you rent me a boat?" I asked.

"Better than that," he said, going behind a wooden counter.

The place was a fisherman's fantasy. Boxes of lures on the walls in bins. A variety of rods and reels as good as you could find along the coast as far up as San Francisco. A windowed cooler full of beer and soft drinks and a sign saying that the proprietor would be happy to prepare your catch and panfry it for you. There were three rustic wooden tables, each with four matching chairs around it. There were no stuffed fish on the wall. Harlan Williams was above that. There was a wooden plaque on the wall into which someone had wood-burned: "It's not the size of the fish that counts, it's the fight he gives you."

Williams was like my father. If a fish gave him a good enough fight, he'd let it go, no matter how big it was or if it was his only catch of the day.

Williams came from behind the counter and handed me a badge.

"Repeat after me," he said. "I, James Rockford."

"I, James Rockford," I repeated.

"Do hereby solemnly and legally swear that I will uphold the laws of this county, state and country as a duly appointed temporary deputy marshal of Big Bear Lake."

I repeated his words and he handed me a badge.

"Have a seat," he said. "You're legal now. At least around here for a day or so. Beer?"

I nodded and sat at one of the tables. Through the window I could see the sun was definitely almost down. Williams came back and took a seat across from me, handing me a bottle and taking a sip from his own.

"You'll be better off rowing across slow when the sun goes all the way down," he said. "We've got a few people from Los Angeles, Fresno, even as far as San Francisco, spending some time here. Their lights will be on and I'll show you what to do. Should be some moon if it doesn't get too cloudy."

"Marshal —" I began.

"And mayor and game warden, to name a few," he amended, taking a drink, "but marshal will do for now considering that you're my deputy."

"Why are you doing all this?" I asked.

"Rockford," he said, examining his bottle.

"I've loved Jackie Romaine since she was a girl coming here with her sister and parents. I asked her to marry me before I went off to college. She said she wanted to be an actress. I have tapes I made or bought of all thirty-one pictures she was in and all three of her television appearances. She was a beauty. I'd still marry her if she'd have me. My own wife died more than twenty years back. I don't want Jamie in Jackie's life. Can't say I'd be heartbroken if he had an accident. But I'm an officer of the state, sworn to uphold the law. Strange things can happen when a violent man like Jamie tries to put up a fight with a legal deputy."

I got the point.

"And if such a deputy needed a good lawyer, I have my shingle from DePaul University back in Illinois and I'm a member of the California bar," he went on. "There aren't that many places like Big Bear Lake left in this country, Rockford. I want this one kept clean and safe along with my friends and family."

"You're pretty sure Hanson's over there?" I said, finishing my beer.

"Someone is," he said. "Someone who covered the windows last night to keep the lights from being seen. Place glowed past midnight."

"Dark enough?" I asked.

"Close enough," said Williams. He handed me a small pocket flashlight. I put it in my pocket. "I'll get you a rowboat and tell you how to find your way. If I don't hear from you by midnight, my son and I will drive on over and see how things are going."

"You're the boss," I said.

"Like it that way on a small level," he said. "Boys up in Fresno tried to get me to run for county or statewide office a few years back. Said no."

Except for the dock lights Williams had turned on, the moon, which kept coming between lazy white clouds, and the dim window lights of a couple of homes, the night was dark. Williams took me to a rowboat and pointed the way.

"Stay away from the shore," he said. "Gets shallow and a little rocky. Go straight for the pier. Go quiet the last thirty or forty yards. Worse comes to worse when you get there, go out on the pier and yell like you've never yelled before. The loons will go crazy. Frogs, too, but I'll hear you. Sound travels fast over the lake."

"Thanks," I said, getting into the aluminum rowboat. "Maybe when I get back we can watch one of Jackie's movies together."

"Maybe," he said. "She was a beauty. Not

a bad actress. Never really got a decent role, though. Remember what I told you."

"Got it," I said as he reached down and pushed the rowboat away from the pier.

I considered another pain pill, had thought about taking one with my beer, but I hadn't wanted to explain it to Harlan Williams. The beer gave me a slight coating for my fear, but my fear was covering a knot of anger. Someone, probably Hanson, had helped frame me for murder. Someone, almost definitely Hanson, had tried to kill me by throwing me through a window. Now Deputy Marshal James Rockford was making his way as silently as he could across Big Bear Lake.

The lake was bigger than it had seemed from the dock, and once something leaped out of the water about ten yards away, something big. I checked my gun and the extra box of cartridges in my pocket and kept rowing.

There was no sound I could hear from the house when I got within about forty yards and started to row even more slowly. My arms were tired and I wasn't rowing all that fast by the middle of the lake. I did my best to ease the rowboat to the small pier without making noise. Still nothing from the house. I crawled up on the pier and tied the rowboat, leaving the oars inside the boat propped against the seat.

Then I headed for the house. There were no lights that I could see as I moved, gun in hand, around the right side of the house. I ducked past a dark window and made my way to the front of the cabin. There were no lights on inside. There was no car parked on the small weeded gravel drive. My eyes were reasonably accustomed to the near-darkness.

With my B-Western revolver in my left hand, I tiptoed up on the wooden porch, moving slowly, hearing the boards creak under me. The door was open. Were they waiting for me inside? Had they parked the car down the road knowing I was coming?

I pushed the door open and stepped inside. A dull patch of light from the moon followed me in. I took the flashlight from my pocket and clicked it on. I found the light switch near the door and turned it on.

When I turned I saw a woodsy room with wooden furniture and a table that had probably been made by Jackie's father. There was a faded, but colorful, woven rug on the floor. On top of the rug, fascinated by something on the log ceiling beam above him, lay Jamie Hanson. I assumed from the blood around his head that had begun to dry that the odds were good he was dead. I also assumed that the brown log the size of a baseball bat and covered with blood had been used to kill him. I moved to his side, went down, touched his neck for a pulse, found nothing but cool clammy dead skin and stood up. I checked the other two rooms in the cabin. Both had double beds. Neither looked as if it had been slept in.

I turned on all the lights and searched the place. I found a single lipstick on top of one of the beds. I decided that I had underestimated Barbie. It could have been a sign of carelessness, but I had the feeling she had left it there to be found. Like Gretel she was leaving a trail of cosmetics to mark her location. I pocketed the lipstick and looked for more. I checked Hanson's pockets. Nothing much. No money. Some ID. No weapon.

Deputy Marshal James Rockford of Big Bear Lake looked around for a phone and found one. I asked the operator for Harlan Williams Boat Rentals, and after three rings Williams came on.

"Rockford," I said. "Hanson's dead. I found him on the floor, head beat in by a log. First stages of rigor."

"Which means," he said calmly, "that he was dead before you got there, providing I come right over and confirm your observation."

"Something like that," I said.

"Second murder in Big Bear Lake history," he said. "First and only other was when I was a kid. Couple rented a cabin, got into a fight and she put a knife in his chest. That was back when I came home from Korea. She pleaded guilty."

"Won't be that easy this time, Marshal," I said.

" 'Fraid it wouldn't be when you showed up," he said. "Rug in the big room?"

"He's lying on it," I said. "Covered with blood."

"My mother weaved that for the Romaines," he said. "I'll be right over."

Less than fifteen minutes later a Jeep pulled up in front of the cabin kicking gravel. Car doors opened and closed and Harlan Williams and his double only twenty-five years younger was at his side.

"Harlan Junior," Williams introduced his son, who stepped forward to shake my hand.

Both of the Williamses looked down at Hanson's body. Senior nodded and Junior went to check the body. He looked over at his father and nodded confirmation of Hanson's death.

"I'll call Jackie in the morning," the elder Williams said. "Maybe if I can get enough of this cleared up, I'll go down to LA and tell her in person. I think I better take your badge back while Harlan Junior calls the state police."

I handed him the badge.

"Now," he said. "While Junior is calling, why don't you and I step out on the porch, look at the moonlight on the water and you tell me what the hell is going on."

I followed him outside while his son made the call.

"Whoever did it was gone by morning," I said.

"Probably," Williams agreed, looking at the water.

"I think it was a guy named Richter, Jerry Richter, who Hanson helped to kidnap a girl."

"What girl?" he asked.

"I've got a client," I said.

"Rockford, you could have come here this morning," he said, "killed Hanson, drove halfway back to Los Angeles and then headed for my place."

"I've got a waitress not far from Bakersfield who'll remember me," I said. "And Jackie Romaine talked to me late this morning."

"Still possible," he said. "Not likely, but possible. You think Jackie's in any danger?"

"No," I said. "Not anymore."

Williams nodded and ran a hand through his hair. Something jumped in the water. We both looked.

"I saw that when I was rowing here," I said. "What the hell fish that size lives in a glacial lake?"

Williams laughed.

"Our secret," he said. "We've got ourselves a monster, just like Loch Ness, but we keep ours a secret. We don't want the *National Enquirer* and marine expeditions tearing up the place followed by tourists with cameras. Officially what you saw was Old Carlos, the giant pike that always gets away. Unofficially, it was Old Carlos all right, but he's no pike."

"You're kidding?"

"Rockford, you think I'd be kidding now?"

"No," I said.

"I've seen him maybe two or three hundred times," Williams said. "Usually at night. I think there may be more than one. They never hurt anyone."

"Your secret is safe with me," I said.

"The girl's name," he said.

"Barbie, Barbie Lewiston," I said. "The city police don't know about it. My client's her uncle."

"You didn't tell the LA police?"

"Not yet," I said, "but I might have to

soon. I'm not too welcome by the LA police. They've got my gun and a body who has a bunch of bullets in him that came from it."

"Now you tell me," he said. "You figure Hanson stole your gun, shot this guy you're talking about and framed you?"

"Yeah," I said. "Hanson or a friend of his named Richter."

"Damned if I don't believe you," he said, scanning the water for another sign of the supposed creature. "Look, I'll make a deal with you. You get in that rowboat, get across the lake, get in your car, go find that girl. My boy and I will say we saw lights out here, came to check and found Hanson's body. Frankly, I am not planning to mourn his loss. I will not lie under oath if they start putting questions to me about visitors, but I've got a feeling Junior and I can handle that. El Swenton of the state police has a place on the lake. He's not going to be all broken up about Hanson getting killed either. Probably figure he came up here with a friend. They got in a fight and . . . one dead son-of-a-bastard with maybe an extra Y chromosome. You keep Jackie's name out of it. I do my best to keep your name out. My advice to you, son, is find out who did it and find out fast, 'cause they're gonna get to Jackie pretty soon and I'm not asking her to hold back anything about you."

"More than fair, Marshal," I said.

He put his hands in his pockets. It wouldn't look too good if he had to testify at some point that he had shaken the hand of a murder suspect before letting him go.

I rowed off as fast as I could. Williams stood on the end of the small Romaine pier watching me. His son came out when I was about a quarter of the way across, and the two of them went back in the house.

Old Carlos, the monster of Big Bear Lake, did not make another appearance. I'd say I made it back across the lake a lot faster than I had rowed to the Romaine pier. I checked my watch. Fifteen minutes. I hobbled for my car and moved fast, bright lights on, hoping I didn't meet a state police car on the dark, winding road. There might be another way to the cabin, but I doubted it.

I took the narrow road and eventually made it back to the double-lane leading back to Los Angeles. A few cars passed me and I passed a few going below the speed limit. Two highway patrol cars did zip by me when I hit the state road. Their lights were on and they were moving fast, probably headed for the Romaine cabin. I joined the normal traffic and headed for Los Angeles.

I was running out of time and ideas.

CHAPTER TWELVE

It was a little after midnight but Gilda's place was open. The fast food signs across the road were all turned off, and there were a couple of rigs parked in front and a tired-looking Richie in his tilted-back Wasco Oil cap pumping gas to a late-model Caddy.

I pulled in next to a pump, waved at Richie, threw him my keys and went inside Gilda's. There were three guys at the counter and two tables with an older couple at one and three young guys and a girl no more than sixteen at the other. The jukebox was on and Patsy Cline was lonesome.

I went to the counter and the thin woman with the pretty freckled face moved down to me, wiping the counter. She looked tired.

"Business is booming," I said.

"Eleven to about one in the morning and then four in the morning till about eight are our busiest times," she said. "Most nights my friend Dolly and her husband take over for me and Richie. Her husband's a cop. Their kid Jason's got the mumps so . . . It's a long day for me and Richie. What'll it be?"

"Four fill-ups, Gigi," called one of the kids, holding up his cup.

"And two peach pies," added one of the others.

"And you?" she asked me.

"Guess I'll go with the coffee and a burger," I said, feeling the stubble on my chin.

"With cheese and onion?" she asked.

"The works," I said.

"Let that beard grow out and it might be on the white side," she said, looking at me. "I'd like that."

I tried to grin, but there wasn't much grin left in me. Gigi took this as rejection. I held out a hand and touched her arm.

"I'd consider it an honor if you'd give me your phone number," I said.

She smiled a weary smile.

"Sure thing," she said, moving off to take care of the customers.

I needed sleep. I needed a pain pill. I took the pill with the first of my three coffees. Sometime during the second cup Richie came in, handed me my keys, and joined the kids at the table till Gigi called him to clear the table from which the old couple had departed. I wondered which way they were headed during the night — running away from Los Angeles or toward it.

I gabbed with Gigi when she had a few

seconds. We talked about earthquakes and riots and rain and mud slides and whether I knew any movie stars. She liked the idea that I was a PI. Normally, I liked the idea, too. I made my own hours, took vacations when I could afford them, met people both savory and as low as ones existing near the bottom of the evolutionary scale. Sometimes I just tracked down deadbeat husbands who owed child support payments or did investigations for insurance companies, but once in a while I came up with a scam case, a major theft or a dead body.

Gigi was fascinated.

"All I do is sling burgers and pie, talk to old truckers and watch the people pile into the Kentucky Fried Chicken across the road. Think I should sell out?"

I shrugged and took a bite of my burger. It was good. I liked Gigi. I liked Richie. I didn't want to think about Jamie Hanson with his head bashed in, his yellow hair and the handwoven carpet covered with blood and his eyes looking up at that cross beam. I didn't want to think of what I would do next or where I might find Barbie and Richter.

"You got a place here I could sleep for a few hours?" I asked.

I knew there had been rooms for truckers

at Gilda's when Rocky was on the road. Rooms and a communal shower.

"Got your choice up those stairs," she said, pointing. "We've got disposable razors and toothbrush-and-toothpaste travel packages. Fresh soap in the shower complete with towels. Rooms lock from the inside. Twenty dollars a night."

"You got a customer," I said wearily.

"I'll have Richie set you up in three," she said. "Everything'll be on your bill in the morning along with my phone number, which you can use when neither of us is as dog-tired as I'm sure we both look."

I nodded and went up the stairs, my gun still in my pocket, my mind echoing with confusion, my knee hurting and my bandaged arm itching under my long-sleeved shirt. The room was neat and clean, the shower hot and the soap fresh. I shaved, having a hell of a time keeping my bandaged arm dry, and stood for a long time with my eyes closed letting the hot water hit my knees and back. There was a half-used tube of Prell on the sink. I shampooed and felt cleaner when I got out of the shower.

I wrapped a towel around me and went to my room, locked the door, put my shorts back on and lay on the bed in the darkness listening to some of the night traffic on the highway a few hundred yards away.

What did I have? Hanson and Richter had taken Barbie. They wanted her to blackmail the person she had heard kill Hill? *Or maybe they planned to hold her for ransom from her uncle.* Maybe they wanted her for other things I didn't want to think about. The way I figured it at that point was that Richter and Hanson had gotten into a fight at the cabin. Richter had taken off with Barbie. Did he have money? Where was he going? Had he already contacted the killer of John Stuart Hill, or had he or Hanson killed Hill? Did Richter have the Chinese bottles? How much time did I have before Harlan Williams had to give up my name, and what had happened to El Swenton of the state police? To the next-to-last question, I answered, "Not much time at all." To the other questions I asked, no answers. Hell, I wasn't even sure if they were the right questions.

I stuck one pillow under my knees, put my head on the other and fell asleep.

In the morning, the sunlight through the window woke me early. I got up groggy and aching from knees to neck, pulled on my pants, took the towel from where I had left it to dry on a wooden chair and hit the washroom. I splashed cold water from the sink in my face and looked at myself in the mirror. I've looked a hell of a lot better. I had my own comb, an ivory gift from Moira, and used it to make myself look semihuman. I brushed my teeth again, went back to my room, and put on the same shirt I had worn the day before.

I could smell the coffee when I came down the stairs.

Gigi and Richie were right there, scrubbed and not particularly busy. The early, early morning trade had already gone.

"Get a few hours' sleep?" I asked.

"We'll take turns getting six or eight hours this afternoon," Gigi said.

I took my usual seat at the counter. Gigi poured me a fresh cup and I smiled my thanks up to her face, which she had taken time with this morning. Her hair was up with a bow and most of her freckles had disappeared under a thin layer of powder. She looked pretty — a little on the thin side, but pretty.

"Got any experience with kidnappers?" I asked.

She laughed.

"Not hardly," she said. "They'd never make a dime taking me or Richie, though God knows what kidnappers do with people

321

these days. You working a kidnapping?"

"I am," I said.

"Woman?"

"Girl," I said.

"Her family got money?" she asked.

"Lots," I said.

"Kidnappers contact them yet?" she asked.

I hadn't considered that possibility. I had only thought of what Richter could get out of the killer. But Barbie's uncle and father were rich enough to buy the Los Angeles Dodgers. And if Richter were the killer of Hanson and Hill, what reason would he have for keeping her alive if she was the witness to his killing Hill or Hanson?"

"Thanks," I said.

"You mean you didn't ask them?" she said with some surprise.

"I've been through one window too many, had one pain pill or more too many and made things more complicated than they might have to be."

I picked up the check. Gigi's name and number were on it. I grinned up at her and put a twenty and a ten on the counter.

"Take care of yourself, Rockford," she said as I headed for the door. "And don't lose that number."

"I won't," I said, thanking Rocky for leading me to Gilda's and Gilda's daughter.

I listened to the radio the rest of the way home — not music, talk radio, with wise-guy, glib young men with lots of opinions, little thought and a whole lot of contempt for their callers. The degree of innocence, stupidity and loneliness out there in radio nowhere conjured up images of retirees in trailers not a hell of a lot different from mine with little to do but listen to the radio in the morning and call in with ideas and opinions even more bigoted and stupid than the hosts. I never bothered to consider why I liked to listen to these shows. I think it has some-thing to do with wanting company while I drive and keeping my mind off what I'd rather think about at a different, maybe deeper level. I wondered if anyone had ever called any of these radio talk guys about a monster in Big Bear Lake.

It was almost ten in the morning when I pulled up to my trailer and found two visi-tors waiting for me inside. I knew who they were from the vehicles parked outside. An-gel's now painted-over van was across the lot. Dennis Becker's private car, a five-year-old blue Buick, was parked right in front of my door.

I got out and took a few steps toward the trailer when I saw Fred Travis, complete with cowboy hat and safari shorts and shirt waving furiously at me. We met about half-way across the lot.

"Last night," he whispered. "Where were you?"

"One of the reasons I live by myself, Fred, is that I don't have to answer questions like that from anyone except the police."

"Well," he said with a sigh, "you had a visitor in a red late-model Nissan just after two in the morning. I didn't think you were home but I wasn't sure, though I didn't see your car. I didn't see the Nissan pull up. I was in the bathroom."

"And he just walked into my trailer?" I asked.

"Seemed to have a key or something," Fred said as he looked toward the beach and across at the steel pier about half a mile away. "Stayed about half an hour."

"Young guy, hair brushed back?" I asked.

Fred shrugged. "It was dark and you forgot to leave your night light on," he said, "but I think so."

"Was there a girl with him?"

"No," Fred said with certainty. "Should I have called the police?"

"The police are here," I said. "Blue Buick."

"About ten minutes ago," Fred said. "One

man about your age. Little bald spot back here. He's been here before."

"The van?"

A sour look crossed Fred's face.

"Came a little after the Buick. Didn't go to your trailer. Wandered toward the beach and out of my vision."

"Good work, Fred," I said, putting my hand on his shoulder.

"Ready to pay the rest of your dues?" he asked. "Connie and I would like to get started with the ads and talking to Realtors."

"Give me a few more days," I said, walking toward my trailer.

"Thursday?" Fred called.

"If I can," I said.

Dennis was sitting behind my desk drinking a cup of coffee he had made with my Braun on the counter. He looked reasonably comfortable as he leaned back and drank. The place was a mess, worse than a mess. Someone — I figured Richter for the job — had tossed the place, not worrying about what he tore or where he threw it. I could see by looking toward the open door that he had done the same in the bedroom.

"I put your desk drawers back, Jimbo," Dennis said. "Coffee's hot."

I poured myself a mug, put a pillow back on my couch and sat.

"It'll take me two or three days and a couple of hundred dollars to get this place back together," I said, looking around.

"You should get a better lock," Dennis suggested. "Any idea who did this or why?"

"Richter," I said. "I think he came to kill me and when I wasn't here started searching."

"For what?"

"Evidence, notes against whoever killed Hill," I guessed.

"You have any — notes? Anything?"

"Nope," I said.

The coffee was too strong, but I drank it.

"I'm on my own time, Jim," Dennis said. "I'm not on shift till noon. Let's say this is a personal call and I failed to notice the sloppy state in which you keep your trailer."

"Let's," I said, looking around.

"I ran checks on the names you gave me," Dennis said, pulling out his notebook. "Richter's got a smooth line and a bad temper. Did a little time for defrauding old ladies out of their savings in a land deal. Made restitution. Out in a few weeks. Couple of arrests for fights that got ugly: one in a bar, one outside of a bar, one in an insurance company office, one in a young lady's apartment. No charges filed. Hence, no convictions, though a few of the people involved did walk away with one or two broken bones and missing teeth."

"Richter's got Barbie Lewiston," I said. "She heard whoever killed Hill. I think he's using her to blackmail the killer and maybe hold her for ransom from her family, whichever comes first with the most money."

"You don't think Richter killed Hill?"

"Barbie would be dead by now," I said. "I saw her in Richter's apartment and his car, alive."

"Let's say I buy that," Dennis said, finishing his coffee and moving to the sink to rinse his cup. "Let's say Captain Diehl buys it. What about James Hanson? He's got a record. Auto theft. Assault. Grand theft."

"I think he and Richter threw me out that window and took off with Barbie Lewiston," I said.

"Hanson's dead," Dennis said, drying his cup and putting it in the blue plastic drainer. "Head beaten in with a log about this time yesterday. Up in Big Bear Lake. I put out a teaser on the names you gave me. His murder came up on the computer first thing this morning when I went in early. Then I decided not to have an early day and came here. Where've you been all night, Jimbo?"

"Big Bear Lake," I said. "Then I slept at

a truck stop called Gilda's not far from Bakersfield."

Dennis nodded and sat behind my desk again. I sipped the strong coffee.

"And . . . ?" Dennis prompted.

"And I found Hanson's body," I admitted. "I got a line that his family owned a cabin up there. I thought he and Richter might have taken the girl up there. I think they did."

"We've got no report of a kidnapping of a Barbie Lewiston," said Dennis. "Checked this morning."

"Uncle thinks she just went away to seek her fortune," I said. "He doesn't know about her being kidnapped. I'll see him, try to talk him into filing a report. The other names?"

Dennis consulted his notebook.

"Dan Cohen, former middle linebacker for five different NFL teams. One Superbowl ring. Square shooter all the way. Picked up once."

"And?"

"Brawl at a gay bar," Dennis said. "A group of skinheads came in with bats and started busting up the place. Cohen started busting up the skinheads. They filed a complaint. The DA told them to take a walk."

"Cohen is gay?"

"Looks that way," Dennis said. "A few

other pickups noted, nothing pursued, all gay-related."

"Sally Brightman?" I asked.

"Drunk and disorderly three times," he said. "Driver's license revoked for a year once. Lots of money from a dead daddy in the pharmaceutical business."

"And?" I prompted.

Dennis sighed and said,

"Corbin is gay, too. No secrets there. No arrests. No convictions. Clean. Dwight Cameron has a few DUIs, but that was a long time ago. Your Doc Lewiston is clean. Hill had a long history of bad behavior, mostly stuff we'd classify as white-collar crime, before he caught a trio of bullets from your gun. Anything else?"

"No," I said. "Thanks, Dennis."

"Jimbo," he said, getting up. "Someone'll probably be picking you up soon about Hanson. It'll go to homicide. I don't know who'll get the call."

"Thanks, Dennis," I said.

Dennis patted my shoulder and left. I poured out what was left of my coffee and was wondering where to start cleaning when Angel came in.

"What did Becker want?" he asked, looking back out the window in case it was some kind of trap. "He looking for me?"

"Angel, I don't have time for you," I said.

He was wearing black slacks and socks and a black long-sleeved shirt: Angel's idea of how to dress when you wanted to look inconspicuous.

"Oh, I bust my liver finding your missing cat and now that I'm going down the tubes with my cat-grooming business, you don't have time for me."

He moved to the sink, poured himself a cup of coffee, drank and looked around.

"This coffee is awful," he said.

"I'm sorry," I said, going to my desk. "Dennis made it."

"Cop coffee," Angel said. "Jimmy, your place has been rousted."

He looked around.

"I noticed, Angel," I said.

In spite of how bad the coffee was, Angel drank it and went on with his complaint.

"A license," he moaned. "I need to apply for a license and meet all kinds of guidelines. Facilities, staff, experience, a vet on retainer. Jimmy, I've already got my business cards printed and a lease on the store. With my record, I'll never get that license, and I'm going to wind up losing money. And I've got a van full of wailing cats I have to keep feeding and . . . Do you know what their cages smell like?"

"I can't begin to imagine, but no matter how they smell, I figure you'll find a way to wind up a little ahead, Angel," I said.

"Well, maybe a little," he said, moving to where I had sat to drink his coffee.

"What I need is someone to front for me fast," he said. "Can't be anyone on the staff, Raul or Consuela."

"Consuela?" I asked.

"Raul's wife; both illegals," he explained.

"No," I said. "I won't front for you, Angel. I wouldn't even if you hadn't lied to me about Douglas."

"Douglas?" he asked. "Who the hell is Douglas?"

"The Self cat you found. The one you told me was stolen by the housekeeper's boyfriend. Douglas showed up on Mrs. Carstairs's doorstep yesterday. He'd spent a few nights on the prowl and found the adventure less favorable than pampering by Olivia Carstairs. You lied to me, Angel."

"She went to the cops?" Angel asked, sitting up.

"No," I said. "She's keeping both cats, and I don't want to know where you got the second. But you lied to me, Angel. There's no chance in hell I'd front for your cat-grooming service."

"I wasn't thinking of you, Jimmy," he said.

"Your record's almost as bad as mine. I was thinking more in the line of one of your neighbors out here or some client of yours that might be feeling enterprising. I don't know anyone straight enough to go to."

"No, Angel," I said. "No."

"I got you the piece," he said.

"You want it back," I said, taking the gun from my pocket and putting it on the desk, "take it. You probably lied about it being legal anyway."

"Jimmy," he said, sounding genuinely hurt. "I wouldn't lie about a thing like that."

"Angel, you'd lie about anything to make a buck or save your skin."

Angel shrugged. The truth was the truth.

"You want some help cleaning up?" he said, looking around.

"You're offering to help me?" I said.

"Yeah," Angel said.

"What's the price?" I asked.

"None," he said. "Let's say it's because I lied about the Carstairs cat. Let's say it's because I know you're in trouble. Let's say I'm hoping but not counting on you coming up with someone who might front for me."

"Thanks, Angel," I said.

"What are friends for?" he asked.

"I often wonder about that," I said.

"I'll start in the bedroom," he said, getting

up. "No, I'll start by making some decent coffee."

Angel actually got up and went to work while I made some calls after checking my machine and finding nothing but a new message from Andy Lewiston.

First, though, I called Carl Corbin. He had been less than cordial at our only meeting and his pal, Richard Lamotta, the star of *Death on a Dark Street*, had been even less cordial. I gave Corbin's secretary my name. She said Corbin was busy right now. I said I was busier, that he had called me, and that I had no plans to call him back or be home all day.

"One moment," she said.

Then Corbin came on the line.

"Rockford?" he asked.

"Right," I said. "What do you want?"

"You've made rudeness a lesser art."

"I work at it," I said. "You have something on your mind?"

"I've been threatened," he said calmly. "By a man whose voice I didn't recognize."

"Yesterday?"

"Yes," said Corbin. "The voice was less than literate and the threat was explicit and promised violence. The call didn't happen to come from someone you know?"

"Not from someone I'd call a friend," I

said. "What did they want?"

"The caller said that if I were asked to go to John Stuart Hill's home and examine his Chinese bottle collection, I should declare it authentic or I would be joining Hill in the cemetery. The call was brief, the caller apparently sincere."

"It wasn't Jerry Richter?" I asked.

"I'd recognize Richter's voice," he said. "Considering your involvement in this matter, I thought —"

"I think the person who called you was a guy named Hanson," I said. "I think Hanson was murdered after he talked to you. How well do you know Dan Cohen?"

"Why do you ask? Because we're both gay?"

"And you both collect Chinese bottles," I said.

"Dan and I have met as collectors," he said. "We've made a few sales and exchanges with each other. That's all."

"Same with Sally Brightman, Crystal Fontaine, Andy Lewiston, Dwight Cameron?"

"The same," he said. "And with Hill, of course."

"I don't think you have to worry about that call," I said. "It's up to you whether you want to authenticate the Hill collection if you're called on by the police, though I don't think it's generally a good idea to lie to the police. It can come back to haunt you. Trust my experience on that one."

"I appreciate the advice," Corbin said. "I'd also appreciate your letting me know when you discover which of my fellow collectors, if any, had Hill murdered, stole his collection and had me threatened by your late Mr. Hanson."

"You're sure it was one of them?" I asked.

"Who else would know I'm a collector and that I might be called in to authenticate Hill's collection?" he asked.

"Good point," I said.

"I've grown reasonably wealthy, well known and powerful by being able to add simple numbers and act like a bastard. I have two vulnerabilities that make me think that I am reasonably human: my passion for others of my gender and my appreciation of those bottles. Find the killer, Rockford, and the Hill collection and I will be grateful."

"A check?" I said.

"Cash," he said.

The line went dead.

I made my calls and was told by every one of the collectors that they had been threatened, including Dwight Cameron and the receiver of my last call, Andy Lewiston. None of them had called the police. Lewiston was calm when I reached him, much too calm, trying to hold himself together. Not only had he been warned about authenticating Hill's collection, he had received a call saying that Barbie would be killed if he did not come up with either a considerable sum of cash or his entire collection of Chinese bottles by tomorrow morning.

Gigi had been right.

"Did you recognize the voice?" I asked.

"Richter," he said. "Jerry Richter. He tried to disguise it, but it was him. He let Barbie come on long enough to say she was all right and hadn't been hurt. She sounded frightened, Rockford."

"Andy," I said. "I think that whether you come up with that money or your collection, Richter and whoever he's working with plan to kill her. We've got to find her first, and we've got to bring in the police. Barbie knows who murdered Hill. I'm pretty certain that it was one of your collector friends."

"Associates," he corrected.

"Associates," I repeated. "And I have an idea I know which one. I strongly suggest that you give me permission to officially tell the police that I'm working for you on trying to find Barbie, and that you call a Lieutenant Dennis Becker of the LAPD, whose number

I'll give you, and tell him the whole story, everything."

"And you?" he asked.

"You hired me to find Barbie," I said. "I talked to her once. I liked her. Richter tried to kill me. I've got three reasons to find her."

"I'll call your Lieutenant Becker," he said.

I gave him Dennis's number and told him to leave a message on my machine if Richter called again and I wasn't in. He agreed and asked me to keep him informed of any progress I might make. Then we hung up.

"Jimmy," Angel said, coming in with a pillow in his hand. "I can't remember if the head of your bed is the right or left."

"Left," I said.

Angel stood there for a beat and said, "Beth, you think she'd front for —"

I was already shaking my head "no." He stopped and went back to the bedroom.

I called Beth, told her I was all right and that Lewiston was going to the police. I told her about Hanson and that if anything happened to me she was to call Dennis and tell him that Angela Woo would testify that Hill's collection had been stolen and replaced by cheap imitations. She agreed and told me that I better come up with something soon before a trial date was set and a jury had to be picked on my portable indict-

337

ment for the murder of John Stuart Hill and, if things went badly, the additional murder of James Hanson, about which I gave her all the details and the name and number of both Jackie Romaine and Big Bear Lake's keeper of the faith Harlan Williams. I left out Old Carlos. My credibility already had enough deficiencies. We hung up and I began to help Angel clean up the mess.

"One more thing, Jimmy," Angel said, coming back out of the bedroom with one of my dresser drawers, which had been ripped out and ransacked. "Before this license thing came up, I talked to some of my clients about coming in with me, you know, putting up their money on a good thing, to make videos on cat care from Angelo Martini, groomer of the cats of the rich and famous. You know, $19.95 with a bonus hair-removing mitt thrown in for ordering today?"

"And?"

"Well," said Angel. "If I can squirm out of this mess and find a front, I can add the video business in. Big money."

I left Angel to clean up and promised him I'd try to think of someone who could front for him in the Feline Finesse business. After all, Raul and Consuela were apparently doing a good job and I didn't see how a video or two could be a danger to owners or pets who might be gullible enough to buy them.

Both Daniel Cohen and Sally Brightman had agreed to meet with me after I'd dropped Andy Lewiston's name. Cohen lived on a road just off Topanga Boulevard. Brightman lived in Reseda.

Cohen was closer. Cohen's house was high in the steep hills near the middle of the canyon and to the left as you headed toward the San Fernando valley. The road Cohen lived on was narrow, twisted and very private. It was unlikely that anyone who wasn't invited or didn't know where he was going would accidentally find himself here. I knew where I was going and I almost didn't find the place. The house was behind a stone wall. The number was clear in white letters. There was no name. I stopped, got out of my Firebird, having pulled as far over as I could to give whoever might be driving past just enough room to get past.

I pushed a button on a speaker and a deep voice said,

"Yes."

"Rockford," I said.

There was a buzz and the gate clicked open. I got back in the car and drove in. The gates closed behind me. The house wasn't big, but it wasn't small either. It was a one-story adobe-style ranch. I figured it for four bedrooms and a pool in back. The house was set back about thirty yards. A new, perfectly polished black Jaguar was parked in front. I pulled in behind the Jaguar. Cohen was waiting for me in the doorway as I got out of the car.

I recognized him from his photographs in the paper and from television. He had done a few guest spots on shows and been on all the late-nights. He was a good interview. He'd made Johnny Carson's show about six or seven times and had recently done a Barbara Walters. The reasons were easy to see when Cohen showed his perfect teeth, movie star looks and Schwarzenegger muscles, which he had the good taste to hide beneath a loose-fitting red polo shirt and dark pants. His mother, who was very much alive and active as a civil rights lawyer, was black. His father, very much dead from an accident widely thought to be a mob hit, had been an attorney for the ACLU. Cohen was a photogenic combination of his parents. Now he was doing weekly on-camera commentary on NFL games, cameos in movies and occasional guest-starring roles on television shows.

He held out his hand. I took it. He didn't do any macho squeezing.

"Good to meet you," he said sincerely. "Sorry about this."

He looked down at his bare feet.

"I was out by the pool reading," he said.

"No need to apologize," I said, following him into the house.

He closed the door and said,

"I suppose you'd like to see my collection before we talk."

"That would be nice," I said. "But to tell the truth I couldn't tell a real from a fake."

We were standing in a large entryway with mosaic tile floors.

"The differences are those between truly great artists whose work almost proves the existence of a god or gods and those that display everything from great skill to the complete fraud. I'll show you."

I followed him through a living room full of what seemed to be antique furniture, all comfortable looking, none quite matching, but all seeming to fit together. There was a window in the room with a view of the pool and the hillside right behind it. Since we were almost at the peak of the canyon, there wasn't much hillside.

The living room was carpeted, but the small room off of it to which he led me was not. He opened the door and hit a switch. The floor was a dark tile. We were surrounded by cabinets with glass fronts, each with hidden lights placed to best illuminate the several hundred bottles inside the cabinets that lined the room.

"Impressive," I said, moving forward to look at some of the bottles.

Birds, bushes, people, forests, odd trees, strange animals, dragons, waterfalls.

"You feel something?" he asked when I turned around to look at him.

I had to admit that I had.

"The room and the lighting would impress you even if they were fakes or inferior works," he said. "But you wouldn't have that feeling."

For the first time since I had been on this case involving a collection of odd people who collected little bottles, I had a sense of what this might be all about.

"The workmanship is truly amazing," Cohen said, looking around with pride. "The dedication to detail, to perfection, to beauty. The time it must have taken for each of these. A test, Rockford. One of these bottles is, in fact, a cheap imitation. I put it out when a so-called collector or expert comes to admire or praise it. I put one out for you. Can you find it?"

I went to the cases. Each bottle stood on a clean glass shelf. I went from bottle to bottle and stopped at one in the third case on the top row.

"That one," I said.

"You're right," he said with a laugh. "You recognized the imitation."

He moved past me, opened the case and handed the bottle to me.

It was a picture of a yellow-beaked bird on the branch of a tree filled with large green leaves.

"It wasn't even painted by hand," he said. "There's a place in Hong Kong that does these. Market's getting bigger. Pretty soon they'll be selling imitation pieces of junk like this on television, Home Shopping."

"Nineteen-ninety-five along with videos on how to care for your cat," I said. "I didn't recognize the fake. When you put it on the shelf before I came in, it left a small line of dust. I'm not a great appreciator of art, but I'm a fair country detective."

Cohen took the bottle from me and grinned, putting his hand on my shoulder. We were about the same size, but I had never thought of the possibility of being in the shape he was in.

"Keep it," he said, handing the bottle back to me. "Memento. Probably worth sixty dollars, maybe even a bit more. You've taught me to be more careful with my little trick in the future."

"Thanks," I said, pocketing the small bottle in the left pocket of my slacks. The gun from Angel was in the right pocket.

I followed him into the living room where he offered to make me a drink.

"I keep it for my guests," he said. "I don't drink. But I have taken the liberty of preparing some fresh lemonade."

"Thanks," I said.

He was gone for only a few seconds, returned, handed me a glass of lemonade with just two ice cubes and took a second glass for himself as he sat, his back to the window. I sat across from him.

"Majored in Oriental Art at Stanford," he said. "Played football on scholarship and got an education. You know all this?"

"I know," I said.

"The call I got about appraising Hill's collection," he said. "I wasn't threatened with death. I was threatened with exposure, exposure of the fact that I am gay. I'm afraid, however, that becomes less of a secret with each day. I've agreed to give another interview with Barbara Walters in which I make this a public revelation."

"Which will end your film and television career?" I asked.

"According to my agent, we should

weather it pretty well. I've already got a book offer of close to a million about my life as a gay football star. A major film company has said it wants to discuss a contract for a series of action films about a gay hero. They already have a series of popular novels featuring such a hero. Satisfied?"

"About what?" I asked.

"That I didn't kill Hill and steal his collection or have someone do it."

"Gut feeling?"

"Gut feeling."

"You're off my list of suspects," I said, "but with a thin line through your name."

"Hill's collection was good, but not great, not worth killing over, at least not by me," he said, looking over his shoulder at the pool. A gull was walking around the edge.

"Is there any collection you would kill over?" I asked.

"No," he said. "There are collections I might kill to save from destruction. One is in Tokyo, another in London, a third in Lyon, several in China and two in Los Angeles."

"The Los Angeles ones?"

"Lewiston's and Cameron's," he said. "Those bottles deserve to outlive the humans who own them and be admired by people who appreciate them for thousands of years. I had a dream once that all the bottles were brought together for an exhibition and there was a sudden unexpected volcano eruption. All the owners died. The bottles were engulfed in the exhibition hall. Then thousands of years in the future during an excavation, a careful and appreciative archaeologist began to dig them intact from the rubble. Before I awoke, I noted that the archaeologist looked surprisingly like me."

"Here's to dreams," I said, holding up my lemonade.

"To dreams," he said, doing the same.

"Two more questions," I said.

He nodded.

"First, given the local collectors, which would you think might go for Hill's collection?"

I handed him the list I had taken from Hill's boat.

"Off the record?"

"Completely," I said.

"Well, on this list, none of them. But if I had to pick I'd go with Cameron, Corbin and Crystal Fontaine. But it could be any of the others too, from anyplace in the world, and my guess is if you ask the others on your list of local collectors, my name would be high on their list. You had another question."

"When Barbara Walters asks you how it felt playing football all those years and hiding the fact that you were gay, what'll you say?"

"When I played, I wasn't straight, I wasn't gay. I was a focused middle linebacker. I don't even think I was quite human. I was an animal on automatic. I loved it. I miss it. I liked hitting and I liked being hit. Blocking a pass or a field goal, sacking a quarterback, a solid tackle for no gain. That's as high as you can get."

I finished the last of my lemonade, handed Cohen my glass and shook his hand, still cool from the lemonade glass.

"Let me know if I can help," he said.

"Maybe one way," I said, suddenly thinking of it. "If someone would kill Hill for his less-than-perfect collection, they might not think twice about stealing another collection or two and not worry about who might get in the way. Could you give a call to the others and tell them to put their collections in a safe place? That includes you. I'd do it, but I don't think they'd all listen to me."

"I will," he said.

He walked me to the door, shook hands again, wished me luck and closed the door.

Less than a minute later I was going back down the narrow canyon road high up Topanga Canyon. I was going about fifteen miles an hour, window open to listen for anyone who might be coming up. I had gone about a hundred yards when I checked my rearview mirror and saw a red Nissan coming down behind me with Jerry Richter at the wheel. He was moving too fast and I had nowhere to go but down and even faster.

It took about five seconds to realize that he meant to run me off the road or into an oncoming car.

CHAPTER THIRTEEN

Just before we came to a sharp curve, the Nissan hit me from behind. I managed to make the turn without going off the road or into the rocky cliffside. Neither was a very good option. On my left, there were the tops of tall trees from the forested hill below leading down to Topanga Boulevard. On my right, a hard rock wall. Behind me was a someone determined to kill me. He had already tried once by throwing me through a window. I had also ignored his warning to stay off the case and stop looking for Barbie. There seemed little likelihood that we might someday become close friends. At the moment, it looked like he wanted me dead and he didn't much care if he took himself with me, but that might have been wishful thinking on my part as I tried to steady my Firebird on the curve and hoped no one in a vehicle large or small would meet me head-on.

I hit my horn, looked through my rear window and felt the rear of my car swerve out over the edge of the narrow road. I didn't go over, no thanks to Richter, who hit me again trying to nudge me over the edge. One of my wheels was churning over the treetops. The other one was just touching unsolid dirt.

My left rear fender must have looked like an aluminum can after a treatment by some macho kid in a bar. He hit me again. This time I could see his face. He looked determined, a man with a job of murder to do.

I tried to stay calm and ease forward slowly, in spite of the fact that Richter's Nissan had backed up for a third try at sending me into the tops of waiting trees. My right wheel caught and I eased forward as he came at me. Then, when I felt something like solid ground beneath both my rear tires, I hit the gas hard and zigzagged around the curve.

Behind me Richter managed to keep from going over the edge after I moved out of his way. Then for an instant I lost sight of him as I went around the curve. I could hear him backing up with a screech and I knew that my chances of making the canyon highway without dealing with Richter were slim to nothing. I hit the brakes, pulled to the right and eased dangerously up on the rocky cliffside, two wheels on the ground, two on the wall. I tumbled out of my door and lay flat on the road next to my car, my six-shooter in hand, as the Nissan came around the curve. He was already traveling too fast and I was too close to my car for him to simply swerve and run me over. If he tried, he would see, or I hoped he would see, that he would hit my car head-on, which might greatly reduce his chances of getting off this road alive unless it was in an ambulance. He came around the curve and I think he saw the gun in my hand.

He skidded, trying to stop, spun around and the red Nissan went flying backward over the edge of the road and into the trees.

I lay there breathing hard for a few seconds, waiting for the sound of Richter's car crashing down the side of the hill, but all I heard was the sound of something heavy cracking the tops of the trees.

I got up, dusted myself off gun still in hand and moved to the side of the road. If I had my camera, I could have taken a picture that could make the *L.A. Times*, network television and the *National Enquirer*.

The Nissan sat about twenty yards below me resting on the tops of some trees. Branches were broken showing yellow-white bark. One of the trees was straining with the brunt of the weight, but there sat the red car about thirty or forty yards above the canyon floor.

While I stood there wondering what to do,

two things happened. First, one of the trees under the Nissan began to creak and complain about the weight of the car. Second, Richter, who was in danger of falling to his death, moved quickly into the passenger seat, which was facing me. The trees beneath his car complained but held as Richter looked up and took three quick shots in my direction.

I backed away fast and was out of his sight when the next wild shot came.

"You're a dead man, Rockford," he screamed. "I warned you."

"Seems to me," I shouted back, putting my gun in my pocket, "that's brave or crazy talk from a man who might very well be dead in a few minutes, not that I'd care all that much since that's what you had in mind for me."

He fired again. The bullet hit high above my head on the hill. I moved to my right, hoping I'd be out of his sight if I looked over the edge. A car was coming slowly up the narrow road. I stood in front of it and flagged it down.

There was a young woman inside with a toddler in a car seat at her side. She was pretty. She was confused. She glanced at my car as I stood in the road and pointed to her right. Her eyes opened wide. I guessed she could see Richter in the Nissan, maybe with a gun in his hand.

"Call the police," I shouted.

Her windows were closed. She was driving a dark Lexus and might not be able to hear me.

"The police," I said. "The fire department. Somebody."

The baby had a pacifier in his mouth. He was looking with mild curiosity at the red car slowly sinking into the trees.

The woman nodded and picked up her car phone. I moved to the edge of the ridge and looked down at Richter. The car was definitely a few feet lower now and tilting distinctly backward.

"You feel like living?" I called.

The woman in the car took another look at the sinking Nissan and at me and took off up the hill past my crazily parked Firebird.

The situation must have begun to sink in, and Richter's anger was quickly being replaced by fear. He raised his weapon in my direction again but didn't shoot.

"Richter," I said. "I could lie down and pick you off with my peashooter. My guess is the police or firemen or both are on the way. They're not all that close. My guess is it's a fifty-fifty gamble whether they get here in time to do you any good and a good chance that they might not be able to figure out how to get you down when they do get here. Personally, I intend to be long gone."

"Rockford," he said. "Do something."

"Well," I said. "I'm a little miffed at your trying to kill me and destroying the rear fender of my car, but I'll make a deal."

"Deal?"

"Throw your gun up here if you can get it this far," I said. "That's for starters."

The trees below him dipped a little more. The gun came flying in my direction, almost hit my shoulder and skidded against the rocks behind me.

"Good start," I said. "Now, did you kill Hanson?"

No answer.

"Richter, it's just my word and yours," I said. "You can deny you said it later. Simple 'yes' or 'no.' "

"No," he said through his teeth. "Now get me out of here."

"Few more questions," I said, looking down at him.

He glanced down through the passenger-side window and didn't like what he saw.

"Ask fast," he said. "For Chrissake, ask fast."

"Is Barbie alive?"

"Yes," he said.

"Where is she?" I asked.

No answer.

"Once more. Where is she?"

"Safe," he said. "That's all you'll get from me. I'll take my chances right here."

"Okay. At least for now. Did you kill John Stuart Hill?"

"No," he said emphatically.

"Did you steal his bottle collection and replace it with cheap ones?"

"No," he said. "What's the point of all this talking, Rockford?"

"Okay," I said. "Let's see if I can get you up so we can take a ride and have a conversation with Lieutenant Becker."

This time the Nissan took a definite turn for the worse. It sunk slowly backward so that the front of the car was now facing upward toward a nice sunny sky.

"Hurry," he shouted.

I went back to my Firebird and opened the trunk with some difficulty. First, it was at an angle. Second, the right rear fender was pushed in against it. I managed to get it open with a blackboard scratch of shrieking.

"What was that?" Richter shouted, out of sight over the edge of the road.

"My knees," I said.

"Move fast, Rockford," he cried. "I'm going down."

"I'm moving as fast as a man can with weak knees and some mean injuries from your throwing me through a window."

"I'm sorry about that," he shouted, the first real touch of panic beginning to show in his voice.

"I'll bet," I said, finding what I was looking for in the trunk and moving back to the edge of the road. It was Rocky's coil of rough braided rope. He'd kept it for small jobs. Now I kept it in my trunk. I didn't know if it was long enough to reach Richter, but I thought it probably was.

"Hurry," he shouted. "Hurry."

"I'm no cowboy," I said, unfurling the rope. "I'm tying the rope to this tat bush and then I'll throw the other end to you and you can swing over and climb up."

I knew there was no way in hell I could just pull Richter up. My knees would buckle. My back would pop and my injured left arm couldn't take the weight.

"Open your door slowly," I said.

Richter looked down. There was sweat on his face and his hair was all over, no longer slicked back. He started to open the door, but the movement sent the car farther back with a creak of breaking branches and flying leaves.

"Okay," I said. "Just open your window all the way."

He did. It took me four throws to get the rope in his hands. Two of the throws were just bad. Two were shaky-handed misses by Richter. Finally he grabbed it tight with both hands.

"Out the window," I said. "You'll probably hit the wall below me pretty hard. Put your feet out and try to hold on."

He nodded, fear on his face, and eased himself out of the car window. As soon as he started his swing, the Nissan suddenly turned on its back, but still it didn't fall. I don't like heights, but I looked down and saw that a stunned Jerry Richter was still clinging to the rope I had thrown him. His pants and shirt were torn by the bushes growing from the side of the hill, and he had lost one shoe.

"Now," I said. "All you have to do is climb up."

"Can't make it," he said. "Arms tired. I feel dizzy."

"Damn," I said aloud and moved to the bush where I had tied the end of the rope. "Give me as much help as you can. Use your feet along the sides, bushes, flowers, anything to help take the weight."

He didn't answer. Far away a siren howled.

"I can't hold on long," Richter called.

"Okay, okay," I said, starting to pull him up by the rope.

He was a big man, not as heavy or as big as me, but big enough, and he wasn't giving me a hell of a lot of help. My knees told me I was an idiot. My back refused to communicate with me. My bandaged arm decided to go nearly numb. All this for a man who wanted to kill me. I pulled. The sirens got closer. I was breathing hard and cursing Richter as I pulled. When I heard him panting and saw his arm reach up, I grabbed it and dragged him over the edge.

He sat for an instant, frightened, tired, clothes torn. He turned his head toward the sound of the approaching sirens.

"You helped me because you want me to talk," he said, still panting.

"One reason."

"Just to save my life?" he said, shaking his head.

"Something like that," I said, looking down at him, trying to hide the tremors in my body.

"And I tried to kill you," he said, looking up at me, confused about who the hell I was and how I thought. "I'm still going to have to kill you."

"Seems a fair exchange for saving your life," I said.

We both looked at the Nissan. It hadn't moved, just nested in the trees facing the sky.

Richter got up. Neither of us was in any mood or condition for a fight.

"Now?" he said.

"We wait for the police," I said.

He didn't answer. He looked around the narrow road and got to his feet. He staggered toward the rocky wall away from the scene of his near-death experience.

At this point, I've got to admit I wasn't thinking all that straight. Shaky, thirsty and more than a little angry with Richter now that he was safe, I stood panting. Richter had calculated well. He leaned against the hill and reached down. I glanced at him and realized that he was reaching for the gun he had thrown up to me. I had been stupid. I hadn't taken the time to pocket the gun or even worry about it.

He came up with it about the same time I came out with mine. The sirens were close now, probably at the bottom of the road.

We were a sad pair for a shoot-out, a tired, battle-scarred veteran with a six-gun that might not even work and a young gunslinger with half a shirt and one shoe.

"I'm taking your car," he said, trying to keep his hand from shaking.

"Nope," I said as he moved toward my tilted Firebird.

He kept his gun on me as he closed the trunk and looked inside the car. My keys were in the ignition. Now or never, I thought, and pulled the trigger. Nothing happened. I looked at Richter. He hadn't heard the click of the hammer coming back but refusing to move forward. I kept the gun aimed at him.

"I still plan to kill you, Rockford," he said.

"So you said."

With his gun on me, he climbed awkwardly into the driver's seat of my car and turned the key. It started a lot smoother for him than it ever did for me. He eased off the side of the hill, the tires hitting the road with a shock that couldn't have done any good to my suspension system.

The sirens were very close now.

Richter took careful aim at me. "I heard it misfire," he said with a grin on his grimy face.

And then he fired as I dived for the bush I had tied the rope to, the rope that had saved Richter's life.

He drove away as I used what little I had left to make it back up on the road. Richter was out of sight. My car was out of sight. I was out of breath when the police car pulled up and two uniformed officers climbed out and came over to me. I was sitting on the road. Both of the policemen were young. Both were black.

"You okay?" one asked. "Ambulance is on the way."

"Artie," the other one said. "Look at this. Son of a bitch."

He moved to the edge of the road and pointed to the Nissan still perched in the treetops.

They both turned to me and Artie said,

"How the hell did you get out of that?"

I tried to talk but could only gasp for a few seconds.

"What the hell happened?" asked the other cop, coming over to me.

"Car, Firebird," I said gasping. "You see one when you came up?"

"Yeah," said Artie. "I think it was a Firebird."

"My car," I panted. "Stolen. Man named Richter."

I gave them my license plate number. Artie wrote it down.

"Call it in," I said, trying to stand up. Artie's partner helped me. "The guy in my car killed someone, tried to kill me. He's a kidnapper and he's armed."

"And who are you?" asked Artie.

"Rockford. Private investigator," I panted.

"You carrying a weapon?" Artie asked suspiciously as an ambulance pulled up and a pair of medics leaped out.

"Antique," I said, pulling out my six-shooter. "It doesn't fire."

Artie's partner took the gun, looked at it, fooled with it and handed it back to me.

"Probably worth a few bucks at an antique sale," he said. "You got papers, I'll buy it myself, get it back in shape."

"Borrowed from a friend," I said as the medics approached, looked at the Nissan, looked at me. "Just admiring it for a few days."

"You're not in good shape, mister," one of the medics said.

She was short, powerful, with no-nonsense black hair brushed straight and cut short.

"Old wounds," I said. "I could use a ride."

"We'll get you checked out at the hospital," the woman said. "You need the stretcher?"

"I can make it," I said.

She took my arm and her partner opened the back door of the ambulance. I climbed in.

"Lie down," the woman commanded.

Artie was at the door.

"Someone'll meet you at the hospital," he

said. "I'm gonna look forward to reading that report."

"Wait. My rope, the one I used to pull him out. It's still tied to a bush back there. I'd like it back."

"Okay," said Artie.

"And call my car in," I said, lying back. "It's stolen by a killer, remember."

"Partner's calling it in now," he said, closing the door. "I'll get your rope and bring it to the hospital."

It was dark. It was cool. I put my good arm over my eyes and rolled with the bumps and turns in the road. It could have been a better morning, but I was alive. There was something to be said for that.

I think I sustained more injuries from the ride to the hospital than I had from my encounter with Richter. When we got to the hospital emergency room, I refused to be carried out on the stretcher. I creaked out at my own pace while the medics stood back with folded arms waiting for me to fall. I was too mad to fall, too mad to let the pain do anything but push me forward.

"Need a phone," I said.

One of the medics nodded. I followed him, my back threatening to give out completely. I found a water fountain in the emergency room where a small black boy sat with a blood red piece of gauze covering his head. A woman sat next to him reading a *People* magazine. She glanced at him from time to time to be sure the boy, who was now watching me, didn't pass out.

I took one of Dr. Lewiston's magic pain pills.

No one tried to stop me. The medics told me to check in at the desk and then went through a pair of double doors.

Artie and his partner came through the double door of the hospital waiting room while I dropped a quarter into the phone.

"Rockford, James," Artie's partner said.

"Right," I agreed, dialing.

"You're out on bail on a murder charge," Artie said.

"I'm aware of that," I said.

"I'll bet you are," said the partner, handing me Rocky's rope.

"Hello, Dennis?" I said as the call went through.

"Jim," he said. "I've been trying to reach you. Beth's been trying to reach you. Lewiston got a ransom call, dollars and place. He won't tell us without talking to you."

"I'm putting an Officer . . ."

"Bates," said Artie's partner.

"Bates on the phone. Richter tried to kill

me. He took my car. These officers have called it in. I'm in the hospital emergency room with a few more aches, tokens of gratitude from Richter for saving his life. I'll tell you all about it when I see you."

"See me now," said Dennis.

I handed the phone to Bates, who identified himself and listened, saying nothing. Finally, he hung up and turned to me.

"You want a doctor to look at you?" he asked.

"No," I said. "I'm a man approaching the brink of poverty. I can do without a hospital bill."

"Suit yourself," said Artie with a shrug. "We're to take you to Lieutenant Becker now."

"That's just where I want to go," I said, welcoming the first effects of the painkiller. I wasn't feeling good, just capable of functioning. "One more call."

"I —" Artie said.

"Okay," Bates said. "Fast one."

I called Beth, left a message on her machine and followed Artie and Bates as we went back to their car. I sat in the back of their car, coiled rope in my lap, as they sat silently. Bates was driving.

I looked out the window, thinking about Barbie, wanting to feel Richter's neck in my hands, dreading the dread of private investigators, especially those with my record. I spent most of my money on automobile insurance. I was listed by insurance companies as super-high risk and only one or two fly-by-nights would accept me after I agreed to a $1,000 deductible. I wondered if Richter had done any more damage to my car out of spite. I wondered if I should just advise Lewiston to pay the money in the hope that Richter would let her go, but I knew that Richter was holding her for more than the ransom from her uncle. He was holding her because she knew, had heard, who had killed Hill with my gun. Richter might try to get the money from Lewiston and pick up another bundle from the killer who, since he or she was a collector and probably had big money, would pay to have Barbie show up dead in one of the cement drainage channels.

I didn't feel like talking either. Bates and Artie parked behind the building and led me up to Dennis's desk. He was on the phone. He nodded at the two uniformed cops that they could leave now.

I thanked them. They didn't quite feel like shaking hands. As they left, I sat in the chair opposite Dennis, rope on my lap. People bustled behind us. A woman's voice behind us screamed, "I can't stand it anymore."

"Lucille," Dennis explained. "Office manager. The copy machine is a dud. Jim, you look terrible, and why the hell are you carrying a rope?"

I told him my story. He took notes and told me that Lewiston had called about his niece's kidnapping. He had advised my client that a tap be set up on his phones. Lewiston had agreed.

Beth showed up and said,

"Jim, you look terrible."

"Thank you, Beth," I said.

"What are you doing here?"

"Giving a statement about my stolen car and the fact that Jerry Richter tried to kill me, twice, once before I saved his life and once after."

Dennis's phone rang. He picked it up.

"Hearing for trial is in three days," Beth said softly, leaning toward me. "I think we've got a good case. It's all too circumstantial. I think the judge will throw it out before it goes to trial unless . . ."

"Unless?" I asked.

"Unless they come up with more evidence against you."

Dennis hung up.

"Good news," he said, folding his hands.

Lucille screamed past behind my back.

"Found your car," Dennis said. "Ran a

computer check when the investigating officers called it in. It was parked on Western near Slauson. In front of both a flower shop and a fireplug. City towed the car as soon as a complaint came in from the flower shop. The computer made the match. Who says the Los Angeles Police Department isn't efficient?"

"My car is in the pound?" I asked.

" 'Fraid so, Jimbo," Dennis said.

"Can you get it out for me? Is it damaged?"

"Between you and the towing people," he said, holding up his hands. "I do my best to keep from getting them mad."

"Great," I said. "I'll have to pay fifty bucks to get my stolen car back, my car whose fender was smashed by a thief, a murderer, a kidnapper and —"

"Seventy-five bucks," Dennis said. "Be sure to bring proof of ownership.

I sat back.

"Let's go, Jim," Beth said, helping me up.

"Jimbo, try to talk Lewiston into cooperating with us," said Dennis. "I've got the feeling that if he pays, he's not getting her back alive. And I've got a feeling he wants to pay in spite of what we tell him to do."

"I have the same feeling," I said. "I'll talk to him."

"Then get to bed," he said.

Dennis's phone rang again. I waved him thanks for finding my car.

Beth drove me to the towing pound, told me her strategy, said something about a software whiz she had had two dates with. I said that was great and she suggested that after I got my car I go home. I said I'd consider it. She waited while I went inside to retrieve my towed car and spent a half hour proving that the damaged Firebird was mine. It cost me $75 to get the car out, keys still in the ignition, and an additional $25 to get an old guy who looked like he was in desperate need of four or five bottles of Milk of Magnesia to move around a dozen cars that were parked in front of mine.

I opened the trunk, which didn't feel much like cooperating, and threw in the rope. I got behind the wheel when I'd managed to close the trunk. The Firebird moved, but there was something wrong with the transmission and the right rear fender was rubbing against my tire, probably shredding it with each turn. I stopped in back of Beth's car, got out and she told me to keep her informed. I promised I would and gave her a kiss through her open window. I had to lean down to kiss her. It didn't help my back.

I drove slowly back to Malibu and the

cove, parking next to Rocky's pickup. I wasn't surprised to find Angel inside eating a sandwich and using my phone. I hadn't seen his van outside. He nodded up at me and went back to his call.

"No doubt," he said, taking a bite of sandwich that looked like packaged bologna on white with mustard, all from my refrigerator. I had no idea how old the bologna was, but Angel led a charmed life.

"Off the phone, Angel," I said.

He put his hand over the mouthpiece and said,

"Almost done, Jimmy." Then he went back to his call and said, "Right, check for the equipment. You can verify it with my bank. I'll be there in the morning. Nice doing business with you."

"I've got it put together, Jimmy," he said slyly.

"That's nice, Angel," I said. "I don't want my name involved and I don't want the details."

I motioned for him to get up, which he did. I went around my desk and reached into my pocket. Amazingly, the cheap bottle with the picture of the bird that Dan Cohen had given me was unscratched. I put it on my desk, sat down and I picked up the phone.

"Got a front for the cat business who also wants to get in on the video deal, the cat videos," he said. "He's even putting up a few dollars to make a demo. With the demo we go to the clients I've picked up and get some big-time investment. Just talked to one of those clients. Angel Martin knows how to come out shouting, 'You can't put me down for long.' "

"Great," I said, checking on Lewiston's phone number.

I got through to Nurse Caples. She put me through to Lewiston.

"Rockford, where are you? They want half a million dollars, cash, unmarked. I can't get that in less than three days."

"I'll be right over," I said.

"The police say they want to set up some kind of trap," he said. "I'm not going to be responsible for what these madmen might do to Barbie. I'm going to have to call my brother about it today. God, I dread that."

"I'm on my way," I said, hanging up.

"Fred Travis," said Angel, finishing his sandwich and smiling. "Your neighbor, convinced him it was a good deal. And it is."

"The gun you gave me, Angel," I said, taking it out and throwing it to him. "It doesn't work. It's an antique."

"Jimmy," he said, raising his right hand.

"I swear to God —"

"Don't be here when I get back," I said. "I plan to tell Travis not to trust you. I have to live binocular distance from him and his wife and I don't need any more enemies. He's a big boy. If he still wants to give you his name and money after I talk to him, I wish you both luck."

I moved slowly across around the desk. There was one message on my machine. I pressed the replay button.

"Guy says he'll 'see you soon,' " said Angel. "Didn't leave his name."

I recognized the voice. Richter. Angel was right: All he said was "I'll see you soon."

I called Lionel and asked him if he was up to fixing my car. He said with the help of his grandson and a friend of theirs they could probably do it. He said he'd be over before the end of the day. I said I'd leave the keys on the floor in the back. I hung up and looked at Angel.

"The Firebird won't run so don't think about taking it," I said. "And I'm taking Rocky's pickup."

"I'm fine for transportation," he said. "I think I'll have a little more to eat before I start lining up some meetings for tomorrow. You need to do some serious grocery shopping, Jimmy."

"Thanks, Angel," I said, heading for the door. "Anything else I can do for you?"

"Nothing I can think of at the moment," he said happily, heading for the refrigerator.

I glanced around the trailer. He had done a good job of cleaning up. I sighed, went out and headed for the pickup. I can't say I was feeling good, but I was feeling, and I was beginning to get an idea I didn't like.

CHAPTER FOURTEEN

There weren't very many pain pills left in the bottle Andy Lewiston had given me, but then again we had not anticipated the amount of pain I was going to suffer. I popped a pill and downed it dry as I drove the pickup on a slight detour on the way to Lewiston's office. The pill was bitter and stuck in my throat for a few seconds, but I got it down. I knew what would go a long way toward curing my ills: catching Jerry Richter, getting him in my hands. Revenge has been underestimated. I've found that it can cure a lot of ailments and even scores, so you can have the sense that you've erased something that can haunt you.

Rocky always used to say, "Let it go, Jimmy."

I'm not saying he was wrong for him, but I was a different animal, and I was in pain and being threatened by a murderer whose life I had just saved. Not to mention that I would be paid with decent knees if I could find the missing Barbie Lewiston, who could also clear me of a murder charge. It had all begun with a green bottle. I didn't bother to wish that I had never seen the bottle; it had happened. I'd do it all again unless I knew what would happen, and you never know.

People are always saying, "If I knew then what I know now . . ." Well, you didn't know it then and I didn't know it then and we did what seemed right or necessary at the time.

I found the flower shop on Western, the one with the fire hydrant in front of it where Richter had dumped my car. Parking wasn't bad at this hour. The shops were getting ready to close. I got out of the pickup as fast as I could and made it to the flower shop just as the woman was locking the front door.

"Pardon me," I said with my gleaming smile.

The woman paused, looked up. She was around sixty, lean, white hair, perfect skin, still a beauty and still Linda Darcy.

"Linda Darcy," I said.

"Correct," she said, standing to face me when the door was firmly locked.

"I had a crush on you when you were on the 'Moppy Doodle Show,' " I said. "Moppy Doodle was a rotten puppet, but you were a beauty from the start."

"Thank you," she said with a polite smile.

"And then you made some movies, one with Rock Hudson," I said, remembering.

She stood with her arms folded, waiting. I stopped in embarrassment and said, "Sorry."

"No," she said, holding up an elegant healthy pink hand. "I was a lousy actress with a great face and a decent body. I went as far as I could go and now I'm doing what I want to do. It's a rare ego booster when someone recognizes me from those days. Now, if you'll excuse me, I'm tired, hungry and have a husband waiting for me in Encino."

"Right," I said. "A little earlier someone parked a car in front of that hydrant."

"And you are?" she asked suspiciously.

"The owner of the car," I said. "The man who parked it there stole it from me."

"I'm sorry," she said. "I was the one who called the police, immediately."

"Did you see the man in the car?" I asked.

"I did," she said. "About thirty-five, dark, good-looking in an untrustworthy way, and he appeared to have just stepped out of an explosion. His shirt was in shreds and he had only one shoe."

"I was wondering why he chose to abandon my car here," I said. "Maybe he knew someone in the neighborhood he could go to or —"

"Two doors down there's a men's shop," she said. "He went in that direction."

"Thanks," I said. "Pleasure to meet you."

She gave me a small smile that showed great teeth.

"I've seen him before," she said.

"The guy who took my car?" I said.

She nodded.

"Once bought some flowers from me," she said. "I didn't get a name. He was bouncy, nervous. That was about a month ago. I saw him once after that when he came into the shop and did a third-rate job of trying to pick me up. Maybe I should have been flattered. I didn't like him and made it clear. I wasn't a second-rate actress for nothing. I've got to go."

"Thanks again," I said.

She turned and walked slowly down the street. There wasn't much in the way of pedestrian traffic even in this neighborhood. Los Angeles is a city of drivers, not walkers. The middle class and well-to-do get their exercise in health clubs and by jogging in carefully selected neighborhoods or in their own home workout rooms. Only the old walked.

Two doors down, where Linda Darcy had

said it would be, was a men's shop, a big men's shop with a sign across the full display window of slacks, suits and shoes ranging from the gaudy to the borderline tasteful. The sign in red letters against a black background gaudily informed the potential customer that this was MOSS'S MEN'S CLOTHING. Straightforward. Refreshing in a town where squeezed-in storefronts called themselves things like "Pierre's School of Modern Dance" and "LaFrance's Suitery."

I went in. There were three men in the shop tidying up and obviously getting ready to close. The place was packed with racks of clothes. There seemed to be signs on all of the racks indicating that everything was marked down from twenty-five to fifty percent.

An older man with a nearly bald head and a graying thatch of hair came toward me. His belly was ample and he wore a shirt, tastefully striped tie and suspenders.

"We're closing," he said, "but if there's something I can help you with?"

"I'm looking for someone," I said.

Solly the Bondsman had my signature for my PI license and the license itself as bond for my possible indictment for murdering John Stuart Hill. So I flashed my grocery check-cashing ID, one with my photograph on it, and put it quickly away as I looked around the shop critically.

"I'm Seymour Moss," he said. "Seymour I. Moss. Seymour E. Moss was my father. He retired from the business five years ago. My son, Seymour L., changed his name to Catt Moss and started running around the world looking for himself. I told him he wasn't missing and when he realized that, he could come back here and be the next Seymour Moss generation. Family's been in the business almost a century. We haven't gotten rich, but it's a living. I talk too much, don't I?"

"A little," I said.

"Keeps a customer friendly," he said softly. "Besides, it's the family curse. I can't stop. What can I do for you?"

"Man came in here earlier, maybe," I said. "Torn shirt. Shoe missing. May have been here before."

"Richter," said Seymour I. Moss with a sigh. "That's his brother, there, by the register. My best salesman. Sells the ladies, who convince their husbands what to buy."

I looked. The man at the register was older than Jerry Richter, a lot older, though there was a family resemblance; both were dark and good looking. This Richter seemed to be in good shape and was dressed like Seymour I. except for the suspenders. Also, his tie was sportier.

"I'd like to talk to him," I said.

"Sure," said Moss, who turned to call, "Mike, man here wants to talk to you."

Mike Richter looked up from the register. We recognized something in each other. You can't hide it from an ex-con. Something about time behind bars leaves a mark on you that other ex-cons can see.

Mike closed the cash register drawer and headed toward me.

"Listen," said Moss, touching my arm, "you get an additional ten percent off of anything in the store. You're a good listener. I've got to go finish closing down."

Mike Richter was a little bigger than his brother and his grip was good — strong, callused, more callused than you'd expect from your average clothing salesman.

"Name's Rockford," I said.

He didn't say anything so I went on,

"Your brother, Jerry, stole my car this morning, not to mention that he tried to kill me, probably killed his partner and kidnapped a girl. Care to tell me what he was doing here?"

"I didn't know about any of that stuff," Richter said with a sigh I believed. "He said he'd been in a car accident nearby. It sounded — Who are you?"

"Rockford, private investigator," I said. "I did time on a con."

"Armed robbery," he said with an intake of breath. "Out six years now. Doing okay here. Clean. Got a wife and a two-year-old."

"Great," I said. "Jerry?"

"He came in for clothes," Richter said with a shrug. "I got him slacks, shirt, socks, clean underwear and shoes. He washed up in the back."

"Who paid for the clothes?"

Richter smiled, just the corner of his mouth.

"I did," he said. "This guy you say he might have taken out, blond, Hanson?"

"That's the fella," I said.

Richter shook his head and looked around the clothes-filled shop as if he thought he'd never see it again.

"Jerry wanted to borrow some money," he said.

Borrow, we both knew, meant "give."

"How much?" I asked.

"Five hundred," Richter said. "I told him I'd have to talk it over with my wife, that I didn't have that kind of money with me and I didn't carry the family checkbook. I told him I might be able to come up with a few hundred by tomorrow, but probably not the whole five hundred."

"He say why he needed it?" I asked.

"Get out of town," Richter said. "Now, thanks to you, I know why."

"I can't tell you to turn your own brother in if he comes back," I said.

"I wouldn't," he said.

"But you'd be doing yourself and maybe him a favor if you didn't give him any money," I said. "I know a captain named Diehl downtown who definitely doesn't like ex-cons and who might come up with the idea that you were aiding a felon in unlawful flight."

"I didn't even know about these things you say he did," said Richter.

"But you know now," I said. "And you believe me."

Richter didn't answer. He looked over at Seymour I. Moss, who was standing back to observe his kingdom before closing down for the night.

"Moss is a good man," Richter said. "Treats me like a son."

"Well," I said. "He didn't have much success with his real one."

"I know," said Richter.

"Your brother say anything about where he was going, what he was going to do? You know anyplace he might be?" I asked.

"No to everything," said Richter. "I only see Jerry maybe once or twice a year when he's in trouble. He comes here. Never to the house. He's never even seen his own niece. But, God help me, he's my brother."

"Thanks," I said, waving at Moss, who waved back. "I'll be back when I'm in the market for some additions to my wardrobe."

I went back to the pickup and drove to the office of Dr. Andrew Lewiston, wondering why Jerry Richter needed five hundred dollars to get out of town when he was about to get a few hundred thousand for Barbie Lewiston. Maybe it was backup money in case everything fell apart and he had to run. Maybe Jerry was close to panic after a near-death experience and was wondering how many lives he had left to gamble with.

Lewiston's office was closed for the day. I peered through the glass window into the reception room. Nothing. I knocked. Doc Lewiston came almost immediately. He was wearing a dark suit and colorful tie. He opened the door, ushered me in and locked the door behind me.

"We're alone," he said. "Staff went home normal time."

He led me back to his office. He looked worried but not panicked, not yet.

"Pills helping?" he said, pointing to a chair

in front of his desk.

"They're helping," I said, sitting.

"Good," he said, moving behind his desk and opening his top drawer.

He looked just as tall, tan, lean and distinguished in a suit as he did in whites. Only now he looked like the perfect chief operating officer for some computer software company. He took a sheet of paper out of his desk and handed it to me. It was typed, short, no date or signature. It read: "Phone booth across the street now. I'll call. Tell no one. You have five minutes or we have one less Barbie Doll."

"My phone is now being monitored by the police," he said. "Whoever left this note knew it. The note came in a plain envelope with my name typed on it. It was marked URGENT, slipped under the front door and someone knocked. My receptionist saw the letter, went to the door, but whoever had left it was gone. She brought it to me and —"

"You ran to the phone booth," I said.

He shook his head yes.

"The phone was ringing when I got to it. I picked it up and was told he wanted two hundred and fifty thousand dollars, tonight. I'm to have it in cash by tonight or he will kill Barbie. I told him I couldn't get that much that fast. He said I had all day and part of the night. He said he didn't believe me. He said that Barbie knew I kept cash in my vault at home, lots of cash. He told me specifically that I should get in touch with you, that you should deliver the money and that he would give you Barbie."

"He wants to kill me, Andy," I said.

"He . . . ?"

"Richter, the one who has Barbie. He wants to kill me. It started out because I seemed to be in his way and now he can't forgive me for saving his life."

"I don't —" Lewiston said.

"Doesn't matter," I said. "You didn't tell the police?"

"No," he said. "I want you to deliver the money and get Barbie."

"Can you get that much money in cash?" I asked.

He reached under his desk and came up with a sturdy red cloth suitcase. It looked reasonably heavy. He put it on the desk.

"It's all in here," he said.

"Where am I supposed to do this and when?" I asked.

"First, a promise that you don't go to the police," he said.

I thought about this one for a long time. We knew Richter's name and that he had taken Barbie. She could probably finger him for both the Hill and Hanson murders. I didn't think she had a chance either way, but maybe Richter was angry enough with me to make a mistake. Maybe he liked Barbie. Maybe he just didn't like the idea of killing a girl. Maybe a lot of things.

"I'm going to need time to get a gun," I said.

He opened another drawer and handed me a gun. It was a Smith & Wesson Model 4046, a double-action only-auto pistol. Compact.

"Keep it in the office and take it home with me at night," he said. "Doctors have, as you know, been the targets of desperate people seeking drugs, and successful surgeons like me have been kidnapped on three occasions in Los Angeles in the last two years. Two of them were found dead. The third was found incoherent and earless. So, if you don't mind, I'd like my gun back as soon as you are finished with it with my fervent hope that you don't have to use it. It is appropriately registered and certainly legal. I will, of course, say that I let you take it. I suppose there might be some minor criminal charge involved in that."

"Possibly," I said, pocketing the gun, thinking of the useless antique Angel had given me. Lewiston's was far from being an antique and was definitely lethal. "I still think the police are our best bet."

"No," said Lewiston. "If you refuse, I'll deliver the money myself and try to explain why you wouldn't come."

"You might just say I was afraid of being shot," I said.

He shrugged. I got up with a sigh and reached for the red cloth bag. Two hundred and fifty thousand dollars is heavy if a lot of it is in small bills, which these seemed to be.

"Where and when?" I asked.

"You know Carbon Canyon Road?" he said. "Where the mineral springs are?"

"Generally," I said.

"Just before you get to the mineral springs, there should be a big sign that says 'Carbon Canyon Road Mineral Springs — three miles straight ahead.' Don't go straight ahead. Take a small road on the left just beyond the sign. Stay on it till you come to a dead end. He should be there with Barbie. Be there just before midnight. Please, Rockford, get her back. We'll try to recover the money when she's safe, but the important thing is to get Barbie back."

"I'll do my best," I said.

I wanted to say, "Remember what you owe me for this. Remember, this was sup-

387

posed to be a simple case of finding a star-struck girl and I was supposed to get new knees." Instead my life had been a couple days of near death, charges of murder and now an encounter with a man who wanted me dead.

"Thank you, Rockford," he said. "Here."

He handed me his business card. On the back he had written his home address and phone number.

"Call me there," he said. "Bring Barbie."

I nodded, gun in one pocket, cloth suitcase in my hand. What happened in Los Angeles, Willy? I didn't know about Willy Loman, but I knew I was walking into a jungle.

I called Beth and told her what was going on. She said as my lawyer she was advising me not to do it, to call Dennis. I knew she'd say that. It was her job and she believed it. She also couldn't tell anyone about it and knew where I was going in case something went wrong.

I drove home with the suitcase on the seat next to me and the doors locked. When I got back to the cove, I waved in the general direction of Fred or Connie Travis and went into my trailer. No Angel. No Dennis. No visitors. I called Lionel, who said he was working with his boys on my car and it

388

should be ready by the next day. I asked him how much it would be. He said it was free, least he could do for the son of his old friend. I pushed and said I wanted to at least cover the parts and something for his boys. I told him I expected a payoff on a case the next day. Lionel reluctantly agreed to charge me three hundred dollars.

A flip of the clasp of the suitcase on my desk and I was looking at what must have been a quarter of a million dollars. I was looking at it when Angel came through the door.

"Angel," I said. "Go away. Don't talk to me about cats or videos or your problems. Don't talk to me about licenses or —"

But he wasn't listening. He had moved forward quickly and was leaning on my desk looking at the open suitcase of bills. His mouth was open. His eyes were wide.

"Jimmy?" he asked.

"Not mine," I said, closing and zipping the case shut and then pressing the clasp.

"Jimmy?" he repeated.

"Angel, it's ransom money I'm delivering tonight," I said.

"How much?"

"A lot," I admitted.

"Looked like a lot of small bills," said Angel. "If this is a ransom deal, your contact isn't going to take the time to count all this, probably doesn't expect the full amount anyway. I'll bet you could pull a few thousand out of there easy and no one would ever know or care."

"No, Angel," I said decisively. "And I thought I told you to knock before you came in here."

"I did knock, Jimmy," he said.

"And you came right in before I could say 'Come in' or 'Stay out.'"

He backed away from the desk a foot or two but couldn't keep his eyes off the suitcase.

"You're feeling touchy right now," he said. "I can understand that. But think it over, Jimmy."

"What did you come here for, Angel?" I asked. "You did a good job cleaning up the place, but you can't stay here tonight."

"I just dropped by to see my best friend," he said, acting hurt. "I'm really here to see my new partner."

"I told you to leave the Travises alone," I said.

"I'm gonna make them rich, Jimmy," Angel said. "And all they need is to front for me and make a small investment in the corporation."

"How small?" I asked, still seated behind my desk.

"Five thousand," he said.

"I'm going to warn them about you, Angel," I said, pointing a finger at him.

"Figured you might," he said seriously. "So I didn't come in here and tell you all this till I got a certified check."

He pulled the check from his pocket and held it up to me.

"I'll give it back," he said, "if you give me seven thousand from that bag. Hell, and you take a few grand for yourself."

"Leave, Angel," I said. "Now. I'm about to risk my life, which I do not like to do, and I don't want my last thought to be about you bilking my neighbors."

"Bilking? We are going to get rich and you could be in on the ground floor," Angel said.

"Angel, with you on the job, the elevator will get to about six, the cable will break and anyone on it with you will plunge into the basement broke."

Angel stood tall with false dignity, turned his back on me and left the trailer. I looked at the small bottle with the tiny yellow-beaked bird on it.

Then I went over how I was going to handle this and came up with lots of dialogue, lots of plans involving sneaking around in the dark or confronting Richter with a line of patter or threats that would turn him into a begging-on-his-knees cow-ard. I didn't believe in any of it.

I watched the clock, tried to eat some eggs and toast with coffee but could only get down one egg and half a slice of toast. The coffee tasted bitter but I thought I might need it. I took a magic pain pill with the coffee and just sat there watching a boxing match on television without the sound. I didn't know who the fighters were. One was black, one was Hispanic. They were prob-ably lightweights and they looked good, but I couldn't keep my mind on the fight. I turned it off. It was still early, but I left. I didn't think it would hurt to be a little early, maybe make sure I could find the road in the dark, look for another way in or out, or find a place to hide when Richter showed up.

The ride wasn't long enough for me. I didn't even feel like arguing with a smug talk radio host who saw conspiracies everywhere in the state and federal government, and I didn't want any music. I drove in silence.

I was well down the canyon road when I knew I was being followed. Whoever it was stayed far behind, but I was sure. I slowed down. So did he. I almost missed the turnoff road three miles from the spring but spotted the sign at the last second and swerved onto the dirt road even though I was about fifteen or twenty minutes early. I turned off my lights and engine. The car following me sped past heading toward the spring. I sat there for a few minutes, turned the engine back on and went down the narrow dirt road that looked as if it ran through a cow patch. There was a decent moon and no clouds so I drove with my lights out, which meant I had to go slowly. I wasn't sure whether I wanted the ride to be long or short. As it was, the ride wasn't long. A car was parked in front of me about half a mile down the road. It looked like another Nissan, Jerry's automobile of choice. I stopped about forty yards in front of it, turned on my lights and saw Richter looking at me in the driver's seat of the other car. He didn't budge.

I didn't see Barbie. Maybe she was in the backseat or tied to a tree out there in the dark. Maybe she was already dead. He didn't move after three minutes or so, so I got out of the pickup without the suitcase but with my hand on the gun.

My plan was to talk to Richter, tell him he'd see the money when I saw the girl, try to get away without getting shot or having to shoot him. I thought I heard the sound of a car far behind me; maybe whoever had been following me figured out what I had

393

done. I was going to be trapped. I walked as fast as I could to Richter's car, watching him to be sure he didn't suddenly pull a gun and start firing, which was unlikely till he saw the money.

As I got closer to him, I could see the smirk on his face. I was getting madder and madder, but he just looked straight ahead at me coming backlit by the lights from Rocky's pickup.

I moved to the driver's side of the car. The window was open. Richter didn't look at me. I didn't see Barbie in the backseat. She might be in the trunk.

"Let's not waste time, Jerry," I said. "Bring out the girl and I go back to my truck and get the money."

Something about the fact that he wouldn't look at me gave me a sick feeling. I opened his door and his body came tumbling out. He toppled over and rolled on his face. There was a hole in the back of his head.

"Barbie?" I called.

No answer in the darkness or from the trunk. I reached into the car, took the ignition key and opened the trunk. Empty.

Something made me turn, a sound, a change in the air. I had the gun Lewiston had given me and I aimed it toward the figure coming toward me. He was backlit but I could make out the form.

"Angel," I said. "What the hell are you doing here?"

"Don't get mad, Jimmy," he said. "I just thought you might be able to use a little backup."

"You thought you might find a way to get your hands on some of that money," I said, putting the gun away.

"Well, that too," he said.

I had been standing between Angel and Richter. Now I stepped forward. Angel saw Richter's body.

"Is he dead?" he asked, frightened.

"Bullet in the head," I said.

"You do it, Jimmy?" he asked.

"Did you hear a gunshot?" I said.

"No," said Angel.

"I could use a more reputable witness," I said. "But this is the only gun I've got and I haven't fired it. Let's go get help."

"Where's the money, Jimmy?" Angel asked.

"In the pickup, Angel," I said. "And I'm turning it over to the police. Every dollar. Now let me give you something to think about. Whoever shot Richter who is lying over there might still be around looking at us, wondering where the money is and considering shooting us both."

Angel got the point. He looked around into the darkness in fear and then turned and ran. He could run. He was already backing his car down the road a few hundred yards behind me when I got in the pickup and took one last look at Richter's body.

It didn't make a hell of a lot of sense. I backed out and headed for the nearest phone to call Dennis, who was asleep, and then to call Andy Lewiston at home, who was definitely not asleep.

I told Dennis I'd be waiting at the entrance to the road and he said he'd have someone come and pick me and the money up.

"You should have brought me in on this, Jimbo," he said, waking up.

"I should have, Dennis," I said.

He hung up.

The first thing I said to Lewiston, who had been waiting for my call, was,

"Richter's dead. I didn't get Barbie. I've got your money and I called the police. Just sit tight, maybe get a few hours' sleep."

"Sleep?" he said. "I'll be sitting at this phone all night."

Then I called Beth and told her what had happened and stopped her before she could say "I told you so." She sounded wide awake. I had the sense that she wasn't alone.

"I'll get dressed and meet you at head-quarters," she said.

I heard a voice, low, definitely male, behind her. Beth was undressed with a visitor in the background. I hung up feeling unreasonably jealous and reasonably sorry for myself.

I went back to the side road leading to the cow patch and sat with one hand on the suitcase thinking and finding all sorts of things that didn't add up.

By the time the local police arrived, checked Richter's body and confiscated the money, the gun Lewiston had given me and my pain pills, I thought I had it figured out, but I doubted if anyone would believe me.

It was nearly three in the morning when I found myself on one end of the table in the conference room next to Captain Diehl's office. More people trickled into the room and sat down with or without coffee. Dennis had entered first, carrying two cups of coffee he must have heated in the microwave from what had been left over that day. He handed me one of the cups. It was definitely left over and probably the last cupful in the pot. Dennis was wearing jeans, sneakers and a green polo shirt his kids had bought him for his last birthday. Captain Diehl was next, bulky, disgruntled, without coffee and without patience. He wore a pair of dark slacks, a pink shirt and a sports jacket with more than a few wrinkles. He had managed to slick back his thick hair with water, but I knew it wouldn't hold. Diehl didn't even bother to look at me. He nodded at Dennis with less than hearty fellowship. Next to arrive was an attorney from the prosecutor's office. He looked sixteen years old, wore glasses and was tall enough to play center for a second-level college. His name was Rory Beeman. He was black and eager. His age or a jolt of something to give him energy kept him bustling and in motion. I tried not to watch. Beth came last. A few strands of her honey-blonde hair had not quite been pinned back and her dark skirt and white blouse were a bit disheveled. I had been sitting there silently waiting for her, hands folded, as each person entered the room. She gave me a look of exasperation.

They all should have beat me here. The cops who had picked me up on the dirt road had gladly agreed to turn me over to the state police, who took over the suitcase, gun and my pills. They let me keep my wallet. They had little to say. Both were veterans. I drove in the patrol car sitting in the back cuffed to the doorknob. The second patrolman drove the pickup. The driver had said nothing in the patrol car, hadn't turned on music or chatted, just looked straight ahead and drove. I should have slept. Tried to but kept thinking thoughts I didn't want to think.

Now I sat at the table looking down at three people who wanted to be in bed, sitting next to my lawyer, who wanted to be undressed and in bed or on some other piece of furniture next to someone else. I wanted to ask her who he was.

"Why didn't you just lock him up for the night?" asked Diehl.

"Possible triple murder," Dennis said, pushing a folder across to Diehl who opened it and looked at the reports. He already knew about Hill. Now he knew about Hanson and Richter.

"You do some traveling to get to your victims," said Diehl. "Must spend a fortune on gas."

"I object to that," said Beth.

"This isn't a trial," said Beeman, opening his briefcase. "It's a witness interrogation. Captain Diehl was making an observation in the form of a question and speculation. I don't believe he expected a response from the suspect."

"We had enough to hold him overnight," Diehl said with a yawn.

"My client wanted to see you immediately," Beth said. "He has information that may save a life."

"That would be a novelty for Rockford," Diehl said.

"Captain, please," Beeman said, putting on a pair of rimless glasses.

At least one person in the room was ready for business.

"My client has a statement to make," said Beth.

"I didn't kill Hill. I didn't kill Hanson. I didn't kill Richter."

"Richter?" asked Diehl.

"One he was bringing the money to," Dennis supplied.

"Why?" asked Diehl, looking at Beeman to be sure each question was within the bounds of official interrogation. The LA police had been bending back and sideways till their noses touched their heels in an effort to avoid mistakes that they'd have to explain later on the witness stand.

"Delivering ransom money for the return of my client's niece," I said.

"You kept the money, killed the kidnapper and lost the girl?" asked Diehl.

"You've got the money. I didn't kill anyone and I didn't find the girl," I admitted.

"Your client was supposed to work with

us," said Diehl, looking at Dennis as if it were all his fault. "He said he would. We could have stopped this killing, caught Richter and made him tell us where the girl is."

"Given your record on such cases, I think my client had some reason to be skeptical about your scenario. Besides, I advised him to go to you with this. He wanted to give it a try."

"Where did you get the gun?" Dennis asked.

"From Lewiston, my client. It's his, protection for his office. He's got drugs there. This is Los Angeles. Enough said on that one?"

"Jim," Beth warned in a whisper.

"Okay," I said. "I'm tired. I've failed and I feel like an ass. I hope that gives you some satisfaction."

"Not enough," said Diehl. "The pills?"

"Given to me by Dr. Lewiston for pain."

"Not a prescription bottle," he said.

"What is this about pills?" I asked. "They're doctor's samples or something. I don't know."

"But you know who killed Hill, Hanson and Richter?" said Diehl.

"No," I said. I had a good idea, but saying it would probably buy me what was left of the night at least in the lockup.

"You have evidence to hold my client?" Beth said.

"His gun killed Hill," Diehl said, holding up a finger. "And he admits returning to Hill's house."

"He's out on bail on that one," said Beth.

"He went all the way up to Big Bear Lake," said Diehl, losing his patience and holding up a second finger. "Rows across the lake and finds the man he claims pushed him out of a window. The man's head is bashed in."

"My client was following a lead to the missing girl he had been hired to find," Beth said. "It is my understanding that the state police have concluded that Hanson was killed hours before my client arrived in Big Bear, found the body and immediately reported in to the town marshal for his cooperation."

"He could have killed Hanson in the afternoon," said Diehl, "driven around and then appeared at the marshal's office pretending he'd just arrived."

"Then the question would be 'Where was Mr. Rockford earlier in the day?'" Beth said. "We are prepared to present very reliable witnesses to his location throughout the day."

I nodded my head knowingly and innocently. I hadn't even talked to her about where I might have been that day.

"Would you like to share some of that information with us?" Beeman asked politely, towering over us.

"Not at this time," said Beth.

"Richter," Diehl said, holding up a third finger. "Rockford was there, had a gun."

"Why would I shoot Richter without finding the girl, put the murder weapon in my pocket and then go call the police."

"You also called your attorney," said Beeman.

"Wouldn't you?" I asked.

Beeman took a note and nodded that he would.

"Look," Beth said. "My client clearly wasn't trying to steal the money or he would have hidden it. Ballistics will show it wasn't the gun he was carrying that killed Richter."

"There was a witness," I said.

Everyone looked at me, including Beth.

"I mean there was someone behind me, backing me up," I said. "He'll testify that he didn't hear any shots fired."

"Can we have the name of this witness?" asked Beeman.

I whispered to Beth. She sighed, shook her head and I turned to the waiting officers of the City of Los Angeles.

"Angel Martin," I said softly.

Dennis put his head in his hands. Diehl smiled. Beeman looked puzzled.

"Angel Martin," explained Dennis, "is an ex-con, a liar, a con man, a thief with a record even longer than Rockford's on the computer. Reports on Martin, Rockford and a few dozen others are highlighted on my computer when they get mentioned in a report. It pulls the report up right away. Martin, at the moment, is awaiting a hearing from the license board. Appears he's been operating an illegal animal care business and misrepresenting himself."

"He's been cleaning cats," I said with some exasperation. "What's that got to do with his being a witness?"

"Credibility," said Beeman. "He's your friend."

"I'm not sure I'd refer to him as 'my friend,' but yes, I know him."

"And he'd lie for you?"

I felt like saying "For a price," but I simply didn't answer.

"Gentlemen," Beth said. "It's almost four in the morning. Do you want to lock up my client for a few hours while I get a release or do you want to let him go home, get some rest and be prepared to aid in your investigation in any way he can?"

"He can walk, Miss Davenport," said Beeman, looking at the reports Diehl had passed over to him. "But he is a witness and still a suspect. And I'm sure that Captain Diehl and Lieutenant Becker would like to talk to him later today when they've had more time to make some inquiries."

"Fair enough," said Beth, rising.

I got up too. Dennis, Diehl and Beeman remained seated. They had things to talk about, like how to nail down one to three murders on me.

"We'll hold the cash until Lewiston comes in to claim it," said Dennis.

"And we'll check to see if those drugs you were carrying are legal," said Diehl. "The gun will go back to Lewiston, providing it's registered and it wasn't used to kill Richter. Lewiston may have to answer some questions about why he let you walk out of his office with a lethal weapon that was registered to him for personal protection."

Beeman didn't seem particularly pleased by Diehl's last remark, but he confined himself to tightening his lips.

Beth and I walked out of the room. She closed the door and didn't say a word till we were outside and sitting in Rocky's pickup. The keys were in the ignition. Beth had miraculously found a cab to the police station but now she needed a ride home, which also gave us time to talk.

"What is going on, Jim?" she said as I pulled out of the lot past parked patrol cars and a few unmarked ones.

"I'm being framed by an amateur," I said.

"Mind telling me who?" she asked.

"When I have a little more," I said.

"All right," she said. "When you drop me off, go home and stay home."

I nodded. I had no intention of going home. I was going to find something that would help keep me awake. In prison, there used to be noise and lights all night. I learned to sleep through that or stay awake through it. I learned to sleep when I could if I had to and keep going for three days without sleep if that was what it took to stay ready for some crazed con who I might have accidentally insulted and who might gain some small degree of revenge by sticking a piece of metal in one of my kidneys.

I nodded to Beth because I figured the police would be coming back for me a lot sooner than she did and I didn't want to be there when they came.

I dropped Beth at her door.

"Do I know him?" I said as she opened the door in front of her apartment building.

"Him?"

"The guy upstairs in your apartment," I said.

"What makes you think . . . ?"

"I'm a detective, remember," I said. "I used to think I was a good one."

"You don't know him," she said. "He's a lawyer. Contracts, not criminal."

I knew some of those too, from working freelance on background checks for possible insurance or contract fraud, but I let it drop. And she was gone.

Sleep was sensible but, under the circumstances, not a good idea. The sun was just about to come up when I drove to Dwight Cameron's house. I wasn't sure whether he owed me a favor or not. I knew I needed one from him.

It was definitely dawn when I stood in front of his door and rang. Before six in the morning, Cameron answered the door clean-shaven, slim, hair brushed and wearing white shorts and shirt and an LA Lakers warm-up zipper jacket. He had a glass of orange juice in his hand.

"Rockford."

"You've correctly identified me," I said.

"You look awful," he said. "Let me get you some juice, squeezed myself, and coffee. My wife is still sleeping."

"Seems a reasonable thing to be doing,"

I said, stepping in. "Yes to the juice and the coffee."

I followed him through the house to an all-white kitchen where he poured me both drinks and I said,

"I think one of your bottle collectors killed three people."

Cameron paused, glass of orange juice now almost empty in his hand.

I drank, gave him more information and told him what I wanted; asked him my questions and got my answers. The answers were pretty much what I had expected.

"How do you know I'm not the killer?" he said.

"It's kind of early," I said, holding back a yawn, starting to feel my morning knee ache and noticing that my back didn't hurt, "but if I can make a call, that'll clear you."

He handed me a cordless white phone that had been hanging on the wall. Dennis answered after two rings.

"I didn't think you'd go home," I said.

"Where are you, Jim?" he said seriously.

"Meaning you sent a car for me and didn't find me home," I said.

"I think you should come right in," he said. "There'll be a warrant out for you within the hour."

"Murder?"

"Murder," he said.

"I'll be in, Dennis, but I've got one or two things to do first."

I hung up.

"I think you're clear," I said, finishing my coffee and accepting his offer of a refill.

Cameron shook his head in confusion and agreed to give me what he knew I wanted. He left the room and was back in less than two minutes with a green Chinese bottle. I was on my way out the door when Mrs. Cameron came down in a white nightgown and robe. I guessed they were both silk. She matched the kitchen where she was probably heading. Her hair billowed back. Cameron and I stood admiring her descent.

"Good luck, Rockford," he said.

"I'll need it," I answered.

The coffee had helped. I wished the police had returned my pills but the pain wasn't nearly as bad as it had been. I hadn't done much running or jumping for the last twenty-four hours and hoped I wouldn't have to do more.

I had a killer to catch and a girl's life to save.

The only thing going for me was the bottle in my pocket Cameron had given me and some definite evidence the killer and I shared.

CHAPTER FIFTEEN

Dr. Andrew Lewiston's house was located in Brentwood on an exclusive street. It was set back with trees around it, an English country manor, three stories, manicured lawn and a low stone fence around the property, making it clear visitors weren't exactly wanted but that they would and could enter if they chose. It all looked very civilized.

I was sure there were houses beyond the trees on either side of and in back of the house a good twenty-five yards away in each direction. I could see the washed stone of one house to the right.

It was seven in the morning when I pulled the pickup in front of the house right behind a new but dusty black Mercedes. I got out and headed toward the door. It opened before I could knock.

Andy Lewiston wore a sports jacket and perfectly coordinated slacks with a white slightly old-fashioned button-down shirt. He was shaved, showered, and he smelled good.

"Alarm system," he explained. "If anyone crosses the property line, the alarm goes off and we can check the video monitor over the front door before we let them in."

"Sounds reasonable," I said. "Can I . . . ?"

I pointed to the interior of the house and he said,

"Of course."

He stepped back to let me in.

"Let's go in here," he said, taking my arm and leading me into a living room whose floor matched the foyer we had come through: dark, inlaid wood, three or four kinds in a repeating pattern of triangles and squares. It was highly polished and the furniture in the living room was, just as I had expected, English-upper-class looking, dark, tasteful, with a fireplace and paintings on the wall of people on horses.

"Well?" he said, sitting in a chair with wooden upholstered arms.

It looked comfortable so I sat in the duplicate opposite him. The back was straight and comfortable, the arms firm and the right height.

"Well what?" I asked.

"What happened?" he said, his dark eyes scanning my face.

"You know a good orthopedic surgeon I can go to who I might come near being able to afford and make periodic payments to," I said.

"I told you, Rockford. Find Barbie and I'll — She's not dead?"

"You tell me, Andy," I said.

"How would I know? That's why I hired you."

"The police work fast on a murder case," I said. "Especially one involving a kidnapping trap they should have been in on. It's over, Andy. You were good, but you're an amateur."

"Rockford," he said, looking at his watch. "I'm supposed to be in surgery right now. Please get to the point. Barbie . . ."

"Is probably alive. I'll give you that. Where are your wife and kids?"

"Alma and the kids spend the month of August with Alma's parents in Yellow Springs," he said.

I shook my head.

"I have a friend with the police," I said. "I may have told you. I called him a little while ago. He says the bullet that killed Richter —"

"Richter's dead?"

"You know damn well he is," I said. "You killed him."

"Rockford, this is . . ."

"The truth," I said. "The bullet from the gun you gave me matched the bullet in Richter's head and my fingerprints are all over the gun. My guess is that they'll put the time of death as somewhere in the afternoon. My guess, if it goes this far, which it won't, is that they'll come to the conclusion, if I don't do anything about it, that I met him early, shot him, went back to you for the cash and back to the murder scene, murder weapon in my pocket. I guess you figured I'd run when I found the body."

"I didn't give you any gun, Rockford," he said so sincerely I almost believed I had lost my mind. "I don't own a gun."

"Not for office protection against crazed drug seekers?" I said.

"No," he insisted.

"You want to tell me the story or should I tell you?" I asked.

He sat silently, a look of sympathy on his face.

"I'm not wired, if that's what you're worried about," I said, opening my shirt and turning around to show him my bare back. "I'll drop my pants if —"

"That won't be necessary," he said, leaning back.

"Okay," I said. "I'll tell it. I did the job for Cameron and he recommended you to work on my knees. Cameron told you that Hanson had taken his bottle. You had probably seen Hanson when he had worked at

Cameron's. In any case, Hanson wasn't hard to find. Later, when you cracked his head, I doubt if there was an excess of brain matter. How'm I doing?"

Lewiston said nothing. I thought I detected just a slight paleness in his cheeks from the sunlight coming through the huge windows whose drapes had been pulled open.

"You found Hanson and made a deal with him to steal Hill's collection," I said. "Maybe the idea was to kill Hanson when he delivered the bottles. And then a fall guy fell into your lap instead, a private investigator with a prison record who had reason to at least dislike Hanson. Maybe even before you met me, you went to my trailer. I had given your receptionist my address. You found my gun. Not too hard. Went back to your office. Saw a few patients and I came in. You sent me off with a list to look for Barbie, a wild-goose chase. Before I found her, you knew I'd be arrested for murder. You went to Hill's house with Hanson and my gun. My guess is that it was you who shot Hill, not Hanson. You took Hill's bottle collection. Then, you went back to your office and left Hanson behind to put in the fake bottles and leave my gun after you made sure there were no prints on it. He was

414

probably about to do just that when Barbie came running out.

"He had no idea what she had heard or seen, but he was sure by the way she was running that she had found the body. Hanson panicked. He was good at that. He grabbed Barbie and probably showed her my gun to keep her quiet. Then he tied and gagged her and put her in the trunk. As it turned out, he did a lousy job of tying her up, but you can't blame him. Hanson was not a Princeton graduate and he didn't like thinking for himself, especially in a situation like this."

"Go on," Lewiston said.

"Am I close?" I said.

"Go on," he repeated softly.

"Then I showed up and he really was in a mess. When I left, he quickly put the cheap bottles on the shelves, wiped his prints from my gun, dropped it near Hill's body and took the money from Hill's wallet.

"At some point before he could ask you what to do about Barbie, she got away. Hanson told you what had happened. What you didn't know was that Barbie would run to Richter.

"My guess is that Barbie told Richter everything. The wrong thing to do, but she didn't know it. Richter called Hanson. Barbie may have recognized his voice, heard you say his name when you were in Hill's house. She could certainly describe him. Richter got in touch with Hanson and told him they could go into business together, charging big dollars to kill Barbie."

"Far ahead," said Lewiston.

"Barbie thought she was hiding safely in Richter's apartment while he and Hanson were calling you and saying they would kill your niece for a quarter of a million dollars. You didn't want her dead. But, then again, you weren't sure you wanted her alive either. You said you'd have to think about it. Richter didn't lie about who he was. He knew you'd recognize his voice. It was all up to you.

"My guess is you canceled whatever you had on schedule and hurried to Richter's, maybe saw me go through the window, saw Hanson, Richter and Barbie come out. You followed them all the way to Big Bear Lake."

"You can guess what you like," he said. "Delusional speculation."

"Not finished," I said. "You went up to Big Bear Lake, smashed Hanson's head in with a log and had a talk with a very frightened Richter. Was Barbie there for all this?"

"Not all of it," Lewiston said, folding his hands.

They were long, delicate and strong hands, a surgeon's hands. They wouldn't be working on me.

"You made a deal with Richter," I said. "He'd get rid of me. Maybe I was just doing a better job than you had thought I would, maybe you thought Barbie had said something to me before Hanson and Richter threw me out of the window. Either way, you made the deal. He agrees to hide Barbie somewhere safe and he agrees to kill me and your niece. The payoff will come as soon as I'm dead. You're still not sure about killing Barbie. Richter agreed. Who wouldn't with Hanson on the floor in front of him, knowing you had killed Hill and having you stand there in front of him with a gun. The rest is more guesswork."

"Guess," said Lewiston.

"When Richter was almost killed trying to kill me in Topanga he decided that the whole thing wasn't worth it and he couldn't trust you anyway. When you gave me the quarter of a million and told me to make the payment and get Barbie back because Richter had called you, a bell went off even in my mind. If Richter was planning to get all that money, why would he go to his brother for a few hundred dollars and say he had to get out of town? You're an important man. He

417

knew you could also be a violent man. There was something I couldn't figure out, but it just hit me. When you gave me the quarter of a million and persuaded me to make the exchange, you had already shot Richter with the gun you gave me. You knew I'd take the gun because Richter had already tried to kill me. What I couldn't figure was why Richter had agreed to meet me down that road.

"You knew the police would get me for his murder," I said. "You knew you'd get your money back because you'd admit that you had sent me with the money. Killing Richter wasn't your idea. You hadn't given me a gun. I'm sure you've got a good enough lawyer so the prosecutor's office won't even consider doing more than asking you a few questions and maybe testifying at my trial. You're a piece of work, Lewiston."

"I'm a good surgeon," he said. "A good husband, a man who is, I admit, obsessed with a particular kind of unique art. My dilemma is that I can't bring myself to kill the only witness to my crime, my brother's daughter. I suppose I'll have to but I'm still trying to find a way to let her live. I can't think of one. It's either that or she testifies against me and I go to jail."

"You've got those good lawyers," I reminded him as he took a pair of surgical gloves from his pocket and expertly put them on. "Barbie could have been wrong about hearing you at Hill's and up at Big Bear Lake talking to Richter."

"No," he said with a sigh, coming up with a gun from behind his back, a gun that had certainly been placed there for just such an emergency. "Barbie won't lie for me. I've been trying to talk her into it. She thinks she loved Richter and he loved her."

"Where is she?" I asked.

"Safe, in this house," he said. "I've got till the end of the day to decide what to do with her. My wife and children will be back in the morning. And now I've got to kill you and . . . It just keeps going on once it starts."

"I've got an offer."

"What kind of offer?" he asked.

I took the green bottle out of my pocket that Dwight Cameron had given me. Lewiston's eyes moved to it.

"You let me live and we figure out a way to get me off these charges. You pay for the lawyers. I keep my mouth shut and you get the bottle. Barbie and I leave the house and she's found in a ditch far from here."

"I can't kill her," he said.

"I'll do the killing," I said.

Lewiston tried not to look at the bottle, the green bottle prize of Dwight Cameron's collection, a more valuable item than anything Lewiston owned. Hanson had tried to steal it for Hill and now I sat with it in my hand.

"Deal?" I asked.

"You wouldn't kill Barbie," he said. "Richter, Hanson, maybe even I would, but not you, definitely not for money, not even to save your own life."

He stopped, stood up and took a step toward me. His plan was simple. He was a surgeon. He knew how close he had to get to make it look like suicide. When he was about a yard in front of me, I threw the bottle. I'd say it went about ten feet up. It was a very high ceiling. Lewiston groaned and turned toward the bottle, took a step toward it while it was still on the way up. As soon as his back was turned, I was out of my chair. I turned him around and hit him twice, once very hard in the stomach, the other time in the right kidney. He went down on his knees and I took the gun from his hand as the green bottle hit the inlaid floor and exploded.

In his pain, Lewiston watched in horror as splinters flew.

"It's a copy," I said. "Worth a few hundred. You would have seen that if I'd let you get close enough. Cameron had it commissioned and kept it on show except for real experts like you who got to see the real thing."

Lewiston's answer was a groan.

I went to the phone, gun aimed at Lewiston and called Dennis. Lewiston and I had little to say while we waited. He managed to make it back to his chair still wearing his surgical gloves. At one point, he said, "I'd never be able to hurt Barbie."

Dennis and a crew arrived in less than fifteen minutes. An alarm went off somewhere in the house and somewhere a video camera was showing two police cars pulling up. I motioned Lewiston toward the front door and we moved through the door, stepping on little pieces of green glass. I told him to open the door. He did and Dennis stepped in. I immediately handed Dennis Lewiston's gun.

"Dr. Lewiston," I said. "This is Lieutenant Becker."

"We've met," said Becker. "We talked about the doctor's missing niece."

"She's somewhere in this house," I said. "When you find her, she'll tell you an interesting story about her uncle murdering three people."

Dennis looked at Lewiston and then at me. He was wondering if he needed a warrant. He decided to take a chance. If he found Barbie, he had cause to search because he believed her life was in immediate danger. A couple of uniformed cops stood next to Lewiston while Dennis and the others searched.

It took them all of five minutes. Dennis and another detective helped Barbie Lewiston down the stairs. She was a frightened wreck who no longer looked younger than her eighteen years.

"He killed them," she cried, looking at her uncle. "He killed them all and he was going to kill me. My uncle was going to kill me."

"Never, Barbie," Lewiston said.

They led Barbie away and Lewiston, holding his stomach where I had punched him, turned to me before they also led him out the door.

"Nathan Spring," he said. "Good man, good orthopedic surgeon, charges reasonably, give you good terms on fixing your legs. I'm sorry."

"Thanks," I said, following them out the door. He was going to get a whole lot sorrier.

I went to Dennis's barbecue on Sunday with Gigi, the waitress from Gilda's truck stop near Bakersfield. I had tried Beth but she was "busy." I knew that "busy" meant the new boyfriend. Moira Green was not the barbecue-in-the-backyard type. That's not quite fair. My guess is she would have fit in quite well. Moira could fit in anywhere, but I had Gigi's number and I remembered her red hair and smile.

She had said "yes" immediately, that Sunday was her day off, and she volunteered to drive herself in to Dennis's house in Tarzana. I insisted on picking her up. I had my Firebird back, and, thanks to Lionel and his crew, it was running better than it ever had before. He wouldn't take three hundred, and he charged me so little I tried to get rid of some of my guilt by taking him, his grandson and the grandson's friend who had worked on the car out to lunch on Saturday. I checked to ask him if they all liked seafood and he said they did. We ate at a place on the ocean, watched the gulls through the window where we were seated and admired the waves. I had the feeling that Lionel had warned the boys not to order anything expensive, but I couldn't prove it. Most of the lunch was spent talking about Rocky, and I think we all had a good time. When Lionel left, I handed him a check for three hundred, asked him to please keep it. He agreed reluctantly and we set a firm date for fishing

423

at a stream he and Rocky had been to last year.

As Gigi said without a blush when I picked her up, she "cleaned up pretty damned good." Her red hair billowed. Her freckles were covered with an invisible face powder and her earrings were bright yellow and went perfectly with her yellow jumper.

"Well," she said after we had gotten into the car. "How do I look?"

"Terrific," I said, meaning it.

The barbecue guests included a few cops and their families, one or two neighbors and some relatives of Dennis's wife. There were lots of kids. They were all noisy. I volunteered to help Dennis, who looked a little silly in his white apron and cap as he worked on hot dogs, chicken and ribs. He would have looked a little less silly if there weren't red felt letters on the apron saying: "Don't mess with the chef. He's armed."

When everyone was served and Dennis was out of his white uniform, he sat down with me on a couple of lawn chairs along his fence. We each had a bottle of beer. Gigi was getting along great with everyone, particularly Dennis's family. I could grow to like Gigi a hell of a lot.

"They found Hill's collection in a vault in Lewiston's house," he said as we watched the kids and adults and listened to laughter. A few clusters of cops were telling war stories near the long lawn table full of potato salad, corn on the cob and coleslaw.

"They've definitely been identified as Hill's by three collectors who knew the collection," said Dennis.

I nodded. I had given Dennis the list of collectors. The police had gone to Dan Cohen and Dwight Cameron.

"This is in confidence, Jim," he said, not looking at me. "Lewiston hired the best defense attorney money can buy. Guy was in overnight and spent a day with Lewiston and his wife. They came up with some plea-bargaining after Lewiston's brother also flew in to get his daughter and see his brother."

"What can they offer, Dennis?"

Dennis sighed, drank deeply and said, still not looking at me, "Barbie Lewiston is an iffy witness. She says she'll testify against her uncle, but who knows what her father wants and who knows if she might not just want to ride away home and try to forget the whole thing. I saw them together. I think the father wants her back home now and turning her back on whatever happened to her in California. I think she'll testify, but . . .

"The prosecutor's office has some doubts

and Lewiston's lawyer is damned good," Dennis went on. "Here's his story. Lewiston didn't kill Hill, Jamie Hanson did. Lewiston wasn't with him, didn't even know him. Barbie did hear a voice, but it was Hanson who had already stolen your gun from the cookie jar. You had a run-in with him over a bottle you recovered from Hanson after he stole it from Cameron, his former employer, a bottle he was going to sell to Hill when you stopped him. So Hanson and his pal Richter decided to set you up. Hanson got your gun, shot Hill, took his bottles, and Richter offered them to Lewiston. Lewiston claims he didn't know they were Hill's collection. He had often bought bottles from Richter. He didn't know Hill was dead. He didn't know Barbie was there or that Richter had her."

"You think that's the way it went down, Dennis?"

"I don't think Hanson had the smarts to set you up, Jim, and he was dead when you got set up later.

"Hanson and Richter go up to Big Bear Lake in case Lewiston figures out that they've killed Hill and sold him Hill's collection. Lewiston's lawyer suggests they fought over the money Lewiston had paid. Richter hits Hanson with a log and goes back to town."

"Caught in the web of circumstance," I said, looking at my beer bottle.

"That's their story," said Dennis. "There's more. Now Richter is getting scared. He's stuck with the girl. Hanson's dead. He goes after you for personal reasons. Remember, Barbie Lewiston's name hasn't been mentioned, won't be in the lawyer's story."

"So Richter just had some kind of grudge against me," I said. "They have any idea what kind of grudge?"

"Richter was angry because he was supposed to be the middleman in the sale of Dwight Cameron's bottle to Hill and you screwed it up."

"That made him want to kill me? Supposedly he had a pile of money from Lewiston for Hill's collection."

"That's Lewiston's lawyer's theory, at least for now," Dennis said. "Just ask his lawyer. Lewiston then gets second thoughts about the collection he bought, wants to return it, get his money back. He gets in touch with Richter, who knows how, says he wants to go back on the deal, feels there's something illegal involved."

"And Andy Lewiston being an upright citizen doesn't want anything to do with possible criminal activity," I said.

"He had hired you to find his missing niece. You were looking. You came up with the story that she had been kidnapped. Lewiston says no one ever told him she had been kidnapped or tried to get ransom money. In fact, Barbie was fine and had been living with a woman named Gail Chernowitz. He didn't own the gun you had that killed Richter, didn't give it to you, doesn't know how you got it. The money in the suitcase was given to you by Richter, who demanded the bottles back. He already had this grudge thing going with you. You said Lewiston would return the bottles immediately at his home. Richter said no. You fought over the suitcase full of money. You shot Richter."

"It's full of holes, Dennis," I said, waving at Gigi who was having a good time, thick paper plate in her hand, a couple of women to talk to.

"It stinks, Jim. A paper bag full of holes, but remember Lewiston's got the best defense lawyer money can buy, the threat of a long trial we might lose, a prime witness who might at this moment be being persuaded to go back to Little Rock. She hasn't made a statement yet. We've got nothing without her."

"So what does Lewiston's lawyer offer?" I asked with a sigh.

"We let Lewiston walk or we go into a trial that will last longer than O.J.'s and end in an acquittal and a suit against the police department."

"What about Richter trying to borrow a few hundred dollars from his brother?" I asked. "He's got a few hundred thousand dollars and he tries to borrow a few hundred to run?"

"Just one of a lot of little things that don't make sense, Jim. But the prosecutor's office is probably going to go for it. Lewiston walks. Barbie goes home with her dad who, by the way, wants nothing more to do with his brother."

"And me?" I asked.

Dennis shrugged.

"I don't know, Jim," he said. "Lewiston's lawyer has volunteered to represent you on the Richter murder charge. I understand his fee will be paid by a protected source."

"A guilty, rich Lewiston," I said.

"My guess is the lawyer will start pushing buttons for you," said Dennis. "Maybe find an airtight alibi for the time of death. You go down for an illegal weapons charge."

"Amazing what being rich can buy you," I said.

"Did I say it stinks?" Dennis asked.

"You did."

"I'm not that far from retirement, Jimbo," Dennis said, looking at his wife. "The day I'm eligible, the house goes on the market and when we sell, we're off to the smallest town we can find in the hills up north, lots of snow."

When the party was over, Gigi gave a lot of hugs and I gave some handshakes. The Beckers invited us to come back some night, just the two of us. Both Gigi and I said that would be great. I drove her to the truck stop near Bakersfield and told her the story.

"Doesn't surprise me any," she said. "Gilda had some stories I didn't believe till I got to be big enough to know what you could and couldn't buy. There wasn't much you couldn't buy, but we were too poor and honest to get the chance. That's the way Gilda wanted it."

"No wonder Rocky liked her," I said.

She didn't invite me in. I did kiss her soft and long at the doorway, but we both wanted this to end, at least today, with the start of a friendship and not a long excuse for me to wind up in her bed. I promised to call and I meant it.

When I got home, it was dark and Fred came running out of his trailer past the Webster trailer, making a beeline right for me.

"Have a nice Sunday, Fred?" I asked.

"Man left a note under your door," he said. "About noon. Big car, rental. That was all."

"Thanks, Fred," I said, moving toward my door.

"No, thanks to you," he said. "Never would have gotten together with your friend Mr. Martin if it weren't for you."

"About that —" I began but Fred cut me off.

"We gave him a check today, a few hours ago," Fred said almost gleefully. I thought he was going to do a Silas Marner or an Ebenezer Scrooge and start rubbing his hands together. "Our investment's already doubled."

"You actually have a check from Mr. Martin?" I asked.

"Yes," said Fred, pulling out a check and showing it to me. Bank check for twenty thousand dollars for the partnership he had sold to the Travises for his video idea. The logo on the check was Feline Finesse Video Corporation.

Angel had found a bigger sucker who put cash upfront and he didn't want the Travises in on a percentage of the action.

"Glad I could help, Fred," I said, patting his shoulder and excusing myself after telling

431

him how happy I was for him and his wife.

The envelope was under the door. I turned on the light. There was nothing written on it. I opened the letter. There was a check for thirteen hundred dollars and signed by Lewiston, but not Andrew. The check had come from Barbie's father. There was also a note, handwritten, unsigned: "With my appreciation for your efforts on behalf of my daughter. I believe this covers five days at your fee of $200 plus a little extra for expenses."

Life is full of surprises. Some good. Some bad. Rocky thought they evened out. I used to think that there was a lot more bad than good, but Rocky said that was just because of my line of work. Maybe he was right.

Lewiston's brother had paid me. Angel had paid the Travises and there were two messages on the machine, one from the office of Dr. Nathan Spring giving me some times when I could make an appointment. Had Andy Lewiston in the middle of everything remembered my knee problem and his recommendation of Nathan Spring? Or were the check and the call from Spring a family suggestion that I let things stand? I expected to hear from Lewiston's lawyer within a few hours if he or one of his assistants wasn't already on my machine.

The second call on my machine was from Angel, who couldn't contain his joy:

— Jimmy, I sold the cat idea to Anson Video Enterprises. They gave me a check on the spot and told me to get right into production. I bought the Travises out; figure to make a lot more. Got a bank account with a corporate name and I'm on my way. Now I need a script, a couple of actors and a director. I told Anson that I had everything lined up. You got any ideas? What about Harvey Freyberg we knew back behind the walls? Didn't he get out after doing eighteen of twenty for manslaughter one? You know how to get in touch with him? I'm a little desperate. But I've got an idea. That Barbie Lewiston. Her name was all over the papers this morning. Mentioned you too. Paper said she had come out here to get in the movies. Good-looking kid. You think you could talk her into being in a couple of my videos? The extra publicity wouldn't hurt either of us. Remember Harvey Freyberg or any other idea. I've got till morning.

I got undressed, took a hot shower for my knees and changed the bandage on my arm. It didn't look so bad considering what Hanson and Richter who had done it to me looked like now.

I was putting on my robe when the phone

rang. It was Dennis.

"You watch the local news?"

"No," I said. "I'm about to go to sleep."

"First story, top of the hour," said Dennis. "Andy Lewiston shot himself. He's dead. He left a note telling the whole story. He cleared you, Jim, and apologized to you, his family, Barbie, his brother and one or two others."

I should have been happy, but I wasn't. I was just tired.

"Thanks, Dennis," I said.

"This one came out right," he said.

"I suppose so," I answered.

"Diehl's gonna be pissed as hell. Thought he had you."

"Thanks again, Dennis. Thanks again for the party," I said and hung up. I didn't turn on the television set.

For some reason, I suddenly thought of Jackie Romaine sitting in front of a television sitcom, her blind eyes dancing, her mouth in a smile. Maybe not. Maybe she was listening to classical music and wondering whether to be happy or sad that her nephew Jamie wouldn't be around to cause any more trouble. I decided to give Harlan Williams up at Big Bear Lake a call in the morning and let him know what was going on. I also decided to call Jackie Romaine and make that appointment with Dr. Nathan Spring, who was sure to take the check in my pocket and a good part of what I planned to earn for the next year.

A light rain was falling. I liked the sound on my new nonleaky roof.

It still wasn't too late. I ate a couple of Oreo cookies from the package in the refrigerator and went out in my robe with a chair to watch the moon and listen to the surf and rain from under the metal canopy on my deck.

I think I fell asleep out there. When I opened my eyes, the rain had stopped. The tip of the sun was just edging over the top of the hills across the highway. The water glowed early-morning gold. My phone was ringing inside. I paid no attention, just sat watching the empty wet beach and the sun and knowing I was going to go back to Big Bear Lake sometime in the hope of getting a good look at Old Carlos the monster. Maybe I'd take Gigi or Lionel. Old Carlos would be a sight worth remembering.

The employees of Thorndike Press hope you have enjoyed this Large Print book. All our Large Print titles are designed for easy reading, and all our books are made to last. Other Thorndike Press Large Print books are available at your library, through selected bookstores, or directly from us.

For information about titles, please call:

(800) 257-5157
To share your comments, please write:

Publisher
Thorndike Press
P.O. Box 159
Thorndike, Maine 04986